WITHDRAWN

NEBULA AWARD STORIES NINE

Nebula Award Stories Nine

SC
NEBU

EDITED BY KATE WILHELM

HARPER & ROW, PUBLISHERS

NEW YORK
EVANSTON
SAN FRANCISCO
LONDON

continued on next page

To Lloyd Biggle,
who deserves more than this.

Contents

Acknowledgments

The editor of an anthology always owes a good deal to many people, and I perhaps more than most, since this is my first. My thanks then to Donna and Bert Emerson, who did so much of the real work; to Lloyd Biggle for always being there with advice when called upon; to Vonda N. McIntyre and Alan Dean Foster, for answering when I called. And thanks to Victoria Schochet, for letting me do it, and to Damon Knight, because he was there if I needed him.

K.W.

Introduction

Conventional wisdom tells us fiction is dying, the short story is dead. Like the statisticians who lop off the extremes that tend to unduly influence results, conventional wisdom chooses to ignore the entire field of science fiction. The fact is science fiction is in a period of exuberant sprawl, appearing in unpredictable places, virtually creating its own markets as it sweeps along. Short science fiction stories are reprinted over and over before the ink on the original has had time to set up permanently. Conventional wisdom says the youth of America doesn't read; our own experience tells us in college after college, when science fiction appears in the catalogue in any form—appreciation courses, overviews, how-to, whatever—the young people rush to fill those classes, and those students have read, and are still reading. Often they are better informed in this area than the teachers. These students are physics majors, sociology majors, anthropology students, mathematicians, English literature majors, musicians, artists. . . . Every field seems represented.

Inevitably one must ask why this surge of interest in a field that has been ghettoized for so long. It may be the answers will vary as much as the definitions of science fiction do, that no simple reason can ever be found, but rather there will be a mosaic of causes inseparably bound together.

Usually a science fiction reader will say he became interested in this field because of its ideas. But the word "ideas" must then be defined before the answer becomes meaningful. When Plato spoke of *ideas* he meant those things that are real, in fact, the only things that are real, not mere shadows of things. Scientists are concerned with *phenomena*, again from the Greeks, meaning "things that seem," or "present themselves to our senses."

When a reader says, "I read science fiction for the ideas," I believe he is talking about the ideas in a Platonic sense. And what are the ideas of science fiction? The future. Space travel, or cosmology. Alternate universes. Time travel. Robots. Marvelous inventions. Immortality. Catastrophes. Aliens. Superman. Other dimensions. Inner space, or the psyche.

These are the ideas that are essential to science fiction. The phenomena change, the basic ideas do not. These ideas are the same philosophical concepts that have intrigued mankind throughout history.

With Francis Bacon's formulation of the scientific method, the separation of science from philosophy began; by now there is little, if any, connection between them. Immortality, as idea, is not investigable by microscope and statistical data analysis; the phenomena of aging, of bacterial disease, of cardiac disease, of modern genetics research are immensely rewarding fields of study. In the process of scientific discovery, the philosophical questions regarding immortality itself were put aside.

One by one the sciences became specialized, became more involved with phenomena that could be tested in the laboratory and, as they developed into the different and separate disciplines that we know today, they left philosophy with little to debate except ethics and morality, which have proven inaccessible to rigorous scientific study. Ethics and morality were not to be debated for long, however, because the school arose, elegantly explicated by Bertrand Russell, that turned philosophy inward to examine the words and syntax it used and had always used. This was the final turn from the great ideas that had stirred men's

passions over the ages. It is hard to become passionately involved
with the logical analysis of syllogisms.

Ideas that are archetypal in their universality, that arouse passions, that inspire people to write dense, eight-hundred-page
books, and other people to read them, don't die; and the concepts
of Plato, Kant, Descartes, Schopenhauer, Bergson are alive and
exciting for this simple reason: the questions they raised are still
waiting answers. And this is what science fiction is about.

In our fiction where the story is about the future, and doesn't
simply use the future as background, whether utopia or dystopia
is described, we are faced instantly with the problem of determi-
nism and free will; the necessity or randomness of historical
change; the opposing propositions concerning the perfectibility of
man or fallen man, whose institutions only can be perfected. From
Plato's *Republic* to More's *Utopia* to Butler's *Erewhon*, to Spencer's utopia that will arise from an industrial state with free trade,
to the utopias we create, we all see the future through the spectacles provided by our own culture. Our reasoning is filtered
through the things we hate about our culture, and the things we
approve, and a host of other things we accept as given without
question.

The ideas in Plato's *Republic* so permeate our thinking that
nearly all the others that have followed seemed designed to refute,
or accept and modify, his basic premises. We build our utopias on
a future Earth, or on other planets, but the standard by which we
judge them was written over two thousand years ago, and to date
has not been surpassed in its thoughtfulness and its comprehen-
siveness.

In the alternate universe story we are trying to cope with the
concept of infinity. No one can really conceive of infinity any more
than he can grasp figures in the billions, or even millions. When
we are provided aids, such as, so many cars bumper to bumper
from here to the moon, that, too, is meaningless. How far is the
moon? How fast is twenty-five thousand miles an hour, the escape
velocity? What we can understand is a personal experience of

distance expressed as time. Twenty-four hours to drive to New York. Twenty minutes to fly to Miami. We count on our fingers and for really tough problems we might use our toes, even our teeth. The macroscopic and the microscopic are beyond our ability to comprehend. Infinity is merely a word. Alternate universe stories attempt to understand. For example, every universal instant (that is, each instant for each person) a new universe comes into being. If a choice is negative here, in another universe it is positive. The changes can be very great or, in another universe born only minutes ago, very slight. It is a way of exploring what would have been if . . . whatever if stands for. It is a way of trying to grasp infinity.

Alternate universe stories offer a rationalization for immortality, because every time we escape death in this universe, in another we die, and conversely, when we finally succumb, there is a universe in which we do not.

The eighteenth-century poet Blake wrote: "To see a world in a grain of sand . . . Hold infinity in the palm of your hand/ And eternity in an hour."

The microscopic world of intelligent beings has passed out of fashion; now we have the alternate universe instead. The phenomena, the tools we use, change; the idea persists.

Kant reasoned time and space out of existence: they are modes of perceiving, or innate characteristics only. There has always been a problem of defining what we mean by "now." As soon as I speak of it, it is gone. If I anticipate it, it is not yet. Bergson said this moment is the culmination of the past becoming the future; time means duration; now is the sum of everything past.

In our dreams and trance states we experience other times, sometimes future times. This led J. S. Dunne to postulate his serial-time theory. Priestley put it this way: events are in pigeon holes that can be entered and left again—the events will be there forever, have always been there.

Or is time simply a symbol, a word we use to mean the process of change? Aging: nonrecurring change; progression of seasons: recurring change. Relativity of time says a space traveler approaching the speed of light will age much less than one remaining on a stationary object—Earth. Are there different rates of time, pockets where time is slower, even flowing backward? In this context we should consider the definition provided by an anonymous writer: "Time is an illusion perpetrated by the manufacturers of space."

Aristotle believed everything is cyclical—we exist in a tape loop that will replay itself endlessly. Asimov's story "Nightfall" explores this theory. Surely this is the most fatalistic philosophical construct of all. Schopenhauer carried it further than Aristotle and was reduced to absolute pessimism.

I will be here at this table drinking from this glass over and over again, he said, and there will be the same suffering, the same injustices in the world. . . . The only way to escape, he wrote, was through suicide. And this, too, would recur endlessly.

Theories about time are practically inexhaustible in the literature of philosophy. And science fiction writers come back to them again and again.

Robot stories have religious overtones; they touch on the problems of ethics and morals. From the Golem of Prague, to the Sorcerer's Apprentice, to Frankenstein, to modern Colossus, the machine doesn't perform as expected. It is flawed by the mistakes of its creator. As the dangers of the world increase, the power of the machine to bring about complete destruction grows more evident. The monster in Frankenstein simply wanted a mate and a place to live in peace in the wilderness. It threatened few people, and only after being denied this basic existence. Colossus has the power of life and death over the entire world. What this fiction asks is: is the thing created responsible for its flaws? In human terms, is man responsible? Why does man have to suffer because of flaws he cannot prevent?

These stories say man is not capable of becoming the Creator—at least not yet—and both man and his creation are doomed in the attempt. Alfred Bester's "Fondly Fahrenheit" demonstrates this inescapably in having master and robot share a psychosis. This line runs through many of the stories: the creator is insane, his creation is insane. Harlan Ellison's "I Have No Mouth and I Must Scream" is another example. There are many.

Side by side with robot stories are those about marvelous inventions, amazing discoveries, spectacular breakthroughs. They examine the same philosophical problems.

They reflect the attitudes that man, in his imperfect state, will build a better mousetrap that will swiftly catch him. Creator and victim of his creation: that is how science fiction looks at man and his wonderful new toys. These stories are concerned with the problem of good and evil, and the impossibility of separating one from the other. Serious writers have been struggling with the problem of good and evil for thousands of years, and there is no solution yet that satisfies everyone. Voltaire created his most memorable comic character, Pangloss, to satirize the then prevalent attitude that everything created by God of necessity must be good, that man is simply too limited in his vision to achieve understanding of the ultimate good that must be derived from that which is only apparently evil.

A modern example of the impossibility of knowing in advance if a product is good or evil is DDT. No one alive today can truly balance the good it has done against the great evils that followed and continue to follow.

So these stories keep alive this cautionary note: man's vision is too narrow to judge the good and evil he is capable of doing, and the best intentions in the world can't insure good results.

Immortality again goes to the heart of philosophy and religion. Man has been proving or disproving immortality for centuries. Kant reasoned that man has an innate morality, *a priori* knowledge of right and wrong. From this he went on to reason that since man's choice of good over evil is seldom sufficiently rewarded, and indeed often brings him injury, it follows that he must be rewarded in an afterlife. Compensation or, in psychological terms, reinforcement is necessary or the trait or action will be extinguished, but morality continues to be practiced. A being capable of fulfilling this reward in an afterlife must exist, and that being, of necessity, is God. This is arguing for immortality in an afterlife, with assumptions of an eschatological design for human beings, a divine goal.

In science fiction the immortality is assumed for this earthly body, and the weight of centuries of belief in the mortality of man comes into question. Is there a divine plan? Is death a long sleep, eternal oblivion? Is there a purpose in the development of intelligence? Immortality stories are elitist by nature. The Greeks believed only their heroes could achieve immortality. We have carried this forward and broadened the definition of hero to include ourselves. The maids and the garbagemen and the elevator operators are not immortal. Would this thwart evolution of the species, and is there such a thing? Is man destined to become godlike in the fullness of time? Are we the bridge to superman?

The immortals of fiction are created with the same flaws that show up in marvelous inventions and robots. Eventually they become bored, or they have a fatal defect after all. Man has a finite capacity for pleasure or pain, for adventure, for anything that might lure one to wish for immortality, and very quickly, measured on the clock of eternity, he would become sated with living. He is forced to reexamine his attitudes and fundamental beliefs.

If intelligence is accidental, and evolution blind, if there is no divine plan after all, then the hedonists' view of man becomes more acceptable, and immortality no longer seems a sin against our own progeny.

This raises another no less grave problem: can intelligence survive without sufficient purpose? And what is sufficient purpose?

No one has to consider this seriously today, but tomorrow we might, or the day after that.

Granting man has evolved, have the changes been gradual, or is man changed abruptly by an outside force, as in *2001*, or by something he does himself? In Darwin's time there was a raging battle between the catastrophists and the gradualists, or evolutionists. The biblical flood was accepted as the first recorded catastrophe that changed mankind. Before the flood man's life-span was measured in hundreds of years; after the flood his life-span was that of modern man. The adherents of catastrophism asked many questions that are still to be answered. Why did the dinosaurs die out? There are theories, but no hard facts. Why did the mammoths stand and freeze to death, with fresh grass in their mouths? Why didn't they try to flee south? What was that cold wind that froze everything in seconds?

The latest battle was fought this century, only twenty years ago, between Velikovsky and his critics who, no matter how they refuted him, could not deny the evidence of worldwide catastrophes: terrible floods, widespread droughts, lands sinking, others rising.

It has been suggested that Darwin's theory of natural selection, expressed by Spencer in the phrase, "survival of the fittest," was eagerly accepted by the rising industrialists who saw in it the perfect justification for their own emerging philosophy of economics.

Nietzsche said if man's destiny is manipulable by man himself, then it is man's duty to prepare for superman through selective breeding. And this thought, taken out of context, without the later disclaimers, culminated in the Nazi pogroms of eradication of the Jews, and the eugenics plan designed to bring forth a thousand years of Aryan supermen. Evolution speeded up through man's intervention.

There are people who today believe eugenics is the answer to many, perhaps even most, of the ills that plague mankind—inferior intelligence, hereditary diseases, and so on.

A new catastrophic ice age could accomplish much the same goal: only the cleverest, strongest, most adaptable, most courageous, most life-oriented would survive, and they would breed a new generation in their image.

William James tells a charming story. A white traveler-explorer in Africa received a newspaper, the first he had seen in months, and he read it word for word, column after column, and even reread parts of it. The puzzled natives watched silently, and when the explorer finally had exhausted the paper and was ready to discard it, the natives asked if they could buy it. He wanted to know what possible use they had for it. And they said it must be powerful eye medicine, or why would he have bathed his eyes in it for so long?

We are all aliens to someone. Even among ourselves, in familiar groups, no one of us can know what another is experiencing, what he thinks, the depth of his sadness, the intensity of his pain, the height of his joy. We are all aliens to each other. We simply are more or less used to the strange behavior of others and try to put up with it with as little friction as possible.

In dealing with extraterrestrial aliens we are not so kind. There are three ways of treating aliens in fiction that seem to repeat endlessly. First, we treat them as cuddly animals, larger-than-life kittens, or koala bears, and feel superior to them. Or we treat them as gods, and fear them, because they might, after all, judge us. Or we treat them as enemies who will get us if we don't get them first. And one wonders, is our xenophobia inherent, or learned? The recent experience with the Tasaday people seems to disprove it is innate. History shows good cause to fear outsiders, strangers. Too many instances of friendly natives being slaughtered by explorers and exploiters have left their imprint. We have all been taught to fear the stranger, the alien. Our treatment of aliens in our fiction seems then to be a justification of an acquired human trait that we recognize as unworthy. Perhaps what the stranger is doing is not mysterious and threatening at all; perhaps he is merely reading the latest news from home because he is lonely.

Of course, our xenophobia also goes back to the belief in a geocentric universe. We are the chosen people, and from biblical days to Descartes, we have known it is not only our right but our duty to master and rule over everything lesser than we. Any nation at war tends to treat the enemy this way, and to reinforce their subhuman status, the enemy is called slopes, gooks, krauts, big nose, redskin. . . .

The geocentric universe theory is dead. The belief that God created man in his image has no scientific basis. The idea that was made not only possible but necessary by these two beliefs, that man is the chosen creature of the universe, lives on, and is examined again and again by writers today.

In fiction superman is doomed. Nietzsche decided the time is not yet right for his appearance. I suspect it never will be right for a solitary superman. He is incontrollable, unpredictable, and a threat, regardless of his intentions. Superman shakes our faith in the laws of nature, and if this goes, it takes everything else with it. It is much easier for primitive people to accept the idea of superman, because they don't believe in the orderliness of nature anyway. Except in the most ephemeral fiction, we create a superman and then damn him for being different and destroy him, or more often, have him destroy himself. We will trim the hair of every Samson we create.

We have to because a technological civilization is grounded in the logic of cause and effect, of order and predictability, and of stability, which can bend a little, but absolutely must not break.

It can be argued if God created man in his image, then superman must have been created by Satanic powers, and it is man's duty to destroy this manifestation of evil. Or, if man evolved from the lesser creatures, and now presumes to create superman, his creation must be flawed, because man is himself imperfect. The creature must be destroyed. Also, it is vastly reassuring to believe all men are created equal, except for those who are naturally inferior to us.

Nowhere on the bell-shaped curve that represents mankind is there room for superman.

In space travel stories we are competing with the astronomers with the two-hundred-inch Palomar telescope, the giant radio telescopes, computers, records that go back thousands of years, and predictions for thousands of years to come. The Incas were astronomers, the Babylonians, some say the Druids, but in spite of the equipment, the respectable age of science, and all the money and man-hours devoted to it, no one knows today how the universe began, how it will end, even *if* it began and is destined to end. There are theories that come and go like the seasons—the Big Bang, all matter was condensed into one mass that exploded, or was exploded, and ever since has been rushing from the scene of the original Big Bang. There is the steady-state theory—nothing has changed or will change. It didn't begin, won't end. The universe has been described as a perfect piece of clockwork, a mechanism wound up by God to tick forever. There is the oscillating-universe theory that says it expands, then contracts, and does this forever. There is the expanding-universe theory that says matter is forever being created and the universe is forever growing larger. Every mythology attempts to explain the creation of Earth, if not the universe. Astronomy was one of the dead sciences for a long time. Everything had been learned that could be, but today it is tumultuous. There are new discoveries that are not understood—quasars, pulsars, black holes, white holes. Space travel stories are exciting news stories, complete with photographs. As news or fiction, space travel brings some of this excitement to the reader, probably more to the writer. The universe is mysterious, awesome, beautiful, and we know practically nothing about it.

Probably a caveman looking at the sky was the first philosopher. There have been flat-earthers, hollow-earthers, the geocentric universe, the heliocentric universe. Slowly we have found our place in the universe, but the questions remain, even as they must have occurred to that first aware caveman. What is it? Why is it?

Historically the psyche has been the battleground of the materialists and the metaphysicians. Is the mind a *tabula rasa,* a blank slate on which can be written what man is to be? Or does the mind contain a system of *a priori* knowledge? Kant said the ultimate nature of reality is conceivable but not knowable. Modern physiological psychologists say there is nothing except the chemical-electrical activities of the physical brain: what we call consciousness is a by-product. Bergson wrote that consciousness is apart from the brain, arising from it, but not necessarily dependent on it. His analogy was this: a coat on a peg is linked to it, and if the peg falls, the coat goes with it, but the coat is not the peg. It exists as a separate thing in itself. It is not an epiphenomenon of the peg. Metaphysics attempts to discover the ultimate nature of reality, and in this sense the innerspace of science fiction is metaphysical fiction.

This isn't a dead issue dragged from the eighteenth century to our contemporary scene. It is very much alive; adherents from the opposing views are still active. The battleground changes, the weapons bear new names. The war is the same. B. F. Skinner, the best known of a host of behaviorists, is persuasive as he demonstrates his results of operant conditioning, and hypothesizes a future in which man can be trained to become whatever the conditioners decide is best for mankind. Not merely become that, but be happy in that role. Noam Chomsky, also active, well known, gathering disciples all the while, seems able to prove, also decisively, the innate structure of the mind with an inherent grasp of language and its grammar. Jean Piaget, working with children, takes this even further, and is able to demonstrate that certain recognizable human characteristics are physiologically determined, among them empathy (which becomes possible no earlier than eight or nine), deductive reasoning, generalizing, and others. No system of rewards and punishment (conditioning) can hasten these developments, if Piaget's theory is correct; moreover, when the child is ready, the latent (innate) ability automatically becomes operational. Potentiality becomes actuality, and each generation spontaneously rediscovers the mental activities that separate *Homo sapiens* from the rest of the animal kingdom.

This is not merely an idle speculation, material for armchair philosophers. Today the biochemists, the psychologists, the behavior modifiers, the neurophysiologists, the analysts, those in ESP research, even nutritionists are all staking out claims in this area.

How much of man is innate, how much is learned behavior? Children's art from around the world reinforces the validity of Jungian archetypes that affect everyone. The way we see our world is innate, and only with training can we view it with the spectacles provided by our separate cultures. That man can be conditioned is a reality also. The battlegrounds have been chosen, the lines drawn, the antagonists are in place. This could well be the fiercest battle of all, involving every one of us.

Lost in the exciting phenomena of discoveries, there remains the basic idea, the basic question: What is man?

These are some of the ideas of science fiction. They aren't new. They have been debated over the centuries, and there have been few enduring answers to the imponderable problems raised by these ideas. No one can be disinterested in them because a new discovery in any of these areas would drastically influence everyone alive today, everyone who will live in the future. An immortality serum discovered tomorrow would alter the lives of everyone on earth. There would be a shift in everything we believe in, and nothing would ever be the same again.

Ask the general public what science fiction is all about and the answer will probably be, the future. In a sense this is correct, but only in that science fiction uses and will continue to use the phenomena of the future, its hardware, its extrapolations, its changing cultures, in order to explore ever again the ideas that have always intrigued mankind. And in this lies its strength. In this lies its appeal to a whole new generation of readers who seem to grasp intuitively that these ideas must be kept alive and that somehow science fiction has found this need and is satisfying it.

KATE WILHELM

Madeira Beach, Florida
February, 1974

NEBULA AWARD STORIES

GENE WOLFE

*The Death
of Doctor Island*

"In my picture of the world there is a vast outer realm and an equally vast inner realm; between these two stands man, facing now one and now the other. . . ." C. G. Jung said that, and he might have been describing Gene Wolfe, who seems frighteningly familiar with both realms. In this story he will take you by the hand and lead you from one to the other with such disarming ease you may never know when the transition occurred. A true Jungian story told in Freudian terms, an exploration into the inner realm, that is what "The Death of Doctor Island" is. And if you recognize yourself as a player, or an aspect of one of the players in that inner realm, don't be surprised. Nothing is accidental.

I have desired to go
    Where springs not fail,
To fields where flies no sharp and sided hail
    And a few lilies blow.

And I have asked to be
    Where no storms come,
Where the green swell is in the havens dumb,
    And out of the swing of the sea.
                    —*Gerard Manley Hopkins*

A grain of sand, teetering on the brink of the pit, trembled and fell in; the ant lion at the bottom angrily flung it out again. For a moment there was quiet. Then the entire pit, and a square meter of sand around it, shifted drunkenly while two coconut palms bent to watch. The sand rose, pivoting at one edge, and the scarred head of a boy appeared—a stubble of brown hair threatened to erase the marks of the sutures; with dilated eyes hypnotically dark he paused, his neck just where the ant lion's had been; then, as though goaded from below, he vaulted up and onto the beach, turned, and kicked sand into the dark hatchway from which he had emerged. It slammed shut. The boy was about fourteen.

For a time he squatted, pushing the sand aside and trying to find the door. A few centimeters down, his hands met a gritty, solid material which, though neither concrete nor sandstone, shared the qualities of both—a sand-filled organic plastic. On it he scraped his fingers raw, but he could not locate the edges of the hatch.

Then he stood and looked about him, his head moving continually as the heads of certain reptiles do—back and forth, with no pauses at the terminations of the movements. He did this constantly, ceaselessly—always—and for that reason it will not often be described again, just as it will not be mentioned that he breathed. He did; and as he did, his head, like a rearing snake's, turned from side to side. The boy was thin, and naked as a frog.

Ahead of him the sand sloped gently down toward sapphire water; there were coconuts on the beach, and seashells, and a scuttling crab that played with the finger-high edge of each dying wave. Behind him there were only palms and sand for a long distance, the palms growing ever closer together as they moved away from the water until the forest of their columniated trunks seemed architectural; like some palace maze becoming as it progressed more and more draped with creepers and lianas with green, scarlet, and yellow leaves, the palms interspersed with bamboo and deciduous trees dotted with flaming orchids until almost at the limit of his sight the whole ended in a spangled wall whose predominant color was black-green.

The boy walked toward the beach, then down the beach until he stood in knee-deep water as warm as blood. He dipped his fingers and tasted it—it was fresh, with no hint of the disinfectants to which he was accustomed. He waded out again and sat on the sand about five meters up from the high-water mark, and after ten minutes, during which he heard no sound but the wind and the murmuring of the surf, he threw back his head and began to scream. His screaming was high-pitched, and each breath ended in a gibbering, ululant note, after which came the hollow, iron gasp of the next indrawn breath. On one occasion he had screamed in this way, without cessation, for fourteen hours and twenty-two minutes, at the end of which a nursing nun with an exemplary record stretching back seventeen years had administered an injection without the permission of the attending physician.

After a time the boy paused—not because he was tired, but in order to listen better. There was, still, only the sound of the wind in the palm fronds and the murmuring surf, yet he felt that he had heard a voice. The boy could be quiet as well as noisy, and he was quiet now, his left hand sifting white sand as clean as salt between its fingers while his right tossed tiny pebbles like beach-glass beads into the surf.

"*Hear me*," said the surf. "*Hear me. Hear me.*"

"I hear you," the boy said.

"Good," said the surf, and it faintly echoed itself: "*Good, good, good.*"

The boy shrugged.

"What shall I call you?" asked the surf.

"My name is Nicholas Kenneth de Vore."

"Nick, *Nick . . . Nick?*"

The boy stood, and turning his back on the sea, walked inland. When he was out of sight of the water he found a coconut palm growing sloped and angled, leaning and weaving among its companions like the plume of an ascending jet blown by the wind. After feeling its rough exterior with both hands, the boy began to climb; he was inexpert and climbed slowly and a little clumsily, but his body was light and he was strong. In time he reached the top, and disturbed the little brown plush monkeys there, who fled chattering into other palms, leaving him to nestle alone among the stems of the fronds and the green coconuts. "I am here also," said a voice from the palm.

"Ah," said the boy, who was watching the tossing, sapphire sky far over his head.

"I will call you Nicholas."

The boy said, "I can see the sea."

"Do you know my name?"

The boy did not reply. Under him the long, long stem of the twisted palm swayed faintly.

"My friends all call me Dr. Island."

"I will not call you that," the boy said.

"You mean that you are not my friend."

A gull screamed.

"But you see, I take you for my friend. You may say that I am not yours, but I say that you are mine. I like you, Nicholas, and I will treat you as a friend."

"Are you a machine or a person or a committee?" the boy asked.

"I am all those things and more. I am the spirit of this island, the tutelary genius."

"Bullshit."

"Now that we have met, would you rather I leave you alone?"

Again the boy did not reply.

"You may wish to be alone with your thoughts. I would like to say that we have made much more progress today than I anticipated. I feel that we will get along together very well."

After fifteen minutes or more, the boy asked, "Where does the light come from?" There was no answer. The boy waited for a time, then climbed back down the trunk, dropping the last five meters and rolling as he hit in the soft sand.

He walked to the beach again and stood staring out at the water. Far off he could see it curving up and up, the distant combers breaking in white foam until the sea became white-flecked sky. To his left and his right the beach curved away, bending almost infinitesimally until it disappeared. He began to walk, then saw, almost at the point where perception was lost, a human figure. He broke into a run; a moment later, he halted and turned around. Far ahead another walker, almost invisible, strode the beach; Nicholas ignored him; he found a coconut and tried to open it, then threw it aside and walked on. From time to time fish jumped, and occasionally he saw a wheeling sea bird dive. The light grew dimmer. He was aware that he had not eaten for some time, but he was not in the strict sense hungry—or rather, he enjoyed his hunger now in the same way that he might, at another time, have gashed his arm to watch himself bleed. Once he said, "Dr. Island!" loudly as he passed a coconut palm, and then later began to chant, "Dr. Island, Dr. Island, Dr. Island," as he walked until the words had lost all meaning. He swam in the sea as he had been taught to swim in the great quartanary treatment tanks on Callisto to improve his coordination, and spluttered and snorted until he learned to deal with the waves. When it was so dark he could see only the white sand and the white foam of the breakers, he drank from the sea and fell asleep on the beach, the right side of his taut, ugly face relaxing first, so that it seemed asleep even while the left eye was open and staring; his head rolling from side to side; the left corner of his mouth preserving, like a death mask, his characteristic expression—angry, remote, tinged with that inhuman quality that is found nowhere but in certain human faces.

When he woke it was not yet light, but the night was fading to a gentle gray. Headless, the palms stood like tall ghosts up and down the beach, their tops lost in fog and the lingering dark. He was cold. His hands rubbed his sides; he danced on the sand and sprinted down the edge of the lapping water in an effort to get warm; ahead of him a pinpoint of red light became a fire, and he slowed.

A man who looked about twenty-five crouched over the fire. Tangled black hair hung over this man's shoulders, and he had a sparse beard; otherwise he was as naked as Nicholas himself. His eyes were dark, and large and empty, like the ends of broken pipes; he poked at his fire, and the smell of roasting fish came with the smoke. For a time Nicholas stood at a distance, watching.

Saliva ran from a corner of the man's mouth, and he wiped it away with one hand, leaving a smear of ash on his face. Nicholas edged closer until he stood on the opposite side of the fire. The fish had been wrapped in broad leaves and mud, and lay in the center of the coals. "I'm Nicholas," Nicholas said. "Who are you?" The young man did not look at him, had never looked at him.

"Hey, I'd like a piece of your fish. Not much. All right?"

The young man raised his head, looking not at Nicholas but at some point far beyond him; he dropped his eyes again. Nicholas smiled. The smile emphasized the disjointed quality of his expression, his mouth's uneven curve.

"Just a little piece? Is it about done?" Nicholas crouched, imitating the young man, and as though this were a signal, the young man sprang for him across the fire. Nicholas jumped backward, but the jump was too late—the young man's body struck his and sent him sprawling on the sand; fingers clawed for his throat. Screaming, Nicholas rolled free, into the water; the young man splashed after him; Nicholas dove.

He swam underwater, his belly almost grazing the wave-rippled sand until he found deeper water; then he surfaced, gasping for breath, and saw the young man, who saw him as well. He dove again, this time surfacing far off, in deep water. Treading water, he could see the fire on the beach, and the young man when he returned to it, stamping out of the sea in the early light. Nicholas then swam until he was five hundred meters or more down the beach, then waded in to shore and began walking back toward the fire.

The young man saw him when he was still some distance off, but he continued to sit, eating pink-tinted tidbits from his fish, watching Nicholas. "What's the matter?" Nicholas said while he was still a safe distance away. "Are you mad at me?"

From the forest, birds warned, "Be careful, Nicholas."

"I won't hurt you," the young man said. He stood up, wiping his oily hands on his chest, and gestured toward the fish at his feet. "You want some?"

Nicholas nodded, smiling his crippled smile.

"Come then."

Nicholas waited, hoping the young man would move away from the fish, but he did not; neither did he smile in return.

"Nicholas," the little waves at his feet whispered, "this is Ignacio."

"Listen," Nicholas said, "is it really all right for me to have some?"

Ignacio nodded, unsmiling.

Cautiously Nicholas came forward; as he was bending to pick up the fish, Ignacio's strong hands took him; he tried to wrench free but was thrown down, Ignacio on top of him. "Please!" he yelled. "Please!" Tears started into his eyes. He tried to yell again, but he had no breath; the tongue was being forced, thicker than his wrist, from his throat.

Then Ignacio let go and struck him in the face with his clenched fist. Nicholas had been slapped and pummeled before, had been beaten, had fought, sometimes savagely, with other boys; but he had never been struck by a man as men fight. Ignacio hit him again and his lips gushed blood.

He lay a long time on the sand beside the dying fire. Consciousness returned slowly; he blinked, drifted back into the dark, blinked again. His mouth was full of blood, and when at last he spit it out onto the sand, it seemed a soft flesh, dark and polymerized in strange shapes; his left cheek was hugely swollen, and he could scarcely see out of his left eye. After a time he crawled to the water; a long time after that, he left it and walked shakily back to the ashes of the fire. Ignacio was gone, and there was nothing left of the fish but bones.

"Ignacio is gone," Dr. Island said with lips of waves.

Nicholas sat on the sand, cross-legged.

"You handled him very well."

"You saw us fight?"

"I saw you; I see everything, Nicholas."

"This is the worst place," Nicholas said; he was talking to his lap.

"What do you mean by that?"

"I've been in bad places before—places where they hit you or squirted big hoses of ice water that knocked you down. But not where they would let someone else—"

"Another patient?" asked a wheeling gull.

"—do it."

"You were lucky, Nicholas. Ignacio is homicidal."

"You could have stopped him."

"No, I could not. All this world is my eye, Nicholas, my ear, and my tongue; but I have no hands."

"I thought you did all this."

"Men did all this."

"I mean, I thought you kept it going."

"It keeps itself going, and you—all the people here—direct it."

Nicholas looked at the water. "What makes the waves?"

"The wind and the tide."

"Are we on Earth?"

"Would you feel more comfortable on Earth?"

"I've never been there; I'd like to know."

"I am more like Earth than Earth now is, Nicholas. If you were to take the best of all the best beaches of Earth, and clear them of all the poisons and all the dirt of the last three centuries, you would have me."

"But this isn't Earth?"

There was no answer. Nicholas walked around the ashes of the fire until he found Ignacio's footprints. He was no tracker, but the depressions in the soft beach sand required none; he followed them, his head swaying from side to side as he walked, like the sensor of a mine detector.

For several kilometers Ignacio's trail kept to the beach; then, abruptly, the footprints swerved, wandered among the coconut palms, and at last were lost on the firmer soil inland. Nicholas lifted his head and shouted, "Ignacio? Ignacio!" After a moment he heard a stick snap, and the sound of someone pushing aside leafy branches. He waited.

"Mum?"

A girl was coming toward him, stepping out of the thicker growth of the interior. She was pretty, though too thin, and appeared to be about nineteen; her hair was blond where it had been most exposed to sunlight, darker elsewhere. "You've scratched yourself," Nicholas said. "You're bleeding."

"I thought you were my mother," the girl said. She was a head taller than Nicholas. "Been fighting, haven't you. Have you come to get me?"

Nicholas had been in similar conversations before and normally would have preferred to ignore the remark, but he was lonely now. He said, "Do you want to go home?"

"Well, I think I should, you know."

"But do you want to?"

"My mum always says if you've got something on the stove you don't want to burn—she's quite a good cook. She really is. Do you like cabbage with bacon?"

"Have you got anything to eat?"

"Not now. I had a thing a while ago."

"What kind of thing?"

"A bird." The girl made a vague little gesture, not looking at Nicholas. "I'm a memory that has swallowed a bird."

"Do you want to walk down by the water?" They were moving in the direction of the beach already.

"I was just going to get a drink. You're a nice tot."

Nicholas did not like being called a "tot." He said, "I set fire to places."

"You won't set fire to this place; it's been nice the last couple of days, but when everyone is sad, it rains."

Nicholas was silent for a time. When they reached the sea, the girl dropped to her knees and bent forward to drink, her long hair falling over her face until the ends trailed in the water, her nipples, then half of each breast, in the water. "Not there," Nicholas said. "It's sandy, because it washes the beach so close. Come on out here." He waded out into the sea until the lapping waves nearly reached his armpits, then bent his head and drank.

"I never thought of that," the girl said. "Mum says I'm stupid. So does Dad. Do you think I'm stupid?"

Nicholas shook his head.

"What's your name?"

"Nicholas Kenneth de Vore. What's yours?"

"Diane. I'm going to call you Nicky. Do you mind?"

"I'll hurt you while you sleep," Nicholas said.

"You wouldn't."

"Yes I would. At St. John's where I used to be, it was zero G most of the time, and a girl there called me something I didn't like, and I got loose one night and came into her cubicle while she was asleep and nulled her restraints, and then she floated around until she banged into something, and that woke her up and she tried to grab, and then that made her bounce all around inside and she broke two fingers and her nose and got blood all over. The attendants came, and one told me—they didn't know then I did it—when he came out his white suit was, like, polka-dot red all over because wherever the blood drops had touched him they soaked right in."

The girl smiled at him, dimpling her thin face. "How did they find out it was you?"

"I told someone and he told them."

"I bet you told them yourself."

"I bet I didn't!" Angry, he waded away, but when he had stalked a short way up the beach he sat down on the sand, his back toward her.

"I didn't mean to make you mad, Mr. de Vore."

"I'm not mad!"

She was not sure for a moment what he meant. She sat down beside and a trifle behind him, and began idly piling sand in her lap.

Dr. Island said, "I see you've met."

Nicholas turned, looking for the voice. "I thought you saw everything."

"Only the important things, and I have been busy on another part of myself. I am happy to see that you two know one another; do you find you interact well?"

Neither of them answered.

"You should be interacting with Ignacio; he needs you."

"We can't find him," Nicholas said.

"Down the beach to your left until you see the big stone, then turn inland. About five hundred meters."

Nicholas stood up, and turning to his right, began to walk away. Diane followed him, trotting until she caught up.

"I don't like," Nicholas said, jerking a shoulder to indicate something behind him.

"Ignacio?"

"The doctor."

"Why do you move your head like that?"

"Didn't they tell you?"

"No one told me anything about you."

"They opened it up"—Nicholas touched his scars—"and took this knife and cut all the way through my corpus . . . corpus . . ."

"Corpus callosum," muttered a dry palm frond.

"—corpus callosum," finished Nicholas. "See, your brain is like a walnut inside. There are the two halves, and then right down in the middle a kind of thick connection of meat from one to the other. Well, they cut that."

"You're having a bit of fun with me, aren't you?"

"No, he isn't," a monkey who had come to the water line to look for shellfish told her. "His cerebrum has been surgically divided; it's in his file." It was a young monkey, with a trusting face full of small, ugly beauties.

Nicholas snapped, "It's in my head."

Diane said, "I'd think it would kill you, or make you an idiot or something."

"They say each half of me is about as smart as both of us were together. Anyway, this half is . . . the half . . . the *me* that talks."

"There are two of you now?"

"If you cut a worm in half and both parts are still alive, that's two, isn't it? What else would you call us? We can't ever come together again."

"But I'm talking to just one of you?"

"We both can hear you."

"Which one answers?"

Nicholas touched the right side of his chest with his right hand. "Me; I do. They told me it was the left side of my brain, that one has the speech centers, but it doesn't feel that way; the nerves cross over coming out, and it's just the right side of me, I talk. Both my ears hear for both of us, but out of each eye we only see half and half—I mean, I only see what's on the right of what I'm looking at, and the other side, I guess, only sees the left, so that's why I keep moving my head. I guess it's like being a little bit blind; you get used to it."

The girl was still thinking of his divided body. She said, "If you're only half, I don't see how you can walk."

"I can move the left side a little bit, and we're not mad at each other. We're not supposed to be able to come together at all, but we do—down through the legs and at the ends of the fingers and then back up. Only I can't talk with my other side because he can't, but he understands."

"Why did they do it?"

Behind them the monkey, who had been following them, said, "He had uncontrollable seizures."

"Did you?" the girl asked. She was watching a sea bird swooping low over the water and did not seem to care.

Nicholas picked up a shell and shied it at the monkey, who skipped out of the way. After half a minute's silence he said, "I had visions."

"Ooh, did you?"

"They didn't like that. They said I would fall down and jerk around horrible, and sometimes I guess I would hurt myself when I fell, and sometimes I'd bite my tongue and it would bleed. But that wasn't what it felt like to me; I wouldn't know about any of those things until afterward. To me it was like I had gone way far ahead, and I had to come back. I didn't want to."

The wind swayed Diane's hair, and she pushed it back from her face. "Did you see things that were going to happen?" she asked.

"Sometimes."

"Really? Did you?"

"Sometimes."

"Tell me about it. When you saw what was going to happen."

"I saw myself dead. I was all black and shrunk up like the dead stuff they cut off in the 'pontic gardens; and I was floating and turning, like in water but it wasn't water—just floating and turning out in space, in nothing. And there were lights on both sides of me, so both sides were bright but black, and I could see my teeth because the stuff"—he pulled at his cheeks—"had fallen off there, and they were really white."

"That hasn't happened yet."

"Not here."

"Tell me something you saw that happened."

"You mean, like somebody's sister was going to get married, don't you? That's what the girls where I was mostly wanted to know. Or were they going to go home; mostly it wasn't like that."

"But sometimes it was?"

"I guess."

"Tell me one."

Nicholas shook his head. "You wouldn't like it, and anyway it wasn't like that. Mostly it was lights like I never saw anyplace else, and voices like I never heard any other time, telling me things there aren't any words for; stuff like that, only now I can't ever go back. Listen, I wanted to ask you about Ignacio."

"He isn't anybody," the girl said.

"What do you mean, he isn't anybody? Is there anybody here besides you and me and Ignacio and Dr. Island?"

"Not that we can see or touch."

The monkey called, "There are other patients, but for the present, Nicholas, for your own well-being as well as theirs, it is best for you to remain by yourselves." It was a long sentence for a monkey.

"What's that about?"

"If I tell you, will you tell me about something you saw that really happened?"

"All right."

"Tell me first."

"There was this girl where I was—her name was Maya. They had, you know, boys' and girls' dorms, but you saw everybody in the rec room and the dining hall and so on, and she was in my psychodrama group." Her hair had been black, and shiny as the lacquered furniture in Dr. Hong's rooms, her skin white like mother-of-pearl, her eyes long and narrow (making him think of cats' eyes) and darkly blue. She was fifteen, or so Nicholas believed— maybe sixteen. *"I'm going home,"* she told him. It was psychodrama, and he was her brother, younger than she, and she was already at home; but when she said this the floating ring of light that gave them the necessary separation from the small doctor-and-patient audience, ceased, by instant agreement, to be Maya's mother's living room and became a visiting lounge. Nicholas/Jerry said: "Hey, that's great! Hey, I got a new bike—when you come home you want to ride it?"

Maureen/Maya's mother said, "Maya, don't. You'll run into something and break your teeth, and you know how much they cost."

"You don't want me to have any fun."

"We do, dear, but *nice* fun. A girl has to be so much more careful —oh, Maya, I wish I could make you understand, really, how careful a girl has to be."

Nobody said anything, so Nicholas/Jerry filled in with, "It has a three-bladed prop, and I'm going to tape streamers to them with little weights at the ends, an' when I go down old thirty-seven B passageway, look out, here comes that old coleslaw grater!"

"Like this," Maya said, and held her legs together and extended her arms, to make a three-bladed bike prop or a crucifix. She had thrown herself into a spin as she made the movement, and revolved slowly, stage center—red shorts, white blouse, red shorts, white blouse, red shorts, no shoes.

Diane asked, "And you saw that she was never going home, she was going to hospital instead, she was going to cut her wrist there, she was going to die?"

Nicholas nodded.

"Did you tell her?"

"Yes," Nicholas said. "No."

"Make up your mind. Didn't you tell her? Now, don't get mad."

"Is it telling, when the one you tell doesn't understand?"

Diane thought about that for a few steps while Nicholas dashed water on the hot bruises Ignacio had left upon his face. "If it was plain and clear and she ought to have understood—that's the trouble I have with my family."

"What is?"

"They won't say things—do you know what I mean? I just say look, just tell me, just tell me what I'm supposed to do, tell me what it is you want, but it's different all the time. My mother says, 'Diane, you ought to meet some boys, you can't go out with him, your father and I have never met him, we don't even know his family at all, Douglas, there's something I think you ought to know about Diane, she gets confused sometimes, we've had her to doctors, she's been in a hospital, try—' "

"Not to get her excited," Nicholas finished for her.

"Were you listening? I mean, are you from the Trojan Planets? Do you know my mother?"

"I only live in these places," Nicholas said, "that's for a long time. But you talk like other people."

"I feel better now that I'm with you; you're really nice. I wish you were older."

"I'm not sure I'm going to get much older."

"It's going to rain—feel it?"

Nicholas shook his head.

"Look." Diane jumped, bunnyrabbit-clumsy, three meters into the air. "See how high I can jump? That means people are sad and it's going to rain. I told you."

"No, you didn't."

"Yes, I did, Nicholas."

He waved the argument away, struck by a sudden thought. "You ever been to Callisto?"

The girl shook her head, and Nicholas said, "I have; that's where they did the operation. It's so big the gravity's mostly from natural mass, and it's all domed in, with a whole lot of air in it."

"So?"

"And when I was there it rained. There was a big trouble at one of the generating piles, and they shut it down and it got colder and colder until everybody in the hospital wore their blankets, just like Amerinds in books, and they locked the switches off on the heaters in the bathrooms, and the nurses and the comscreen told you all the time it wasn't dangerous, they were just rationing power to keep from blacking out the important stuff that was still running. And then it rained, just like on Earth. They said it got so cold the water condensed in the air, and it was like the whole hospital was right under a shower bath. Everybody on the top floor had to come down because it rained right on their beds, and for two nights I had a man in my room with me that had his arm cut off in a machine. But we couldn't jump any higher, and it got kind of dark."

"It doesn't always get dark here," Diane said. "Sometimes the rain sparkles. I think Dr. Island must do it to cheer everyone up."

"No," the waves explained, "or at least not in the way you mean, Diane."

Nicholas was hungry and started to ask them for something to eat, then turned his hunger in against itself, spat on the sand, and was still.

"It rains here when most of you are sad," the waves were saying, "because rain is a sad thing, to the human psyche. It is that, that sadness, perhaps because it recalls to unhappy people their own tears, that palliates melancholy."

Diane said, "Well, I know sometimes I feel better when it rains."

"That should help you to understand yourself. Most people are soothed when their environment is in harmony with their emotions, and anxious when it is not. An angry person becomes less angry in a red room, and unhappy people are only exasperated by sunshine and birdsong. Do you remember:

> And, missing thee, I walk unseen
> On the dry smooth-shaven green
> To behold the wandering moon,
> Riding near her highest noon,
> Like one that had been led astray
> Through the heaven's wide pathless way?"

The girl shook her head.

Nicholas said, "No. Did somebody write that?" and then, "You said you couldn't do anything."

The waves replied, "I can't—except talk to you."

"You make it rain."

"Your heart beats; I sense its pumping even as I speak—do you control the beating of your heart?"

"I can stop my breath."

"Can you stop your heart? Honestly, Nicholas?"

"I guess not."

"No more can I control the weather of my world, stop anyone from doing what he wishes, or feed you if you are hungry; with no need of volition on my part your emotions are monitored and averaged, and our weather responds. Calm and sunshine for tranquillity, rain for melancholy, storms for rage, and so on. This is what mankind has always wanted."

Diane asked, "What is?"

"That the environment should respond to human thought. That is the core of magic and the oldest dream of mankind; and here, on me, it is fact."

"So that we'll be well?"

Nicholas said angrily, "You're not sick!"

Dr. Island said, "So that some of you, at least, can return to society."

Nicholas threw a seashell into the water as though to strike the mouth that spoke. "Why are we talking to this thing?"

"Wait, tot, I think it's interesting."

"Lies and lies."

Dr. Island said, "How do I lie, Nicholas?"

"You said it was magic—"

"No, I said that when humankind has dreamed of magic, the wish behind that dream has been the omnipotence of thought. Have you never wanted to be a magician, Nicholas, making palaces spring up overnight, or riding an enchanted horse of ebony to battle with the demons of the air?"

"I am a magician—I have preternatural powers, and before they cut us in two—"

Diane interrupted him. "You said you averaged emotions. When you made it rain."

"Yes."

"Doesn't that mean that if one person was really, terribly sad, he'd move the average so much he could make it rain all by himself? Or whatever? That doesn't seem fair."

The waves might have smiled. "That has never happened. But if it did, Diane, if one person felt such deep emotion, think how great her need would be. Don't you think we should answer it?"

Diane looked at Nicholas, but he was walking again, his head swinging, ignoring her as well as the voice of the waves. "Wait," she called. "You said I wasn't sick; I am, you know."

"No, you're not."

She hurried after him. "Everyone says so, and sometimes I'm so confused, and other times I'm boiling inside, just boiling. Mum says if you've got something on the stove you don't want to have burn, you just have to keep one finger on the handle of the pan and it won't, but I can't, I can't always find the handle or remember."

Without looking back the boy said, "Your mother is probably sick; maybe your father, too, I don't know. But you're not. If they'd just let you alone you'd be all right. Why shouldn't you get upset, having to live with two crazy people?"

"Nicholas!" She grabbed his thin shoulders. "That's not true!"

"Yes, it is."

"I am sick. Everyone says so."

"I don't; so 'everyone' just means the ones that do—isn't that right? And if you don't either, that will be two; it can't be everyone then."

The girl called, "Doctor? Dr. Island?"

Nicholas said, "You aren't going to believe that, are you?"

"Dr. Island, is it true?"

"Is what true, Diane?"

"What he said. Am I sick?"

"Sickness—even physical illness—is relative, Diane; and complete health is an idealization, an abstraction, even if the other end of the scale is not."

"You know what I mean."

"You are not physically ill." A long, blue comber curled into a line of hissing spray reaching infinitely along the sea to their left and right. "As you said yourself a moment ago, you are sometimes confused, and sometimes disturbed."

"He said if it weren't for other people, if it weren't for my mother and father, I wouldn't have to be here."

"Diane . . ."

"Well, is that true or isn't it?"

"Most emotional illness would not exist, Diane, if it were possible in every case to separate oneself—in thought as well as circumstance—if only for a time."

"Separate oneself?"

"Did you ever think of going away, at least for a time?"

The girl nodded, then as though she were not certain Dr. Island could see her, said, "Often, I suppose; leaving the school and getting my own compartment somewhere—going to Achilles. Sometimes I wanted to so badly."

"Why didn't you?"

"They would have worried. And anyway, they would have found me, and made me come home."

"Would it have done any good if I—or a human doctor—had told them not to?"

When the girl said nothing Nicholas snapped, "You could have locked them up."

"They were functioning, Nicholas. They bought and sold; they worked, and paid their taxes—"

Diane said softly, "It wouldn't have done any good anyway, Nicholas; they are inside me."

"Diane was no longer functioning: she was failing every subject at the university she attended, and her presence in her classes, when she came, disturbed the instructors and the other students. You were not functioning either, and people of your own age were afraid of you."

"That's what counts with you, then. Functioning."

"If I were different from the world, would that help you when you got back into the world?"

"You are different." Nicholas kicked the sand. "Nobody ever saw a place like this."

"You mean that reality to you is metal corridors, rooms without windows, noise."

"Yes."

"That is the unreality, Nicholas. Most people have never had to endure such things. Even now, this—my beach, my sea, my trees —is more in harmony with most human lives than your metal corridors; and here, I am your social environment—what individuals call 'they.' You see, sometimes if we take people who are troubled back to something like me, to an idealized natural setting, it helps them."

"Come on," Nicholas told the girl. He took her arm, acutely conscious of being so much shorter than she.

"A question," murmured the waves. "If Diane's parents had been taken here instead of Diane, do you think it would have helped them?"

Nicholas did not reply.

"We have treatments for disturbed persons, Nicholas. But, at least for the time being, we have no treatment for disturbing persons." Diane and the boy had turned away, and the waves' hissing and slapping ceased to be speech. Gulls wheeled overhead, and once a red-and-yellow parrot fluttered from one palm to another. A monkey running on all fours like a little dog approached them, and Nicholas chased it, but it escaped.

"I'm going to take one of those things apart someday," he said, "and pull the wires out."

"Are we going to walk all the way 'round?" Diane asked. She might have been talking to herself.

"Can you do that?"

"Oh, you can't walk all around Dr. Island; it would be too long, and you can't get there anyway. But we could walk until we get back to where we started—we're probably more than halfway now."

"Are there other islands you can't see from here?"

The girl shook her head. "I don't think so; there's just this one big island in this satellite, and all the rest is water."

"Then if there's only the one island, we're going to have to walk all around it to get back to where we started. What are you laughing at?"

"Look down the beach, as far as you can. Never mind how it slips off to the side—pretend it's straight."

"I don't see anything."

"Don't you? Watch." Diane leaped into the air, six meters or more this time, and waved her arms.

"It looks like there's somebody ahead of us, way down the beach."

"Uh-huh. Now look behind."

"Okay, there's somebody there, too. Come to think of it, I saw someone on the beach when I first got here. It seemed funny to see so far, but I guess I thought they were other patients. Now I see two people."

"They're us. That was probably yourself you saw the other time, too. There are just so many of us to each strip of beach, and Dr. Island only wants certain ones to mix. So the space bends around. When we get to one end of our strip and try to step over, we'll be at the other end."

"How did you find out?"

"Dr. Island told me about it when I first came here." The girl was silent for a moment, and her smile vanished. "Listen, Nicholas, do you want to see something really funny?"

Nicholas asked, "What?" As he spoke, a drop of rain struck his face.

"You'll see. Come on, though. We have to go into the middle instead of following the beach, and it will give us a chance to get under the trees and out of the rain."

When they had left the sand and the sound of the surf, and were walking on solid ground under green-leaved trees, Nicholas said, "Maybe we can find some fruit." They were so light now that he had to be careful not to bound into the air with each step. The rain fell slowly around them, in crystal spheres.

"Maybe," the girl said doubtfully. "Wait, let's stop here." She sat down where a huge tree sent twenty-meter wooden arches over dark, mossy ground. "Want to climb up there and see if you can find us something?"

"All right," Nicholas agreed. He jumped, and easily caught hold of a branch far above the girl's head. In a moment he was climbing in a green world, with the rain pattering all around him; he followed narrowing limbs into leafy wildernesses where the cool water ran from every twig he touched, and twice found the empty nests of birds, and once a slender snake, green as any leaf with a head as long as his thumb; but there was no fruit. "Nothing," he said, when he dropped down beside the girl once more.

"That's all right, we'll find something."

He said, "I hope so," and noticed that she was looking at him oddly, then realized that his left hand had lifted itself to touch her right breast. It dropped as he looked, and he felt his face grow hot. He said, "I'm sorry."

"That's all right."

"We like you. He—over there—he can't talk, you see. I guess I can't talk either."

"I think it's just you—in two pieces. I don't care."

"Thanks." He had picked up a leaf, dead and damp, and was

tearing it to shreds; first his right hand tearing while the left held the leaf, then turnabout. "Where does the rain come from?" The dirty flakes clung to the fingers of both.

"Hmm?"

"Where does the rain come from? I mean, it isn't because it's colder here now, like on Callisto; it's because the gravity's turned down some way, isn't it?"

"From the sea. Don't you know how this place is built?"

Nicholas shook his head.

"Didn't they show it to you from the ship when you came? It's beautiful. They showed it to me—I just sat there and looked at it, and I wouldn't talk to them, and the nurse thought I wasn't paying any attention, but I heard everything. I just didn't want to talk to her. It wasn't any use."

"I know how you felt."

"But they didn't show it to you?"

"No, on my ship they kept me locked up because I burned some stuff. They thought I couldn't start a fire without an igniter, but if you have electricity in the wall sockets, it's easy. They had a thing on me—you know?" He clasped his arms to his body to show how he had been restrained. "I bit one of them, too—I guess I didn't tell you that yet: I bite people. They locked me up, and for a long time I had nothing to do, and then I could feel us dock with something, and they came and got me and pulled me down a regular companionway for a long time, and it just seemed like a regular place. Then they stuck me full of Tranquil-C—I guess they didn't know it doesn't hardly work on me at all—with a pneumo-gun, and lifted a kind of door thing and shoved me up."

"Didn't they make you undress?"

"I already was. When they put the ties on me I did things in my clothes and they had to take them off me. It made them mad." He grinned unevenly. "Does Tranquil-C work on you? Or any of that other stuff?"

"I suppose they would, but then I never do the sort of thing you do anyway."

"Maybe you ought to."

"Sometimes they used to give me medication that was supposed to cheer me up; then I couldn't sleep, and I walked and walked, you know, and ran into things and made a lot of trouble for everyone; but what good does it do?"

Nicholas shrugged. "Not doing it doesn't do any good either—I mean, we're both here. My way, I know I've made them jump; they shoot that stuff in me and I'm not mad any more, but I know what it is and I just think what I would do if I *were* mad, and I do it, and when it wears off I'm glad I did."

"I think you're still angry somewhere, deep down."

Nicholas was already thinking of something else. "This island says Ignacio kills people." He paused. "What does it look like?"

"Ignacio?"

"No, I've seen him. Dr. Island."

"Oh, you mean when I was in the ship. The satellite's round of course, and all clear except where Dr. Island is, so that's a dark spot. The rest of it's temperglass, and from space you can't even see the water."

"That *is* the sea up there, isn't it?" Nicholas asked, trying to look up at it through the tree leaves and the rain. "I thought it was when I first came."

"Sure. It's like a glass ball, and we're inside, and the water's inside, too, and just goes all around up the curve."

"That's why I could see so far out on the beach, isn't it? Instead of dropping down from you like on Callisto it bends up so you can see it."

The girl nodded. "And the water lets the light through, but filters out the ultraviolet. Besides, it gives us thermal mass, so we don't heat up too much when we're between the sun and the Bright Spot."

"Is that what keeps us warm? The Bright Spot?"

Diane nodded again. "We go around in ten hours, you see, and that holds us over it all the time."

"Why can't I see it, then? It ought to look like Sol does from the

Belt, only bigger; but there's just a shimmer in the sky, even when it's not raining."

"The waves diffract the light and break up the image. You'd see the Focus, though, if the air weren't so clear. Do you know what the Focus is?"

Nicholas shook his head.

"We'll get to it pretty soon, after this rain stops. Then I'll tell you."

"I still don't understand about the rain."

Unexpectedly, Diane giggled. "I just thought—do you know what I was supposed to be? While I was going to school?"

"Quiet," Nicholas said.

"No, silly. I mean what I was being trained to do, if I graduated and all that. I was going to be a teacher, with all those cameras on me and tots from everywhere watching and popping questions on the two-way. Jolly time. Now I'm doing it here, only there's no one but you."

"You mind?"

"No, I suppose I enjoy it." There was a black-and-blue mark on Diane's thigh, and she rubbed it pensively with one hand as she spoke. "Anyway, there are three ways to make gravity. Do you know them? Answer, clerk."

"Sure; acceleration, mass, and synthesis."

"That's right; motion and mass are both bendings of space, of course, which is why Zeno's paradox doesn't work out that way, and why masses move toward each other—what we call falling— or at least try to; and if they're held apart it produces the tension we perceive as a force and call weight and all that rot. So naturally if you bend the space direct, you synthesize a gravity effect, and that's what holds all that water up against the translucent shell— there's nothing like enough mass to do it by itself."

"You mean"—Nicholas held out his hand to catch a slow-moving globe of rain—"that this is water from the sea?"

"Right-o, up on top. Do you see, the temperature differences in the air make the winds, and the winds make the waves and surf you saw when we were walking along the shore. When the waves break they throw up these little drops, and if you watch you'll see that even when it's clear they go up a long way sometimes. Then if the gravity is less they can get away altogether, and if we were on the outside they'd fly off into space; but we aren't, we're inside, so all they can do is go across the center, more or less, until they hit the water again, or Dr. Island."

"Dr. Island said they had storms sometimes, when people got mad."

"Yes. Lots of wind, and so there's lots of rain, too. Only the rain then is because the wind tears the tops off the waves, and you don't get light like you do in a normal rain."

"What makes so much wind?"

"I don't know. It happens somehow."

They sat in silence, Nicholas listening to the dripping of the leaves. He remembered then that they had spun the hospital module, finally, to get the little spheres of clotting blood out of the air; Maya's blood was building up on the grills of the purification intake ducts, spotting them black, and someone had been afraid they would decay there and smell. He had not been there when they did it, but he could imagine the droplets settling, like this, in the slow spin. The old psychodrama group had already been broken up, and when he saw Maureen or any of the others in the rec room they talked about Good Old Days. It had not seemed like Good Old Days then except that Maya had been there.

Diane said, "It's going to stop."

"It looks just as bad to me."

"No, it's going to stop—see, they're falling a little faster now, and I feel heavier."

Nicholas stood up. "You rested enough yet? You want to go on?"

"We'll get wet."

He shrugged.

"I don't want to get my hair wet, Nicholas. It'll be over in a minute."

He sat down again. "How long have you been here?"

"I'm not sure."

"Don't you count the days?"

"I lose track a lot."

"Longer than a week?"

"Nicholas, don't ask me, all right?"

"Isn't there anybody on this piece of Dr. Island except you and me and Ignacio?"

"I don't think there was anyone but Ignacio before you came."

"Who is he?"

She looked at him.

"Well, who is he? You know me—us—Nicholas Kenneth de Vore; and you're Diane who?"

"Phillips."

"And you're from the Trojan Planets, and I was from the Outer Belt, I guess, to start with. What about Ignacio? You talk to him sometimes, don't you? Who is he?"

"I don't know. He's important."

For an instant, Nicholas froze. "What does that mean?"

"Important." The girl was feeling her knees, running her hands back and forth across them.

"Maybe everybody's important."

"I know you're just a tot, Nicholas, but don't be so stupid. Come on, you wanted to go, let's go now. It's pretty well stopped." She stood, stretching her thin body, her arms over her head. "My knees are rough—you made me think of that. When I came here they were still so smooth, I think. I used to put a certain lotion on them. Because my Dad would feel them, and my hands and elbows, too, and he'd say if they weren't smooth nobody'd ever want me; Mum wouldn't say anything, but she'd be cross after, and they used to come and visit, and so I kept a bottle in my room and I used to put it on. Once I drank some."

Nicholas was silent.

"Aren't you going to ask me if I died?" She stepped ahead of him, pulling aside the dripping branches. "See here, I'm sorry I said you were stupid."

"I'm just thinking," Nicholas said. "I'm not mad at you. Do you really know anything about him?"

"No, but look at it." She gestured. "Look around you; someone *built* all this."

"You mean it cost a lot."

"It's automated, of course, but still . . . well, the other places where you were before—how much space was there for each patient? Take the total volume and divide it by the number of people there."

"Okay, this is a whole lot bigger, but maybe they think we're worth it."

"Nicholas . . ." She paused. "Nicholas, Ignacio is homicidal. Didn't Dr. Island tell you?"

"Yes."

"And you're fourteen and not very big for it, and I'm a girl. Who are they worried about?"

The look on Nicholas's face startled her.

After an hour or more of walking they came to it. It was a band of withered vegetation, brown and black and tumbling, and as straight as if it had been drawn with a ruler. "I was afraid it wasn't going to be here," Diane said. "It moves around whenever there's a storm. It might not have been in our sector any more at all."

Nicholas asked. "What is it?"

"The Focus. It's been all over, but mostly the plants grow back quickly when it's gone."

"It smells funny—like the kitchen in a place where they wanted me to work in the kitchen once."

"Vegetables rotting, that's what that is. What did you do?"

"Nothing—put detergent in the stuff they were cooking. What makes this?"

"The Bright Spot. See, when it's just about overhead the curve of the sky and the water up there make a lens. It isn't a very good lens—a lot of the light scatters. But enough is focused to do this. It wouldn't fry us if it came past right now, if that's what you're wondering, because it's not that hot. I've stood right in it, but you want to get out in a minute."

"I thought it was going to be about seeing ourselves down the beach."

Diane seated herself on the trunk of a fallen tree. "It was, really. The last time I was here it was further from the water, and I suppose it had been there a long time, because it had cleared out a lot of the dead stuff. The sides of the sector are nearer here, you see; the whole sector narrows down like a piece of pie. So you could look down the Focus either way and see yourself nearer than you could on the beach. It was almost as if you were in a big, big room, with a looking-glass on each wall, or as if you could stand behind yourself. I thought you might like it."

"I'm going to try it here," Nicholas announced, and he clambered up one of the dead trees while the girl waited below, but the dry limbs creaked and snapped beneath his feet, and he could not get high enough to see himself in either direction. When he dropped to the ground beside her again, he said, "There's nothing to eat here either, is there?"

"I haven't found anything."

"They—I mean, Dr. Island wouldn't just let us starve, would he?"

"I don't think he could do anything; that's the way this place is built. Sometimes you find things, and I've tried to catch fish, but I never could. A couple of times Ignacio gave me part of what he had, though; he's good at it. I bet you think I'm skinny, don't you? But I was a lot fatter when I came here."

"What are we going to do now?"

"Keep walking, I suppose, Nicholas. Maybe go back to the water."

"Do you think we'll find anything?"

From a decaying log, insect stridulations called, "Wait."

Nicholas asked, "Do *you* know where anything is?"

"Something for you to eat? Not at present. But I can show you something much more interesting, not far from here, than this clutter of dying trees. Would you like to see it?"

Diane said, "Don't go, Nicholas."

"What is it?"

"Diane, who calls this 'the Focus,' calls what I wish to show you 'the Point.' "

Nicholas asked Diane, "Why shouldn't I go?"

"I'm not going. I went there once anyway."

"I took her," Dr. Island said. "And I'll take you. I wouldn't take you if I didn't think it might help you."

"I don't think Diane liked it."

"Diane may not wish to be helped—help may be painful, and often people do not. But it is my business to help them if I can, whether or not they wish it."

"Suppose I don't want to go?"

"Then I cannot compel you; you know that. But you will be the only patient in this sector who has not seen it, Nicholas, as well as the youngest; both Diane and Ignacio have, and Ignacio goes there often."

"Is it dangerous?"

"No. Are you afraid?"

Nicholas looked questioningly at Diane. "What is it? What will I see?"

She had walked away while he was talking to Dr. Island, and was now sitting cross-legged on the ground about five meters from where Nicholas stood, staring at her hands. Nicholas repeated, "What will I see, Diane?" He did not think she would answer.

She said, "A glass. A mirror."

"Just a mirror?"

"You know how I told you to climb the tree here? The Point is where the edges come together. You can see yourself—like on the beach—but closer."

Nicholas was disappointed. "I've seen myself in mirrors lots of times."

Dr. Island, whose voice was now in the sighing of the dead leaves, whispered, "Did you have a mirror in your room, Nicholas, before you came here?"

"A steel one."

"So that you could not break it?"

"I guess so. I threw things at it sometimes, but it just got puckers in it." Remembering dimpled reflections, Nicholas laughed.

"You can't break this one either."

"It doesn't sound like it's worth going to see."

"I think it is."

"Diane, do you still think I shouldn't go?"

There was no reply. The girl sat staring at the ground in front of her. Nicholas walked over to look at her and found a tear had washed a damp trail down each thin cheek, but she did not move when he touched her. "She's catatonic, isn't she," he said.

A green limb just outside the Focus nodded. "Catatonic schizophrenia."

"I had a doctor once that said those names—like that. They didn't mean anything." (The doctor had been a therapy robot, but a human doctor gave more status. Robots' patients sat in doorless booths—two and a half hours a day for Nicholas: an hour and a half in the morning, an hour in the afternoon—and talked to something that appeared to be a small, friendly food freezer. Some people sat every day in silence, while others talked continually, and for such patients as these the attendants seldom troubled to turn the machines on.)

"He meant cause and treatment. He was correct."

Nicholas stood looking down at the girl's streaked, brown-blond head. "What *is* the cause? I mean for her."

"I don't know."

"And what's the treatment?"

"You are seeing it."

"Will it help her?"

"Probably not."

"Listen, she can hear you, don't you know that? She hears everything we say."

"If my answer disturbs you, Nicholas, I can change it. It will help her if she wants to be helped; if she insists on clasping her illness to her it will not."

"We ought to go away from here," Nicholas said uneasily.

"To your left you will see a little path, a very faint one. Between the twisted tree and the bush with the yellow flowers."

Nicholas nodded and began to walk, looking back at Diane several times. The flowers were butterflies, who fled in a cloud of color when he approached them, and he wondered if Dr. Island had known. When he had gone a hundred paces and was well away from the brown and rotting vegetation, he said, "She was sitting in the Focus."

"Yes."

"Is she still there?"

"Yes."

"What will happen when the Bright Spot comes?"

"Diane will become uncomfortable and move, if she is still there."

"Once in one of the places I was in there was a man who was like that, and they said he wouldn't get anything to eat if he didn't get up and get it, they weren't going to feed him with the nose tube any more; and they didn't, and he died. We told them about it and they wouldn't do anything and he starved to death right there, and when he was dead they rolled him off onto a stretcher and changed the bed and put somebody else there."

"I know, Nicholas. You told the doctors at St. John's about all that, and it is in your file; but think: well men have starved themselves—yes, to death—to protest what they felt were political injustices. Is it so surprising that your friend killed himself in the same way to protest what he felt as a psychic injustice?"

"He wasn't my friend. Listen, did you really mean it when you said the treatment she was getting here would help Diane if she wanted to be helped?"

"No."

Nicholas halted in mid-stride. "You didn't mean it? You don't think it's true?"

"No. I doubt that anything will help her."

"I don't think you ought to lie to us."

"Why not? If by chance you become well you will be released, and if you are released you will have to deal with your society, which will lie to you frequently. Here, where there are so few individuals, I must take the place of society. I have explained that."

"Is that what you are?"

"Society's surrogate? Of course. Who do you imagine built me? What else could I be?"

"The doctor."

"You have had many doctors, and so has she. Not one of them has benefited you much."

"I'm not sure you even want to help us."

"Do you wish to see what Diane calls 'the Point'?"

"I guess so."

"Then you must walk. You will not see it standing here."

Nicholas walked, thrusting aside leafy branches and dangling creepers wet with rain. The jungle smelled of the life of green things; there were ants on the tree trunks, and dragonflies with hot, red bodies and wings as long as his hands. "Do you want to help us?" he asked after a time.

"My feelings toward you are ambivalent. But when you wish to be helped, I wish to help you."

The ground sloped gently upward, and as it rose became somewhat more clear, the big trees a trifle farther apart, the underbrush spent in grass and fern. Occasionally there were stone outcrops to be climbed, and clearings open to the tumbling sky. Nicholas asked, "Who made this trail?"

"Ignacio. He comes here often."

"He's not afraid, then? Diane's afraid."

"Ignacio is afraid, too, but he comes."

"Diane says Ignacio is important."

"Yes."

"What do you mean by that? Is he important? More important than we are?"

"Do you remember that I told you I was the surrogate of society? What do you think society wants, Nicholas?"

"Everybody to do what it says."

"You mean conformity. Yes, there must be conformity, but something else, too—consciousness."

"I don't want to hear about it."

"Without consciousness, which you may call sensitivity if you are careful not to allow yourself to be confused by the term, there is no progress. A century ago, Nicholas, mankind was suffocating on Earth; now it is suffocating again. About half of the people who have contributed substantially to the advance of humanity have shown signs of emotional disturbance."

"I told you, I don't want to hear about it. I asked you an easy question—is Ignacio more important than Diane and me—and you won't tell me. I've heard all this you're saying. I've heard it fifty, maybe a hundred times from everybody, and it's lies; it's the regular thing, and you've got it written down on a card somewhere to read out when anybody asks. Those people you talk about that went crazy, they went crazy because while they were 'advancing humanity,' or whatever you call it, people kicked them out of their rooms because they couldn't pay, and while they were getting thrown out you were making other people rich that had never done anything in their whole lives except think about how to get that way."

"Sometimes it is hard, Nicholas, to determine before the fact—or even at the time—just who should be honored."

"How do you know if you've never tried?"

"You asked if Ignacio was more important than Diane or yourself. I can only say that Ignacio seems to me to hold a brighter promise of a full recovery coupled with a substantial contribution to human progress."

"If he's so good, why did he crack up?"

"Many do, Nicholas. Even among the inner planets space is not a kind environment for mankind; and our space, trans-Martian space, is worse. Any young person here, anyone like yourself or Diane who would seem to have a better-than-average chance of adapting to the conditions we face, is precious."

"Or Ignacio."

"Yes, or Ignacio. Ignacio has a tested IQ of two hundred and ten, Nicholas. Diane's is one hundred and twenty. Your own is ninety-five."

"They never took mine."

"It's on your records, Nicholas."

"They tried to and I threw down the helmet and it broke; Sister Carmela—she was the nurse—just wrote down something on the paper and sent me back."

"I see. I will ask for a complete investigation of this, Nicholas."

"Sure."

"Don't you believe me?"

"I don't think you believed me."

"Nicholas, Nicholas . . ." The long tongues of grass now beginning to appear beneath the immense trees sighed. "Can't you see that a certain measure of trust between the two of us is essential?"

"Did you believe me?"

"Why do you ask? Suppose I were to say I did; would you believe that?"

"When you told me I had been reclassified."

"You would have to be retested, for which there are no facilities here."

"If you believed me, why did you say retested? I told you I haven't ever been tested at all—but anyway you could cross out the ninety-five."

"It is impossible for me to plan your therapy without some estimate of your intelligence, Nicholas, and I have nothing with which to replace it."

The ground was sloping up more sharply now, and in a clearing the boy halted and turned to look back at the leafy film, like algae over a pool, beneath which he had climbed, and at the sea beyond. To his right and left his view was still hemmed with foliage, and ahead of him a meadow on edge (like the square of sand through which he had come, though he did not think of that), dotted still with trees, stretched steeply toward an invisible summit. It seemed to him that under his feet the mountainside swayed ever so slightly. Abruptly he demanded of the wind, "Where's Ignacio?"

"Not here. Much closer to the beach."

"And Diane?"

"Where you left her. Do you enjoy the panorama?"

"It's pretty, but it feels like we're rocking."

"We are. I am moored to the temperglass exterior of our satellite by two hundred cables, but the tide and the currents none the less impart a slight motion to my body. Naturally this movement is magnified as you go higher."

"I thought you were fastened right onto the hull; if there's water under you, how do people get in and out?"

"I am linked to the main air lock by a communication tube. To you when you came, it probably seemed an ordinary companionway."

Nicholas nodded and turned his back on leaves and sea and began to climb again.

"You are in a beautiful spot, Nicholas; do you open your heart to beauty?" After waiting for an answer that did not come, the wind sang:

> "The mountain wooded to the peak, the lawns
> And winding glades high up like ways to Heaven,
> The slender coco's drooping crown of plumes,
> The lightning flash of insect and of bird,
> The lustre of the long convolvuluses
> That coil'd around the stately stems, and ran
> Ev'n to the limit of the land, the glows
> And glories of the broad belt of the world,
> All these he saw."

"Does this mean nothing to you, Nicholas?"

"You read a lot, don't you?"

"Often, when it is dark, everyone else is asleep and there is very little else for me to do."

"You talk like a woman; are you a woman?"

"How could I be a woman?"

"You know what I mean. Except, when you were talking mostly to Diane, you sounded more like a man."

"You haven't yet said you think me beautiful."

"You're an Easter egg."

"What do you mean by that, Nicholas?"

"Never mind." He saw the egg as it had hung in the air before him, shining with gold and covered with flowers.

"Eggs are dyed with pretty colors for Easter, and my colors are beautiful—is that what you mean, Nicholas?"

His mother had brought the egg on visiting day, but she could never have made it. Nicholas knew who must have made it. The gold was that very pure gold used for shielding delicate instruments; the clear flakes of crystallized carbon that dotted the egg's surface with tiny stars could only have come from a laboratory high-pressure furnace. How angry he must have been when she told him she was going to give it to him.

"It's pretty, isn't it, Nicky?"

It hung in the weightlessness between them, turning very slowly with the memory of her scented gloves.

"The flowers are meadowsweet, fraxinella, lily of the valley, and moss rose—though I wouldn't expect you to recognize them, darling." His mother had never been below the orbit of Mars, but she pretended to have spent her girlhood on Earth; each reference to the lie filled Nicholas with inexpressible fury and shame. The egg was about twenty centimeters long and it revolved, end over end, in some small fraction more than eight of the pulse beats he felt in his cheeks. Visiting time had twenty-three minutes to go.

"Aren't you going to look at it?"

"I can see it from here." He tried to make her understand. "I can see every part of it. The little red things are aluminum oxide crystals, right?"

"I mean, look *inside*, Nicky."

He saw then that there was a lens at one end, disguised as a dewdrop in the throat of an asphodel. Gently he took the egg in his hands, closed one eye, and looked. The light of the interior was not, as he had half-expected, gold-tinted, but brilliantly white, deriving from some concealed source. A world surely meant for Earth shone within, as though seen from below the orbit of the moon—indigo sea and emerald land. Rivers brown and clear as tea ran down long plains.

His mother said, "Isn't it pretty?"

Night hung at the corners in funereal purple, and sent long shadows like cold and lovely arms to caress the day; and while he watched and it fell, long-necked birds of so dark a pink that they were nearly red trailed stilt legs across the sky, their wings making crosses.

"They are called flamingos," Dr. Island said, following the direction of his eyes. "Isn't it a pretty word? For a pretty bird, but I don't think we'd like them as much if we called them sparrows, would we?"

His mother said, "I'm going to take it home and keep it for you. It's too nice to leave with a little boy, but if you ever come home again it will be waiting for you. On your dresser, beside your hairbrushes."

Nicholas said, "Words just mix you up."

"You shouldn't despise them, Nicholas. Besides having great beauty of their own, they are useful in reducing tension. You might benefit from that."

"You mean you talk yourself out of it."

"I mean that a person's ability to verbalize his feelings, if only to himself, may prevent them from destroying him. Evolution teaches us, Nicholas, that the original purpose of language was to ritualize men's threats and curses, his spells to compel the gods; communication came later. Words can be a safety valve."

Nicholas said, "I want to be a bomb; a bomb doesn't need a safety valve." To his mother, "Is that South America, Mama?"

"No, dear, India. The Malabar Coast on your left, the Coromandel Coast on your right, and Ceylon below." Words.

"A bomb destroys itself, Nicholas."

"A bomb doesn't care."

He was climbing resolutely now, his toes grabbing at tree roots and the soft, mossy soil; his physician was no longer the wind but a small brown monkey that followed a stone's throw behind him. "I hear someone coming," he said.

"Yes."

"Is it Ignacio?"

"No, it is Nicholas. You are close now."

"Close to the Point?"

"Yes."

He stopped and looked around him. The sounds he had heard, the naked feet padding on soft ground, stopped as well. Nothing seemed strange; the land still rose, and there were large trees, widely spaced, with moss growing in their deepest shade, grass where there was more light. "The three big trees," Nicholas said, "they're just alike. Is that how you know where we are?"

"Yes."

In his mind he called the one before him "Ceylon"; the others were "Coromandel" and "Malabar." He walked toward Ceylon, studying its massive, twisted limbs; a boy naked as himself walked out of the forest to his left, toward Malabar—this boy was not looking at Nicholas, who shouted and ran toward him.

The boy disappeared. Only Malabar, solid and real, stood before Nicholas; he ran to it, touched its rough bark with his hand, and then saw beyond it a fourth tree, similar, too, to the Ceylon tree, around which a boy peered with averted head. Nicholas watched him for a moment, then said, "I see."

"Do you?" the monkey chattered.

"It's like a mirror, only backwards. The light from the front of me goes out and hits the edge, and comes in the other side, only I can't see it because I'm not looking that way. What I see is the light from my back, sort of, because it comes back this way. When

I ran, did I get turned around?"

"Yes, you ran out the left side of the segment, and of course returned immediately from the right."

"I'm not scared. It's kind of fun." He picked up a stick and threw it as hard as he could toward the Malabar tree. It vanished, whizzed over his head, vanished again, slapped the back of his legs. "Did this scare Diane?"

There was no answer. He strode farther, palely naked boys walking to his left and right, but always looking away from him, gradually coming closer.

"Don't go farther," Dr. Island said behind him. "It can be dangerous if you try to pass through the Point itself."

"I see it," Nicholas said. He saw three more trees, growing very close together, just ahead of him; their branches seemed strangely intertwined as they danced together in the wind, and beyond them there was nothing at all.

"You can't actually go through the Point," Dr. Island Monkey said. "The tree covers it."

"Then why did you warn me about it?" Limping and scarred, the boys to his right and left were no more than two meters away now; he had discovered that if he looked straight ahead he could sometimes glimpse their bruised profiles.

"That's far enough, Nicholas."

"I want to touch the tree."

He took another step, and another, then turned. The Malabar boy turned, too, presenting his narrow back, on which the ribs and spine seemed welts. Nicholas reached out both arms and laid his hands on the thin shoulders, and as he did, felt other hands—the cool, unfeeling hands of a stranger, dry hands too small—touch his own shoulders and creep upward toward his neck.

"Nicholas!"

He jumped sidewise away from the tree and looked at his hands, his head swaying. "It wasn't me."

"Yes, it was, Nicholas," the monkey said.

"It was one of them."

"You are all of them."

In one quick motion Nicholas snatched up an arm-long section of fallen limb and hurled it at the monkey. It struck the little creature, knocking it down, but the monkey sprang up and fled on three legs. Nicholas sprinted after it.

He had nearly caught it when it darted to one side; as quickly, he turned toward the other, springing for the monkey he saw running toward him there. In an instant it was in his grip, feebly trying to bite. He slammed its head against the ground, then catching it by the ankles swung it against the Ceylon tree until at the third impact he heard the skull crack, and stopped.

He had expected wires, but there were none. Blood oozed from the battered little face, and the furry body was warm and limp in his hands. Leaves above his head said, "You haven't killed me, Nicholas. You never will."

"How does it work?" He was still searching for wires, tiny circuit cards holding micrologic. He looked about for a sharp stone with which to open the monkey's body, but could find none.

"It is just a monkey," the leaves said. "If you had asked, I would have told you."

"How did you make him talk?" He dropped the monkey, stared at it for a moment, then kicked it. His fingers were bloody, and he wiped them on the leaves of the tree.

"Only my mind speaks to yours, Nicholas."

"Oh," he said. And then, "I've heard of that. I didn't think it would be like this. I thought it would be in my head."

"Your record shows no auditory hallucinations, but haven't you ever known someone who had them?"

"I knew a girl once . . ." He paused.

"Yes?"

"She twisted noises—you know?"

"Yes."

"Like, it would just be a service cart out in the corridor, but she'd hear the fan, and think . . ."

"What?"

"Oh, different things. That it was somebody talking, calling her."

"Hear them?"

"What?" He sat up in his bunk. "Maya?"

"They're coming after me."

"Maya?"

Dr. Island, through the leaves, said, "When I talk to you, Nicholas, your mind makes any sound you hear the vehicle for my thoughts' content. You may hear me softly in the patter of rain, or joyfully in the singing of a bird—but if I wished I could amplify what I say until every idea and suggestion I wished to give would be driven like a nail into your consciousness. Then you would do whatever I wished you to."

"I don't believe it," Nicholas said. "If you can do that, why don't you tell Diane not to be catatonic?"

"First, because she might retreat more deeply into her disease in an effort to escape me; and second, because ending her catatonia in that way would not remove its cause."

"And thirdly?"

"I did not say 'thirdly,' Nicholas."

"I thought I heard it—when two leaves touched."

"Thirdly, Nicholas, because both you and she have been chosen for your effect on someone else; if I were to change her—or you —so abruptly, that effect would be lost." Dr. Island was a monkey again now, a new monkey that chattered from the protection of a tree twenty meters away. Nicholas threw a stick at him.

"The monkeys are only little animals, Nicholas; they like to follow people, and they chatter."

"I bet Ignacio kills them."

"No, he likes them; he only kills fish to eat."

Nicholas was suddenly aware of his hunger. He began to walk.

He found Ignacio on the beach, praying. For an hour or more, Nicholas hid behind the trunk of a palm watching him, but for a long time he could not decide to whom Ignacio prayed. He was

kneeling just where the lacy edges of the breakers died, looking
out toward the water; and from time to time he bowed, touching
his forehead to the damp sand; then Nicholas could hear his voice,
faintly, over the crashing and hissing of the waves. In general,
Nicholas approved of prayer, having observed that those who
prayed were usually more interesting companions than those who
did not; but he had also noticed that though it made no difference
what name the devotee gave the object of his devotions, it was
important to discover how the god was conceived. Ignacio did not
seem to be praying to Dr. Island—he would, Nicholas thought,
have been facing the other way for that—and for a time he wondered if he were not praying to the waves. From his position
behind him he followed Ignacio's line of vision out and out, wave
upon wave into the bright, confused sky, up and up until at last
it curved completely around and came to rest on Ignacio's back
again; and then it occurred to him that Ignacio might be praying
to himself. He left the palm trunk then and walked about halfway
to the place where Ignacio knelt, and sat down. Above the sounds
of the sea and the murmuring of Ignacio's voice hung a silence so
immense and fragile that it seemed that at any moment the entire
crystal satellite might ring like a gong.

After a time Nicholas felt his left side trembling. With his right
hand he began to stroke it, running his fingers down his left arm,
and from his left shoulder to the thigh. It worried him that his left
side should be so frightened, and he wondered if perhaps that
other half of his brain, from which he was forever severed, could
hear what Ignacio was saying to the waves. He began to pray
himself, so that the other (and perhaps Ignacio, too) could hear,
saying not quite beneath his breath, "Don't worry, don't be afraid,
he's not going to hurt us, he's nice, and if he does we'll get him;
we're only going to get something to eat, maybe he'll show us how
to catch fish, I think he'll be nice this time." But he knew, or at
least felt he knew, that Ignacio would not be nice this time.

Eventually Ignacio stood up; he did not turn to face Nicholas,
but waded out to sea; then, as though he had known Nicholas was

behind him all the time (though Nicholas was not sure he had been heard—perhaps, so he thought, Dr. Island had told Ignacio), he gestured to indicate that Nicholas should follow him.

The water was colder than he remembered, the sand coarse and gritty between his toes. He thought of what Dr. Island had told him—about floating—and that a part of her must be this sand, under the water, reaching out (how far?) into the sea; when she ended there would be nothing but the clear temperglass of the satellite itself, far down.

"Come," Ignacio said. "Can you swim?" Just as though he had forgotten the night before. Nicholas said yes, he could, wondering if Ignacio would look around at him when he spoke. He did not.

"And do you know why you are here?"

"You told me to come."

"Ignacio means *here*. Does this not remind you of any place you have seen before, little one?"

Nicholas thought of the crystal gong and the Easter egg, then of the microthin globes of perfumed vapor that, at home, were sometimes sent floating down the corridors at Christmas to explode in clean dust and a cold smell of pine forests when the children struck them with their hopping-canes; but he said nothing.

Ignacio continued, "Let Ignacio tell you a story. Once there was a man—a boy, actually—on the Earth, who—"

Nicholas wondered why it was always men (most often doctors and clinical psychologists, in his experience) who wanted to tell you stories. Jesus, he recalled, was always telling everyone stories, and the Virgin Mary almost never, though a woman he had once known who thought she was the Virgin Mary had always been talking about her son. He thought Ignacio looked a little like Jesus. He tried to remember if his mother had ever told him stories when he was at home, and decided that she had not; she just turned on the comscreen to the cartoons.

"—wanted to—"

"—tell a story," Nicholas finished for him.

"How did you know?" Angry and surprised.

"It was you, wasn't it? And you want to tell one now."

"What you said was not what Ignacio would have said. He was going to tell you about a fish."

"Where is it?" Nicholas asked, thinking of the fish Ignacio had been eating the night before, and imagining another such fish, caught while he had been coming back, perhaps, from the Point, and now concealed somewhere waiting the fire. "Is it a big one?"

"It is gone now," Ignacio said, "but it was only as long as a man's hand. I caught it in the big river."

Huckleberry—"I know, the Mississippi; it was a catfish. Or a sunfish."—*Finn*.

"Possibly that is what you call them; for a time he was as the sun to a certain one." The light from nowhere danced on the water. "In any event he was kept on that table in the salon in the house where life was lived. In a tank, but not the old kind in which one sees the glass, with metal at the corner. But the new kind in which the glass is so strong, but very thin, and curved so that it does not reflect, and there are no corners, and a clever device holds the water clear." He dipped up a handful of sparkling water, still not meeting Nicholas's eyes. "As clear even as this, and there were no ripples, and so you could not see it at all. My fish floated in the center of my table above a few stones."

Nicholas asked, "Did you float on the river on a raft?"

"No, we had a little boat. Ignacio caught this fish in a net, of which he almost bit through the strands before he could be landed; he possessed wonderful teeth. There was no one in the house but him and the other, and the robots; but each morning someone would go to the pool in the patio and catch a goldfish for him. Ignacio would see this goldfish there when he came down for his breakfast, and would think, 'Brave goldfish, you have been cast to the monster, will you be the one to destroy him? Destroy him and you shall have his diamond house forever.' And then the fish, who had a little spot of red beneath his wonderful teeth, a spot like a cherry, would rush upon that young goldfish, and for an instant the water would be all clouded with blood."

"And then what?" Nicholas asked.

"And then the clever machine would make the water clear once more, and the fish would be floating above the stones as before, the fish with the wonderful teeth, and Ignacio would touch the little switch on the table, and ask for more bread, and more fruit."

"Are you hungry now?"

"No, I am tired and lazy now; if I pursue you I will not catch you, and if I catch you—through your own slowness and clumsiness— I will not kill you, and if I kill you I will not eat you."

Nicholas had begun to back away, and at the last words, realizing that they were a signal, he turned and began to run, splashing through the shallow water. Ignacio ran after him, much helped by his longer legs, his hair flying behind his dark young face, his square teeth—each white as a bone and as big as Nicholas's thumbnail—showing like spectators who lined the railings of his lips.

"Don't run, Nicholas," Dr. Island said with the voice of a wave. "It only makes him angry that you run." Nicholas did not answer, but cut to his left, up the beach and among the trunks of the palms, sprinting all the way because he had no way of knowing Ignacio was not right behind him, about to grab him by the neck. When he stopped it was in the thick jungle, among the boles of the hardwoods, where he leaned, out of breath, the thumping of his own heart the only sound in an atmosphere silent and unwaked as Earth's long, prehuman day. For a time he listened for any sound Ignacio might make searching for him; there was none. He drew a deep breath then and said, "Well, that's over," expecting Dr. Island to answer from somewhere; there was only the green hush.

The light was still bright and strong and nearly shadowless, but some interior sense told him the day was nearly over, and he noticed that such faint shades as he could see stretched long, horizontal distortions of their objects. He felt no hunger, but he had fasted before and knew on which side of hunger he stood; he was not as strong as he had been only a day past, and by this time next day he would probably be unable to outrun Ignacio. He should, he now realized, have eaten the monkey he had killed; but his stomach revolted at the thought of the raw flesh, and he did not know how he might build a fire, although Ignacio seemed to have done so the night before. Raw fish, even if he were able to catch a fish, would be as bad, or worse, than raw monkey; he remembered his effort to open a coconut—he had failed, but it was surely not impossible. His mind was hazy as to what a coconut might contain, but there had to be an edible core, because they were eaten in books. He decided to make a wide sweep through the jungle that would bring him back to the beach well away from Ignacio; he had several times seen coconuts lying in the sand under the trees.

He moved quietly, still a little afraid, trying to think of ways to open the coconut when he found it. He imagined himself standing before a large and raggedly faceted stone, holding the coconut in both hands. He raised it and smashed it down, but when it struck it was no longer a coconut but Maya's head; he heard her nose cartilage break with a distinct, rubbery snap. Her eyes, as blue as the sky above Madhya Pradesh, the sparkling blue sky of the egg, looked up at him, but he could no longer look into them, they retreated from his own, and it came to him quite suddenly that Lucifer, in falling, must have fallen up, into the fires and the coldness of space, never again to see the warm blues and browns and greens of Earth: *I was watching Satan fall as lightning from heaven.* He had heard that on tape somewhere, but he could not remember where. He had read that on Earth lightning did not come down from the clouds, but leaped up from the planetary surface toward them, never to return.

"Nicholas."

He listened, but did not hear his name again. Faintly water was babbling; had Dr. Island used that sound to speak to him? He walked toward it and found a little rill that threaded a way among the trees, and followed it. In a hundred steps it grew broader, slowed, and ended in a long blind pool under a dome of leaves.

Diane was sitting on moss on the side opposite him; she looked up as she saw him, and smiled.

"Hello," he said.

"Hello, Nicholas. I thought I heard you. I wasn't mistaken after all, was I?"

"I didn't think I said anything." He tested the dark water with his foot and found that it was very cold.

"You gave a little gasp, I fancy. I heard it, and I said to myself, *that's Nicholas,* and I called you. Then I thought I might be wrong, or that it might be Ignacio."

"Ignacio was chasing me. Maybe he still is, but I think he's probably given up by now."

The girl nodded, looking into the dark waters of the pool, but did not seem to have heard him. He began to work his way around to her, climbing across the snakelike roots of the crowding trees. "Why does Ignacio want to kill me, Diane?"

"Sometimes he wants to kill me, too," the girl said.

"But why?"

"I think he's a bit frightened of us. Have you ever talked to him, Nicholas?"

"Today I did a little. He told me a story about a pet fish he used to have."

"Ignacio grew up all alone; did he tell you that? On Earth. On a plantation in Brazil, way up the Amazon—Dr. Island told me."

"I thought it was crowded on Earth."

"The cities are crowded, and the countryside closest to the cities. But there are places where it's emptier than it used to be. Where Ignacio was, there would have been Red Indian hunters two or three hundred years ago; when he was there, there wasn't anyone, just the machines. Now he doesn't want to be looked at, doesn't want anyone around him."

Nicholas said slowly, "Dr. Island said lots of people wouldn't be sick if only there weren't other people around all the time. Remember that?"

"Only there are other people around all the time; that's how the world is."

"Not in Brazil, maybe," Nicholas said. He was trying to remember something about Brazil, but the only thing he could think of was a parrot singing in a straw hat from the comview cartoons; and then a turtle and a hedgehog that turned into armadillos for the love of God, Montressor. He said, "Why didn't he stay there?"

"Did I tell you about the bird, Nicholas?" She had been notlistening again.

"What bird?"

"I have a bird. Inside." She patted the flat stomach below her small breasts, and for a moment Nicholas thought she had really found food. "She sits in here. She has tangled a nest in my entrails, where she sits and tears at my breath with her beak. I look healthy to you, don't I? But inside I'm hollow and rotten and turning brown, dirt and old feathers, oozing away. Her beak will break through soon."

"Okay." Nicholas turned to go.

"I've been drinking water here, trying to drown her. I think I've swallowed so much I couldn't stand up now if I tried, but she isn't even wet, and do you know something, Nicholas? I've found out I'm not really me, I'm her."

Turning back Nicholas asked, "When was the last time you had anything to eat?"

"I don't know. Two, three days ago. Ignacio gave me something."

"I'm going to try to open a coconut. If I can I'll bring you back some."

When he reached the beach, Nicholas turned and walked slowly back in the direction of the dead fire, this time along the rim of dampened sand between the sea and the palms. He was thinking about machines.

There were hundreds of thousands, perhaps millions, of machines out beyond the belt, but few or none of the sophisticated servant robots of Earth—those were luxuries. Would Ignacio, in

Brazil (whatever that was like), have had such luxuries? Nicholas thought not; those robots were almost like people, and living with them would be like living with people. Nicholas wished that he could speak Brazilian.

There had been the therapy robots at St. John's; Nicholas had not liked them, and he did not think Ignacio would have liked them either. If he had liked his therapy robot he probably would not have had to be sent here. He thought of the chipped and rusted old machine that had cleaned the corridors—Maya had called it Corradora, but no one else ever called it anything but *Hey!* It could not (or at least did not) speak, and Nicholas doubted that it had emotions, except possibly a sort of love of cleanliness that did not extend to its own person. "You will understand," someone was saying inside his head, "that motives of all sorts can be divided into two sorts." A doctor? A therapy robot? It did not matter. "Extrinsic and intrinsic. An extrinsic motive has always some further end in view, and that end we call an intrinsic motive. Thus when we have reduced motivation to intrinsic motivation we have reduced it to its simplest parts. Take that machine over there."

What machine?

"Freud would have said that it was fixated at the latter anal stage, perhaps due to the care its builders exercised in seeing that the dirt it collects is not released again. Because of its fixation it is, as you see, obsessed with cleanliness and order; compulsive sweeping and scrubbing palliate its anxieties. It is a strength of Freud's theory, and not a weakness, that it serves to explain many of the activities of machines as well as the acts of persons."

Hello there, Corradora.

And hello, Ignacio.

My head, moving from side to side, must remind you of a radar scanner. My steps are measured, slow, and precise. I emit a scarcely audible humming as I walk, and my eyes are fixed, as I swing my head, not on you, Ignacio; but on the waves at the edge of sight, where they curve up into the sky. I stop ten meters short of you, and I stand.

You go, I follow, ten meters behind. What do I want? Nothing.

Yes, I will pick up the sticks, and I will follow—five meters behind.

"Break them, and put them on the fire. Not all of them, just a few."

Yes.

"Ignacio keeps the fire here burning all the time. Sometimes he takes the coals of fire from it to start others, but here, under the big palm log, he has a fire always. The rain does not strike it here. Always the fire. Do you know how he made it the first time? Reply to him!"

"No."

"No, *Patrão!*"

" 'No, *Patrão.*' "

"Ignacio stole it from the gods, from Poseidon. Now Poseidon is dead, lying at the bottom of the water. Which is the top. Would you like to see him?"

"If you wish it, *Patrão.*"

"It will soon be dark, and that is the time to fish; do you have a spear?"

"No, *Patrão.*"

"Then Ignacio will get you one."

Ignacio took a handful of the sticks and thrust the ends into the fire, blowing on them. After a moment Nicholas leaned over and blew, too, until all the sticks were blazing.

"Now we must find you some bamboo, and there is some back here. Follow me."

The light, still nearly shadowless, was dimming now, so that it seemed to Nicholas that they walked on insubstantial soil, though he could feel it beneath his feet. Ignacio stalked ahead, holding up the burning sticks until the fire seemed about to die, then pointing the ends down, allowing it to lick upward toward his hand and come to life again. There was a gentle wind blowing out toward the sea, carrying away the sound of the surf and bringing a damp coolness; and when they had been walking for several minutes, Nicholas heard in it a faint, dry, almost rhythmic rattle.

Ignacio looked back at him and said, "The music. The big stems talking; hear it?"

They found a cane a little thinner than Nicholas's wrist and piled the burning sticks around its base, then added more. When it fell, Ignacio burned through the upper end, too, making a pole about as long as Nicholas was tall, and with the edge of a seashell scraped the larger end to a point. "Now you are a fisherman," he said. Nicholas said, "Yes, *Patrão*," still careful not to meet his eyes.

"You are hungry?"

"Yes, *Patrão*."

"Then let me tell you something. Whatever you get is Ignacio's, you understand? And what he catches, that is his, too. But when he has eaten what he wants, what is left is yours. Come on now, and Ignacio will teach you to fish or drown you."

Ignacio's own spear was buried in the sand not far from the fire; it was much bigger than the one he had made for Nicholas. With it held across his chest he went down to the water, wading until it was waist high, then swimming, not looking to see if Nicholas was following. Nicholas found that he could swim with the spear by putting all his effort into the motion of his legs, holding the spear in his left hand and stroking only occasionally with his right. "You breathe," he said softly, "and watch the spear," and after that he had only to allow his head to lift from time to time.

He had thought Ignacio would begin to look for fish as soon as they were well out from the beach, but the Brazilian continued to swim, slowly but steadily, until it seemed to Nicholas that they must be a kilometer or more from land. Suddenly, as though the lights in a room had responded to a switch, the dark sea around them became an opalescent blue. Ignacio stopped, treading water and using his spear to buoy himself.

"Here," he said. "Get them between yourself and the light."

Open-eyed, he bent his face to the water, raised it again to breathe deeply, and dove. Nicholas followed his example, floating belly-down with open eyes.

All the world of dancing glitter and dark island vanished as

though he had plunged his face into a dream. Far, far below him
Jupiter displayed its broad, striped disk, marred with the spreading Bright Spot where man-made silicone enzymes had stripped
the hydrogen from methane for kindled fusion: a cancer and a
burning infant sun. Between that sun and his eyes lay invisible a
hundred thousand kilometers of space, and the temperglass shell
of the satellite; hundreds of meters of illuminated water, and in it
the spread body of Ignacio, dark against the light, still kicking
downward, his spear a pencil line of blackness in his hand.

Involuntarily Nicholas's head came up, returning to the universe of sparkling waves, aware now that what he had called
"night" was only the shadow cast by Dr. Island when Jupiter and
the Bright Spot slid beneath her. That shadow line, indetectable
in air, now lay sharp across the water behind him. He took breath
and plunged.

Almost at once a fish darted somewhere below, and his left arm
thrust the spear forward, but it was far out of reach. He swam after
it, then saw another, larger, fish farther down and dove for that,
passing Ignacio surfacing for air. The fish was too deep, and he had
used up his oxygen; his lungs aching for air, he swam up, wanting
to let go of his spear, then realizing at the last moment that he
could, that it would only bob to the surface if he released it. His
head broke water and he gasped, his heart thumping; water struck
his face and he knew again, suddenly, as though they had ceased
to exist while he was gone, the pulsebeat pounding of the waves.

Ignacio was waiting for him. He shouted, "This time you will
come with Ignacio, and he will show you the dead sea god. Then
we will fish."

Unable to speak, Nicholas nodded. He was allowed three more
breaths; then Ignacio dove and Nicholas had to follow, kicking
down until the pressure sang in his ears. Then through blue water
he saw, looming at the edge of the light, a huge mass of metal
anchored to the temperglass hull of the satellite itself; above it,
hanging lifelessly like the stem of a great vine severed from the
root, a cable twice as thick as a man's body; and on the bottom,

sprawled beside the mighty anchor, a legged god that might have
been a dead insect save that it was at least six meters long. Ignacio
turned and looked back at Nicholas to see if he understood; he did
not, but he nodded, and with the strength draining from his arms,
surfaced again.

After Ignacio brought up the first fish, they took turns on the
surface guarding their catch, and while the Bright Spot crept
beneath the shelving rim of Dr. Island, they speared two more,
one of them quite large. Then when Nicholas was so exhausted he
could scarcely lift his arms, they made their way back to shore, and
Ignacio showed him how to gut the fish with a thorn and the edge
of a shell, and reclose them and pack them in mud and leaves to
be roasted by the fire. After Ignacio had begun to eat the largest
fish, Nicholas timidly drew out the smallest, and ate for the first
time since coming to Dr. Island. Only when he had finished did
he remember Diane.

He did not dare to take the last fish to her, but he looked cov-
ertly at Ignacio, and began edging away from the fire. The Brazilian seemed not to have noticed him. When he was well into the
shadows he stood, backed a few steps, then—slowly, as his instincts
warned him—walked away, not beginning to trot until the distance between them was nearly a hundred meters.

He found Diane sitting apathetic and silent at the margin of the
cold pool, and had some difficulty persuading her to stand. At last
he lifted her, his hands under her arms pressing against her thin
ribs. Once on her feet she stood steadily enough, and followed him
when he took her by the hand. He talked to her, knowing that
although she gave no sign of hearing she heard him, and that the
right words might wake her to response. "We went fishing—Ignacio showed me how. And he's got a fire, Diane, he got it from
a kind of robot that was supposed to be fixing one of the cables that
holds Dr. Island, I don't know how. Anyway, listen, we caught
three big fish, and I ate one and Ignacio ate a great big one, and
I don't think he'd mind if you had the other one, only say, 'Yes,
Patrão,' and 'No, *Patrão*,' to him—he likes that, and he's only used

to machines. You don't have to smile at him or anything—just look at the fire, that's what I do, just look at the fire."

To Ignacio, perhaps wisely, he at first said nothing at all, leading Diane to the place where he had been sitting himself a few minutes before and placing some scraps from his fish in her lap. When she did not eat he found a sliver of the tender, roasted flesh and thrust it into her mouth. Ignacio said, "Ignacio believed that one dead," and Nicholas answered, "No, *Patrão.*"

"There is another fish. Give it to her."

Nicholas did, raking the gob of baked mud from the coals to crack with the heel of his hand, and peeling the broken and steaming fillets from the skin and bones to give to her when they had cooled enough to eat; after the fish had lain in her mouth for perhaps half a minute she began to chew and swallow, and after the third mouthful she fed herself, though without looking at either of them.

"Ignacio believed that one dead," Ignacio said again.

"No, *Patrão,*" Nicholas answered, and then added, "Like you can see, she's alive."

"She is a pretty creature, with the firelight on her face—no?"

"Yes, *Patrão,* very pretty."

"But too thin." Ignacio moved around the fire until he was sitting almost beside Diane, then reached for the fish Nicholas had given her. Her hands closed on it, though she still did not look at him.

"You see, she knows us after all," Ignacio said. "We are not ghosts."

Nicholas whispered urgently, "Let him have it."

Slowly Diane's fingers relaxed, but Ignacio did not take the fish. "I was only joking, little one," he said. "And I think not such a good joke after all." Then when she did not reply, he turned away from her, his eyes reaching out across the dark, tossing water for something Nicholas could not see.

"She likes you, *Patrão,*" Nicholas said. The words were like swallowing filth, but he thought of the bird ready to tear through

Diane's skin, and Maya's blood soaking in little round dots into the white cloth, and continued. "She is only shy. It is better that way."

"You. What do you know?"

At least Ignacio was no longer looking at the sea. Nicholas said, "Isn't it true, *Patrão?*"

"Yes, it is true."

Diane was picking at the fish again, conveying tiny flakes to her mouth with delicate fingers; distinctly but almost absently she said, "Go, Nicholas."

He looked at Ignacio, but the Brazilian's eyes did not turn toward the girl, nor did he speak.

"Nicholas, go away. Please."

In a voice he hoped was pitched too low for Ignacio to hear, Nicholas said, "I'll see you in the morning. All right?"

Her head moved a fraction of a centimeter.

Once he was out of sight of the fire, one part of the beach was as good to sleep on as another; he wished he had taken a piece of wood from the fire to start one of his own and tried to cover his legs with sand to keep off the cool wind, but the sand fell away whenever he moved, and his legs and his left hand moved without volition on his part.

The surf, lapping at the rippled shore, said, "That was well done, Nicholas."

"I can feel you move," Nicholas said. "I don't think I ever could before except when I was high up."

"I doubt that you can now; my roll is less than one one-hundredth of a degree."

"Yes, I can. You wanted me to do that, didn't you? About Ignacio."

"Do you know what the Harlow effect is, Nicholas?"

Nicholas shook his head.

"About a hundred years ago Dr. Harlow experimented with monkeys who had been raised in complete isolation—no mothers, no other monkeys at all."

"Lucky monkeys."

"When the monkeys were mature he put them into cages with normal ones; they fought with any that came near them, and sometimes they killed them."

"Psychologists always put things in cages; did he ever think of turning them loose in the jungle instead?"

"No, Nicholas, though we have . . . Aren't you going to say anything?"

"I guess not."

"Dr. Harlow tried, you see, to get the isolate monkeys to breed —sex is the primary social function—but they wouldn't. Whenever another monkey of either sex approached they displayed aggressiveness, which the other monkeys returned. He cured them finally by introducing immature monkeys—monkey children—in place of the mature, socialized ones. These needed the isolate adults so badly that they kept on making approaches no matter how often or how violently they were rejected, and in the end they were accepted, and the isolates socialized. It's interesting to note that the founder of Christianity seems to have had an intuitive grasp of the principle—but it was almost two thousand years before it was demonstrated scientifically."

"I don't think it worked here," Nicholas said. "It was more complicated than that."

"Human beings are complicated monkeys, Nicholas."

"That's about the first time I ever heard you make a joke. You like not being human, don't you?"

"Of course. Wouldn't you?"

"I always thought I would, but now I'm not sure. You said that to help me, didn't you? I don't like that."

A wave higher than the others splashed chill foam over Nicholas's legs, and for a moment he wondered if this were Dr. Island's reply. Half a minute later another wave wet him, and another, and he moved farther up the beach to avoid them. The wind was stronger, but he slept despite it, and was awakened only for a moment by a flash of light from the direction from which he had come; he tried to guess what might have caused it, thought of Diane and Ignacio throwing the burning sticks into the air to see the arcs of fire, smiled—too sleepy now to be angry—and slept again.

Morning came cold and sullen; Nicholas ran up and down the beach, rubbing himself with his hands. A thin rain, or spume (it was hard to tell which), was blowing in the wind, clouding the light to gray radiance. He wondered if Diane and Ignacio would mind if he came back now and decided to wait, then thought of fishing so that he would have something to bring when he came; but the sea was very cold and the waves so high they tumbled him, wrenching his bamboo spear from his hand. Ignacio found him dripping with water, sitting with his back to a palm trunk and staring out toward the lifting curve of the sea.

"Hello, you," Ignacio said.

"Good morning, *Patrão.*"

Ignacio sat down. "What is your name? You told me, I think, when we first met, but I have forgotten. I am sorry."

"Nicholas."

"Yes."

"*Patrão,* I am very cold. Would it be possible for us to go to your fire?"

"My name is Ignacio; call me that."

Nicholas nodded, frightened.

"But we cannot go to my fire, because the fire is out."

"Can't you make another one, *Patrão?*"

"You do not trust me, do you? I do not blame you. No, I cannot make another—you may use what I had, if you wish, and make one after I have gone. I came only to say good-bye."

"You're leaving?"

The wind in the palm fronds said, "Ignacio is much better now. He will be going to another place, Nicholas."

"A hospital?"

"Yes, a hospital, but I don't think he will have to stay there long."

"But . . ." Nicholas tried to think of something appropriate. At St. John's and the other places where he had been confined, when people left, they simply left, and usually were hardly spoken of once it was learned that they were going and thus were already tainted by whatever it was that froze the smiles and dried the tears of those outside. At last he said, "Thanks for teaching me how to fish."

"That was all right," Ignacio said. He stood up and put a hand on Nicholas's shoulder, then turned away. Four meters to his left the damp sand was beginning to lift and crack. While Nicholas watched, it opened on a brightly lit companionway walled with white. Ignacio pushed his curly black hair back from his eyes and went down, and the sand closed with a thump.

"He won't be coming back, will he?" Nicholas said.

"No."

"He said I could use his stuff to start another fire, but I don't even know what it is."

Dr. Island did not answer. Nicholas got up and began to walk back to where the fire had been, thinking about Diane and wondering if she was hungry; he was hungry himself.

He found her beside the dead fire. Her chest had been burned away, and lying close by, near the hole in the sand where Ignacio must have kept it hidden, was a bulky nuclear welder. The power pack was too heavy for Nicholas to lift, but he picked up the welding gun on its short cord and touched the trigger, producing a two-meter plasma discharge, which he played along the sand until Diane's body was ash. By the time he had finished the wind was whipping the palms and sending stinging rain into his eyes, but he collected a supply of wood and built another fire, bigger and bigger until it roared like a forge in the wind. "He killed her!" he shouted to the waves.

"YES." Dr. Island's voice was big and wild.

"You said he was better."

"HE IS," howled the wind. "YOU KILLED THE MONKEY THAT

WANTED TO PLAY WITH YOU, NICHOLAS—AS I BELIEVED IGNACIO
WOULD EVENTUALLY KILL YOU, WHO ARE SO EASILY HATED, SO
DIFFERENT FROM WHAT IT IS THOUGHT A BOY SHOULD BE. BUT
KILLING THE MONKEY HELPED YOU, REMEMBER? MADE YOU BET-
TER. IGNACIO WAS FRIGHTENED BY WOMEN; NOW HE KNOWS
THAT THEY ARE REALLY VERY WEAK, AND HE HAS ACTED UPON
CERTAIN FANTASIES AND FINDS THEM BITTER."

"You're rocking," Nicholas said. "Am I doing that?"

"YOUR THOUGHT."

A palm snapped in the storm; instead of falling, it flew crashing
among the others, its fronded head catching the wind like a sail.
"I'm killing you," Nicholas said. "Destroying you." The left side of
his face was so contorted with grief and rage that he could scarcely
speak.

Dr. Island heaved beneath his feet. "NO."

"One of your cables is already broken—I saw that. Maybe more
than one. You'll pull loose. I'm turning this world, isn't that right?
The attitude rockets are tuned to my emotions, and they're spin-
ning us around, and the slippage is the wind and the high sea, and
when you come loose nothing will balance any more."

"NO."

"What's the stress on your cables? Don't you know?"

"THEY ARE VERY STRONG."

"What kind of talk is that? You ought to say something like: 'The
D-twelve cable tension is twenty-billion kilograms' force. WARN-
ING! WARNING! Expected time to failure is ninety-seven seconds!
WARNING!' *Don't you even know how a machine is supposed to
talk?*" Nicholas was screaming now, and every wave reached farther up the beach than the last, so that the bases of the most
seaward palms were awash.

"GET BACK, NICHOLAS. FIND HIGHER GROUND. GO INTO THE
JUNGLE." It was the crashing waves themselves that spoke.

"I won't."

A long serpent of water reached for the fire, which hissed and
sputtered.

"GET BACK!"

"I won't!"

A second wave came, striking Nicholas calf-high and nearly extinguishing the fire.

"ALL THIS WILL BE UNDER WATER SOON. GET BACK!"

Nicholas picked up some of the still-burning sticks and tried to carry them, but the wind blew them out as soon as he lifted them from the fire. He tugged at the welder, but it was too heavy for him to lift.

"GET BACK!"

He went into the jungle, where the trees lashed themselves to leafy rubbish in the wind and broken branches flew through the air like debris from an explosion; for a while he heard Diane's voice crying in the wind; it became Maya's, then his mother's or Sister Carmela's, and a hundred others; in time the wind grew less, and he could no longer feel the ground rocking. He felt tired. He said, "I didn't kill you after all, did I?" but there was no answer. On the beach, when he returned to it, he found the welder half buried in sand. No trace of Diane's ashes, nor of his fire. He gathered more wood and built another, lighting it with the welder.

"Now," he said. He scooped aside the sand around the welder until he reached the rough understone beneath it, and turned the flame of the welder on that; it blackened and bubbled.

"No," Dr. Island said.

"Yes." He was bending intently over the flame, both hands locked on the welder's trigger.

"Nicholas, stop that." When he did not reply, "Look behind you." There was a splashing louder than the crashing of the waves, and a groaning of metal. He whirled and saw the great, beetle-like robot Ignacio had shown him on the sea floor. Tiny shellfish clung to its metal skin, and water, faintly green, still poured from its body. Before he could turn the welding gun toward it, it shot forward hands like clamps and wrenched it from him. All up and down the beach similar machines were smoothing the sand and repairing the damage of the storm.

"That thing was dead," Nicholas said. "Ignacio killed it."

It picked up the power pack, shook it clean of sand, and turning, stalked back toward the sea.

"That is what Ignacio believed, and it was better that he believed so."

"And you said you couldn't do anything, you had no hands."

"I also told you that I would treat you as society will when you are released, that that was my nature. After that, did you still believe all I told you? Nicholas, you are upset now because Diane is dead—"

"You could have protected her!"

"—but by dying she made someone else—someone very important—well. Her prognosis was bad; she really wanted only death, and this was the death I chose for her. You could call it the death of Dr. Island, a death that would help someone else. Now you are alone, but soon there will be more patients in this segment, and you will help them, too—if you can—and perhaps they will help you. Do you understand?"

"No," Nicholas said. He flung himself down on the sand. The wind had dropped, but it was raining hard. He thought of the vision he had once had, and of describing it to Diane the day before. "This isn't ending the way I thought," he whispered. It was only a squeak of sound far down in his throat. "Nothing ever turns out right."

The waves, the wind, the rustling palm fronds and the pattering rain, the monkeys who had come down to the beach to search for food washed ashore, answered, "Go away—go back—don't move."

Nicholas pressed his scarred head against his knees, rocking back and forth.

"Don't move."

For a long time he sat still while the rain lashed his shoulders and the dripping monkeys frolicked and fought around him. When at last he lifted his face, there was in it some element of personality which had been only potentially present before, and with this an emptiness and an expression of surprise. His lips moved, and the sounds were the sounds made by a deaf-mute who tries to speak.

"Nicholas is gone," the waves said. "Nicholas, who was the right side of your body, the left half of your brain, I have forced into catatonia; for the remainder of your life he will be to you only what you once were to him—or less. Do you understand?"

The boy nodded.

"We will call you Kenneth, silent one. And if Nicholas tries to come again, Kenneth, you must drive him back—or return to what you have been."

The boy nodded a second time, and a moment afterward began to collect sticks for the dying fire. As though to themselves the waves chanted:

> "Seas are wild tonight . . .
> Stretching over Sado island
> Silent clouds of stars."

There was no reply.

EDWARD BRYANT

Shark

Shark: symbol of terror. It is the same throughout the world. Shark is the enemy, to be killed, or fled, but never ignored. You stand on the beach and see the fin in the distance, and even knowing you are safe, the feeling comes. Shark: fear. A racial memory perhaps, of a time when we coexisted in the oceans, when shark was synonymous with death. And Ed Bryant, a Wyoming man, growing to adulthood where the mountain lion or bear might have been the symbol of terror, understands the feeling that comes to the pit of the stomach when you see that fin at sea.

@

@

The war came and left, but returned for him eighteen years later.

Folger should have known when the clouds of smaller fish disappeared. He should have guessed, but he was preoccupied, stabilizing the cage at ten meters, then sliding out the upper hatch. Floating free, he stared into the gray-green South Atlantic. Nothing. With his tongue, he keyed the mike embedded in his mouthpiece. The sonex transmitter clipped to his tanks coded and beamed the message: "Query—Valerie—location." He repeated it. Electronics crackled in his ear, but there was no response.

Something moved to his right—something a darker gray, a darker green than the water. Then Folger saw the two dark eyes. Her body took form in the murk. A blunt torpedo shape gliding, she struck impossibly fast.

It was Folger's mistake and nearly fatal. He had hoped she would circle first. The great white shark bore straight in, mouth grinning open. Folger saw the teeth, only the teeth, rows of ragged white. "Query—" he screamed into the sonex.

Desperately he brought the shark billy in his right hand forward. The great white shape, jaws opening and closing, triangular teeth knifing, whipped past soundlessly.

Folger lifted the billy—tried to lift it—saw the blood and the white ends protruding below his elbow and realized he was seeing surgically sawed bone.

The shock made everything deceptively easy. Folger reached behind him, felt the cage, and pulled himself up toward the hatch. The shark flowed into the distance.

One-handed, it was difficult entering the cage. He was half through the hatch and had turned the flotation control all the way up when he blacked out.

Her name, like that of half the other women in the village, was Maria. For more than a decade she had kept Folger's house. She cleaned, after a fashion. She cooked his two meals each day, usually boiled potatoes or mutton stew. She loved him with a silent, bitter, unrequited passion. Over all the years, they had never talked of it. They were not lovers; each night after fixing supper, she returned to her clay-and-stone house in the village. Had Folger taken a woman from the village, Maria would have knifed both of them as they slept. That problem had never arisen.

"People for you," said Maria.

Folger looked up from his charts. "Who?"

"No islanders."

Folger hadn't had an off-island visitor since two years before, when a Brazilian journalist had come out on the semiannual supply boat.

"You want them?" said Maria.

"Can I avoid it?"

Maria lowered her voice. "Government."

"Shit," said Folger. "How many?"

"Just two. You want the gun?" The sawed-off twelve-gauge, swathed in oilcloth, leaned in the kitchen closet.

"No." Folger sighed. "Bring them in."

Maria muttered something as she turned back through the doorway.

"What?"

She shook her matted black hair. "One is a woman!" she spat.

Valerie came to his quarters later in the afternoon. The project manager had already spoken to Folger. Knowing what she would say, Folger had two uncharacteristically stiff drinks before she arrived. "You can't be serious," was the first thing he said.

She grinned. "So they told you."

He said, "I can't allow it."

The grin vanished. "Don't talk as though you owned me."

"I'm not, I'm just—" He floundered. "Damn it, it's a shock."

She took his hand and drew him down beside her on the couch. "Would I deny your dreams?"

His voice pleaded. "You're my lover."

Valerie looked away. "It's what I want."

"You're crazy."

"You can be an oceanographer," she said. "Why can't I be a shark?"

Maria ushered in the visitors with ill grace. "Get along," she said out in the hallway. "Señor Folger is a busy man."

"We will not disturb him long," said a woman's voice.

The visitors, as they entered, had to duck to clear the doorframe. The woman was nearly two meters in height; the man half a head taller. Identically clad in gray jumpsuits, they wore identical smiles. They were—Folger searched for the right word—extreme. Their hair was too soft and silkily pale; their eyes too obviously blue, teeth too white and savage.

The pair looked down at Folger. "I am Inga Lindfors," said the woman. "My brother, Per." The man nodded slightly.

"Apparently you know who I am," said Folger.

"You are Marcus Antonius Folger," Inga Lindfors said.

"It was supposed to be Marcus Aurelius," Folger said irrelevantly. "My father never paid close attention to the classics."

"The fortune of confusion," said Inga. "I find Mark Antony the more fascinating. He was a man of decisive action."

Bewildered, Maria stared from face to face.

"You were a component of the Marine Institute on East Falkland," said Per.

"I was. It was a long time ago."

"We wish to speak with you," said Inga, "as representatives of the Protectorate of Old America."

"So? Talk."

"We speak officially."

"Oh." Folger smiled at Maria. "I must be alone with these people."

The island woman looked dubiously at the Lindfors. "I will be in the kitchen," she said.

"It is a formidable journey to Tres Rocas," said Per. "Our airboat left Cape Pembroke ten hours ago. Unfavorable winds."

Folger scratched himself and said nothing.

Inga laughed, a young girl's laugh in keeping with her age. "Marcus Antonius Folger, you've been too long away from American civilization."

"I doubt it," said Folger. "You've obviously gone to a lot of trouble to find me. Why?"

Why?

She always asked him questions when they climbed the rocks above the headland. Valerie asked and Folger answered and usually they both learned. Why was the Falklands's seasonal temperature range only ten degrees; what were quasars; how did third-generation computers differ from second; how dangerous were manta rays; when would the universe die? Today she asked a new question:

"What about the war?"

He paused, leaning into a natural chimney. "What do you mean?" The cold passed into his cheek, numbed his jaw, made the words stiff.

Valerie said, "I don't understand the war."

"Then you know what I know." Folger stared down past the rocks to the sea. How do you explain masses of people killing other people? He could go through the glossary—primary, secondary, tertiary targets; population priorities; death-yields—but so what? It didn't give credence or impact to the killing taking place on the land, in space, and below the seas.

"I don't know anything," said Valerie somberly. "Only what they tell us."

"Don't question them," said Folger. "They're a little touchy."

"But why?"

"The Protectorate remembers its friends," said Per.

Folger began to laugh. "Don't try to snow me. At the peak of my loyalty to the Protectorate—or what the Protectorate was then —I was apolitical."

"Twenty years ago, that would have been treason."

"But not now," said Inga quickly. "Libertarianism has made a great resurgence."

"So I hear. The boat brings magazines once in a while."

"The years of reconstruction have been difficult. We could have used your expertise on the continent."

"I was used here. Occasionally I find ways to help the islanders."

"As an oceanographer?"

Folger gestured toward the window. "The sea makes up most of their environment. I'm useful."

"With your talent," said Per, "It's such a waste here."

"Then, too," Folger continued, "I help with the relics."

"Relics?" said Inga uncertainly.

"War surplus. Leftovers. Look." Folger picked up a dried, leathery rectangle from the table and tossed it to Per. He looked at the object, turning it over and over.

"Came from a killer whale. Got him last winter with a harpoon and shaped charge. Damn thing had stove in three boats, killed two men. Now read the other side."

Per examined the piece of skin closely. Letters and numerals had been deeply branded. "USMF-$_{343}$."

"See?" said Folger. "Weapons are still out there. He was part of the lot the year before I joined the Institute. Not especially sophisticated, but he had longevity."

"Do you encounter many?" said Inga.

Folger shook his head. "Not too many of the originals."

The ketch had been found adrift with no one aboard. It had put out early that morning for Dos, one of the two small and uninhabited companions of Tres Rocas. The three men aboard had been expecting to hunt seal. The fishermen who discovered the derelict

*also found a bloody axe and severed sections of tentacle as thick
as a man's forearm.*

*So Folger trolled along the route of the unlucky boat in his
motorized skiff for three days. He searched a vast area of choppy,
gray water, an explosive harpoon never far from his hand. Early
on the fourth afternoon a half-dozen dark-green tentacles poked
from the sea on the port side of the boat. Folger reached with his
left hand for the harpoon. He didn't see the tentacle from star-
board that whipped and tightened around his chest and jerked
him over the side.*

*The chill of the water stunned him. Folger had a quick, surreal-
istic glimpse of intricately weaving tentacles. Two eyes, each as
large as his fist, stared without malice. The tentacle drew him
toward the beak.*

*Then a gray shadow angled below Folger. Razor teeth scythed
through flesh. The tentacle was cut; Folger drifted.*

*The great white shark was at least ten meters long. Its belly was
uncharacteristically dappled. The squid wrapped eager arms
around the thrashing shark. The two fish sank into the darker
water below Folger.*

*Lungs aching, he broke the surface less than a meter from the
skiff. He always trailed a ladder from the boat. It made things
easier for a one-armed man.*

"Would you show us the village?" said Inga.

"Not much to see."

"We would be pleased by a tour anyway. Have you time?"

Folger reached for his coat. Inga moved to help him put it on.
"I can do it," said Folger.

"There are fine experts in prosthesis on the continent," said Per.

"No, thanks," said Folger.

"Have you thought about a replacement?"

"Thought about it. But the longer I thought, the better I got
without one. I had a few years to practice."

"It was in the war, then?" asked Inga.

"Of course it was in the war."

On their way out, they passed the kitchen. Maria looked up sullenly over the scraps of bloody mutton on the cutting board. Her eyes fixed on Inga until the blonde moved out of sight along the hall.

A light, cold rain was falling as they walked down the trail to the village. "Rain is the only thing I could do without here," said Folger. "I was raised in California."

"We will see California after we finish here," said Inga. "Per and I have a leave. We will get our antirad injections and ski the Sierras. At night we will watch the Los Angeles glow."

"Is it beautiful?"

"The glow is like seeing the aurora borealis every night," said Per.

Folger chuckled. "I always suspected L.A.'s future would be something like that."

"The half-life will see to the city's immortality," said Inga.

Per smiled. "We were there last year. The glow appears cold. It is supremely erotic."

In the night, in a bed, he asked her, "Why do you want to be a shark?"

She ran her nails delicately along the cords of his neck. "I want to kill people, eat them."

"Any people?"

"Just men."

"Would you like me to play analyst?" said Folger. She bit his shoulder hard. "Goddammit!" He flopped over. "Is there any blood?" he demanded.

Valerie brushed the skin with her hand. "You're such a coward."

"My threshold of pain's low," said Folger. "Sweetie."

"Don't call me Sweetie," she said. "Call me Shark."

"Shark."

They made love in a desperate hurry.

The descent steepened, the rain increased, and they hurried. They passed through a copse of stunted trees and reached the ruts of a primitive road.

"We have flash-frozen beefsteaks aboard the airboat," said Inga.

"That's another thing I've missed," Folger said.

"Then you must join us for supper."

"As a guest of the Protectorate?"

"An honored guest."

"Make mine rare," said Folger. "Very rare."

The road abruptly descended between two bluffs and overlooked the village. It was called simply the village because there were no other settlements on Tres Rocas and so no cause to distinguish. Several hundred inhabitants lived along the curve of the bay in small, one-story houses, built largely of stone.

"It's so bleak," said Inga. "What do people do?"

"Not much," said Folger. "Raise sheep, hunt seals, fish. When there were still whales, they used to whale. For recreation, the natives go out and dig peat for fuel."

"It's quite a simple existence," said Per.

"Uncomplicated," Folger said.

"If you could be anything in the sea," said Valerie, "what would it be?"

Folger was always discomfited by these games. He usually felt he chose wrong answers. He thought carefully for a minute or so. "A dolphin, I suppose."

In the darkness, her voice dissolved in laughter. "You lose!"

He felt irritation. "What's the matter now?"

"Dolphins hunt in packs," she said. "They gang up to kill sharks. They're cowards."

"They're not. Dolphins are highly intelligent. They band together for cooperative protection."

Still between crests of laughter: "Cowards!"

On the outskirts of the village they encountered a dozen small, dirty children playing a game. The children had dug a shallow pit about a meter in diameter. It was excavated close enough to the beach so that it quickly filled with a mixture of ground-seepage and rainwater.

"Stop," said Per. "I wish to see this."

The children stirred the muddy water with sticks. Tiny, thumb-sized fishes lunged and snapped at one another, burying miniature teeth in the others' flesh. The children stared up incuriously at the adults, then returned their attention to the pool.

Inga bent closer. "What are they?"

"Baby sharks," said Folger. "They hatch alive in the uterus of their mother. Some fisherman must have bagged a female sand tiger who was close to term. He gave the uterus to the kids. Fish won't live long in that pool."

"They're fantastic," Per breathed. For the first time since Folger had met him, he showed emotion. "So young and so ferocious."

"The first one hatched usually eats the others in the womb," said Folger.

"It's beautiful," said Inga. "An organism that is born fighting."

The sibling combat in the pit had begun to quiet. A few sand tiger babies twitched weakly. The children nudged them with the sticks. When there was no response, the sticks rose and fell violently, splashing the water and mashing the fish into the sand.

"The islanders hate sharks," Folger said.

She awoke violently, choking off a scream and blindly striking out at him. Folger held her wrists, pulled her against him, and then began to stroke her hair. Her trembling slowly subsided.

"Bad dreams?"

She nodded, her hair working softly against his jaw.

"Was I in them?"

"No," she said. "Maybe. I don't know. I don't think so."

"What happened?"

She hesitated. "I was swimming. They—some people pulled me out of the water. They put me on a concrete slab by the pier. There was no water, no sea—" She swallowed. "God, I want a drink."

"I'll fix you one," he said.

"They pulled me out. I lay there and felt the ocean drain away. And then I felt things tear loose inside me. There was nothing supporting my heart and liver and intestines and everything began to pull away from everything else. God, it hurts—"

Folger patted her head. "I'll get you a drink."

"So?" said Per. "Sharks aren't particularly aggressive, are they?"

"Not until after the war," said Folger. "Since then there's been continual skirmishing. Both the villagers and the sharks hunt the same game. Now they've started to hunt each other."

"And," said Inga, "there has been you."

Folger nodded. "I know the sea predators better. After all, that was my job."

The children, bored with the dead-shark pool, followed the adults toward the village. They gawked at the Lindfors. One of the more courageous boys reached tentatively toward Inga's hair as it blew back in the wind.

"Vayan!" shouted Folger. "All of you, move!" The children reluctantly withdrew. "They're accustomed to whites," he said, "but blondes are a novelty."

"Fascinating," said Inga. "It is like an enclave of a previous century."

The road widened slightly and became the village's main street, still unpaved, and winding down along the edge of the sea. Folger saw the aluminum bulk of an airboat tied to a pier, incongruous between two fishing ketches. "You come alone?" he said.

"Just the two of us," said Inga.

Per put his hand lightly on her wrist. "We're quite effective as a team," he said.

They passed a dark-stone house, its door swung open to the wind. Rain blew across the threshold.

"Abandoned?" said Inga.

"Quaint old island custom," said Folger. "Catholicism's a little diluted here. Priest only comes twice a year." He pointed at the open door. "The man who lived there died at sea a couple days ago. Family'll keep the door open, no matter what, for a week. It's so his soul can find shelter until it's shunted to heaven or hell."

Per said, "What happened to the man?"

"He was fishing," Folger said. "Friends saw it all. A great white shark got him."

Closer now:

"Dolphin!"

"Shark!"

They lay together.

"I wish we had more time," said Inga. "I should like to hunt a shark."

"Perhaps on some future leave," said Per.

"And that's about it for the village," said Folger. "There isn't much more to see, unless you enjoy native crafts like dipping tallow candles or carding wool."

"It's incredible," said Inga. "The only time I have seen anything remotely like this was in prereconstruction America."

Folger said, "You don't look that old."

"I was barely into puberty. The Protectorate brought our father from Copenhagen. He is a design engineer in hydroelectrics. He worked on the Oklahoma Sea projects."

They stood on a rough plank pier beyond one horn of the crescent of houses. Per tapped a boot on the wood to shake loose some of the mud. "I still can't see how you endure this place, Folger."

Half asleep, Folger said. "Some day when the war is over, we'll get a place by the ocean. There's still some great country north of San Francisco. We'll have a house among the trees, on a mountainside overlooking the beach. Maybe we'll make it a stone tower, like Robinson Jeffers built."

Close to his ear, Valerie said, "A tower would be nice."

"You'll be able to read all day, and swim, and we'll never have any visitors we don't want."

"It's a fine dream for you," Valerie whispered.

"I came as jetsam," Folger said.

The three of them stood silently for a few minutes, watching clouds darker than the water spill in from the west. Triangular shapes took form on the horizon. Folger squinted. "Fishermen are coming in." After another minute he said, "Tour's over."

"I know," said Inga.

"—hoping. I kept hoping." Folger raised himself on one elbow. "You really are going to go through with it."

The fishing boats neared the breakwater. Folger and the others could hear the faint cries of the crewmen. "Why are you here?" he said.

Per Lindfors laid a comradely hand on Folger's shoulder. "We came here to kill you."

Folger smiled. What other response could there be?

"Tell me how it works," said Valerie.

They paused on a steel catwalk overlooking the catch pens. In the tank immediately below, two divers warily manhandled a five-meter great blue in an oval path. If water weren't forced over the shark's gill surfaces, the fish would suffocate. The water glittered in the glare of arc lights. Beyond the pens, the beacon on Cape Pembroke blinked its steady twelve pulses per minute.

"I know the general techniques," said Folger. "But it's not my specialty. I'm strictly mapping and logistics."

"I don't need apologies," said Valerie.

"Excuse me while I violate the National Security Act." Folger turned to face her. "Most of the technology is borrowed from the brothers upstairs on the orbital platforms. Everybody's been doing secret work with cyborgs. Somewhere along the line, somebody got the bright idea of importing it underwater."

"The Marine Forces," said Valerie.

"Right. The bureaucrats finally realized that the best weapons for fighting undersea wars already existed in the ocean. They were weapons that had been adapted for that purpose for more than a hundred million years. All that was needed were guidance systems."

Valerie said wistfully, "Sharks."

"Sharks and killer whales; squid; to a degree, dolphins. We're considering a few other species."

"I want to know how it's done."

"Primarily by direct transplant. Surgical modification. Nerve grafts are partially electronic. Is that what you wanted to know?"

She stared down at the docile shark in the tank. "There's no coming back, is there?"

"We'll probably use your old body to feed the new one."

"So kill me. Do I rate a reason why?"

"Not if your execution had been scheduled now," said Inga. "It would not have been merciful to alert you in advance. Such cheap melodrama is forbidden by Protectorate codes."

Folger snorted. "Isn't all this overly Machiavellian?"

"Not at all. We were given considerable latitude on this assignment. We wished to be sure of doing the right thing."

"—come down to the point of whether or not I'll stop you from doing this." Wind off the headland deadened his words.

"Can you stop me?" Valerie's voice was flat, without challenge. He didn't answer.

"Would you?" Valerie kissed him gently on the side of the throat. "Here's a Hindu proverb for you. The woman you love, you must not possess."

He said in a whisper, without looking at her, "I love you."

"If you're not going to kill me," Folger said, "I've got work to do."

"Folger, what is your fondest wish?"

He stared at her with enigmatic eyes. "You can't give it to me."

"Wealth?" said Per. "Recognition? You had a considerable reputation before the war."

"When we leave," said Inga, "we want you to return with us."

Folger looked slowly from one to the other. "Leave the island?"

"A center for deep Pacific studies is opening on Guam," Inga said. "The directorship is yours."

"I don't believe any of this," said Folger. "I'm in my fifties, and even considering the postwar chaos, I'm a decade behind my field."

"Some refresher study at the University of San Juan," said Per.

Inga said, "Reconstruction is not all that complete. Genius is uncommon. You are needed, Folger."

"Death or a directorship," said Folger.

Folger spoke to the project manager in a sterile cubicle off the operating theater. "What are her chances?"

"For survival? Excellent."

"I mean afterward."

The project manager drew deeply on his extinguished pipe. "Can't say. Test data's been spotty."

"Christ, Danny!" Folger swung around. "Don't double-talk me. What's that mean?"

The project manager evaded Folger's eyes. "A high proportion of the test subjects haven't returned from field trials. The bio boys think it may have something to do with somatic memory, cellular retention of the old, nonhuman personality."

"And you didn't tell us anything about this?"

"Security, Marc." The project manager looked uncomfortable. "I never know from day to day what's under wraps. You know, we haven't had radio reception for twelve days now. Nobody knows—"

"I swear, Danny, if anything happens to her—"

The pipe dropped from the project manager's open mouth. "But she's a volunteer—"

It was the first time Folger had ever struck another human being.

"Elections are approaching on the continent," said Inga.

"Free?"

"Of course," said Per.

"Reasonably," said Inga. "Within the needs of reconstruction."

A crowd of children scampered past. Further down the beach, the fishermen began to unload the day's catch.

"Do you remember a man named Diaz-Gomide?" said Per.

"No."

"He is a Brazilian journalist."

"Yes," said Folger. "About two years ago, right?"

Per nodded. "He is not only a journalist, but also a higher-up in the opposition party. He is their shadow minister of information."

"Señor Diaz-Gomide has proved a great embarrassment to the present administration," said Inga.

"The same regime that's been in power for a quarter century," said Folger.

Inga made a noncommittal gesture. "Someone had to keep order through the war and after."

"The point is," said Per, "that this Diaz-Gomide has been disseminating historical lies on behalf of his party."

"Let me guess," said Folger. He walked slowly toward the end of the pier and the Lindfors followed. "He has disclosed terrible things about the government in connection with the Marine Institute on East Falkland."

"Among other fabrications," said Per.

Folger stopped with his toes overhanging the water. "He alleged that inhuman experiments were carried on, that the brains of unwilling or unknowing subjects were transplanted into the bodies of sea creatures."

"Something like that, except he couched it in less clinical language."

"Down the rabbit hole." Folger shook his head slowly. "What do you want from me—a disclaimer?"

Inga said, "We suspect Diaz-Gomide grossly distorted your statements in the interview. It would be well if you set the record straight."

"The Marine Forces experiments have been greatly exaggerated," said Per.

"Probably not," said Folger.

They stared at each other.

Folger floated in the center of the holding tank. The whisper of the regulator sounded extraordinarily loud in his ears. He turned to follow the great white shark as it slowly circled, its eye continually focused on Folger. The shark—he found difficulty ascribing it her name—moved fluidly, weaving, head traveling from side to side slowly with the rhythm of its motion through the water.

She—he made the attempt—she was beautiful; implacably, savagely so. He had seldom been this close to a shark. He watched silently her body crease with a thousand furrows, every movement emphasizing musculature. He had never seen beauty so deadly.

After a time, he tried the sonex. "Valerie—inquiry—what is it like?"

The coded reply came back and unscrambled. "Marc—never know—mass&bulk&security—better."

He sent: "Inquiry—happy?"

"Yes."

They exchanged messages for a few minutes more. He asked, "Inquiry—what will they do with you?"

"Assigned soldier—picket duty—Mariana Trench."

"Inquiry—when?"

"Never—never soldier—run away first."

"So," said Folger. "Recant or die?"

"We would like to see you take the directorship of the research center on Guam," said Inga.

Folger found the paper among other poems scattered like dry leaves in Valerie's room:

> *"In the void, inviolate*
> *from what she was*
> *is*
> *and will be"*

He went outside to the catch pens. From the catwalk he looked into the tank. The shark circled ceaselessly. She swung around to his side and Folger watched the dark back, the mottled gray and white belly slide by. He watched until darkness fell.

"Do I get time to consider the offer?" Folger asked.

The Lindfors looked at each other, considering.

"I was never good at snap decisions."

"We would like to tidy up this affair—" said Per.

"I know." Folger said. "Skiing the Sierras."

"Would twelve hours be sufficient?"

"Time enough to consult my Book of Changes."

"Do you really?" Inga's eyes widened fractionally.

"Treason," Per said.

"No. No more. My mystical phase played through."

"Then we can expect your decision in the morning?"

"Right."

"And now it is time for supper," said Inga. "Shall we go to the boat? I remember, Folger. Very rare."

"No business during dinner?"

"No," Inga promised.

"Your goddam girl," said the project manager. Soaked through with sea water and reeking of contraband liquor, he sloshed into Folger's quarters. "She got away."

Folger switched on the lamp by the bunk and looked up sleepily. "Danny? What? Who got away?"

"Goddam girl."

"Valerie?" Folger swung his legs off the bed and sat up.

"Smashed the sea-gate. Let loose half the tanks. We tried to head her off in the channel."

"Is she all right?"

"All right?" The project manager cupped his hands over his face. "She stove in the boat. Got Kendall and Brooking. You never saw so much blood."

"Christ!"

"Hell of it was," said the project manager, "we really needed her in the morning."

"For what?"

"Really needed her," the project manager repeated. He staggered out of the room and disappeared in the hall.

Folger answered his own question the following day. Through devious channels of information, he learned that Valerie had been scheduled for vivisection.

That night, Folger climbed the mountain above his house. He felt he was struggling through years as much as brush and mud. The top of the mountain was ragged, with no proper peak. Folger picked a high point and spread his slicker over damp rock. He sat in the cold and watched the dark Atlantic. He looked up and picked out the Southern Cross. A drizzle began.

"Well, hell," he said, and climbed back down the mountain.

Folger took an Institute launch out beyond the cape and anchored. He lowered the cage, then donned his scuba gear. He said into the sonex: "Query—Valerie—location."

Later that morning, Folger suffered his loss.

Maria shook him awake in the morning. Folger awakened reluctantly, head still full of gentle spirals over glowing coral. The water had been warm; he had needed no suit or equipment. Endless, buoyant flight—

"Señor Folger, you must get up. It has been seen."

His head wobbled as she worried his shoulder with insistent fingers. "Okay, I'm awake." He yawned. "What's been seen?"

"The big white one," Maria said. "The one that killed Manuel Padilla three days ago. It was sighted in the bay soon after the sun rose."

"Anybody try anything?" Folger asked.

"No. They were afraid. It is at least ten meters long."

Folger yawned again. "Hell of a way to start a morning."

"I have food for you."

Folger made a face. "I had steak last night. Real beef. Have you ever tasted beef?"

"No, Señor."

Maria accompanied him down the mountain to the village. She insisted upon carrying some of the loose gear; the mask, a box of twelve-gauge shells, a mesh sack of empty jars. Folger filled the jars with sheep's blood at the village butcher shop. He checked his watch; it was seven o'clock.

The skiff was tied up at the end of the second pier. The aluminum airboat glittered in the sun as they passed it. Inga Lindfors stood very still on the bridge. "Good morning, Folger," she called.

"Good morning," said Folger.

"Your answer?"

Folger appraised her for a moment. "No," he said, walking on.

The carcinogenic spread of the war finally and actively engulfed the Falkland Islands. The systemic integrity of the Institute was violated. Many components scattered; some stayed to fight.

Folger, his stump capped with glossy scar tissue, had already said his good-byes.

Suspended in the cold, gray void, Folger realized he was hyperventilating. He floated free, willing himself to relax, letting his staccato breathing find a slower, smoother rhythm. Beside him, a line trailed up to the rectangular blur of the skiff's hull. Tied to the nylon rope were a net and the unopened jars of sheep's-blood bait.

Folger checked his limited arsenal. Tethered to his left wrist was the underwater gun. It was a four-foot aluminum tube capped with a firing mechanism and a waterproof shotgun shell. A shorter, steel-tipped shark billy was fixed to a bracket tied to the stump of Folger's right arm.

Something intruded on his peripheral vision and he looked up.

Arrogant and sure, the two deadly shadows materialized out of the murk. The Lindfors wore only mask, fins, and snorkel. They appeared armed only with knives.

Folger saw them and raised the shark gun in warning. Per Lindfors grinned, his teeth very white. With slow, powerful strokes, he and his sister approached Folger from either side.

Disregarding Inga for the moment, Folger swung the muzzle of the shark gun toward Per. Per batted it aside with his free hand as Folger pulled the trigger. The concussion seemed to stun only Folger. Still smiling, Per extended his knife-hand.

Inga screamed in the water. Per disregarded Folger's weak attempt to fend him off with the billy and began to stroke for the surface. Folger turned his head.

A clownish face rushed at him. Folger stared at the teeth. The pointed nose veered at the last moment as the shark brushed by and struck at Per. The jaws cleanly sliced away Per's left arm and half his chest. The fish doubled back upon itself and made another strike. Per's legs, separate and trailing blood, tumbled slowly through the water.

Then Folger remembered Inga. He turned in the water and saw half her torso and part of her head, a swatch of silky hair spread out fanlike behind the corpse.

He looked back at the shark. It turned toward him slowly and began to circle, eerily graceful for its immense size. A dark eye fixed him coldly.

Folger held the metal billy obliquely in front of his chest. The tether of the shark gun had broken with the recoil.

The shark and Folger inspected each other. He saw the mottled coloration of the shark's belly. He thought he saw a Marine Forces code branded low on the left flank. He keyed the sonex:

"Query—Valerie—query—Valerie."

The shark continued to circle. Folger abruptly realized the shark was following an inexorably diminishing spiral.

"Query—Valerie—I am Folger."

"Folger." An answer came back. "Valerie."

"I am Folger," he repeated.

"Folger" came the reply. "Love/hunger—hunger/love."

"Valerie—love."

"Hunger—love." The shark suddenly broke out of her orbit and drove at Folger. The enormous jaws opened, upper jaw sliding forward, triangular teeth ready to shear.

Folger hopelessly raised the billy. The jaws closed empty and the shark swept by. She was close enough to touch had Folger wished. The shark drove toward the open sea and Folger swam for the surface.

He tossed the yarrow sticks for an hour. Eventually he put them away, along with the book. Folger sat at the table until the sun rose. He heard Maria's footsteps outside on the stone walk. He listened to the sound of her progress through the outside door, the kitchen, and the hall.

"Señor Folger, you didn't sleep?"

"I'm getting old," he said.

Maria was excited. "The great white one is back."

"Oh?"

"The fishermen fear to go out."

"That's sensible."

"Señor, you must kill it."

"Must I?" Folger grinned. "Fix me some tea."

She turned toward the kitchen.

"Maria, you needn't come up tonight to fix supper."

After his usual meager breakfast, Folger gathered together his gear and walked out the front door of the house. He hesitated on the step.

You become what you live.

She lived shark.

He said into the wind, "What do you want me to do? Carve a cenotaph here on the mountain?"

"What, Señor?" said Maria.

"Let's go." They started toward the trail. "Hold it," said Folger. He walked back to the house and opened the front door to the wind and rain. He chocked it with a rock. Then he climbed down the path to the sea.

GEORGE R. R. MARTIN

With Morning Comes Mistfall

If you could go to Loch Ness tomorrow and prove or disprove conclusively the existence of the monster, would you? Should you? When all the questions are answered, when all the superstitions are stilled, when science has unraveled all the mysteries, what will we do? Would you want to live in such a time? Would we be able to live then?

I was early to breakfast that morning, the first day after landing. But Sanders was already out on the dining balcony when I got there. He was standing alone by the edge, looking out over the mountains and the mists.

I walked up behind him and muttered hello. He didn't bother to reply. "It's beautiful, isn't it?" he said, without turning.

And it was.

Only a few feet below balcony level the mists rolled, sending ghostly breakers to crash against the stones of Sanders's castle. A thick white blanket extended from horizon to horizon, cloaking everything. We could see the summit of the Red Ghost, off to the north; a barbed dagger of scarlet rock jabbing into the sky. But that was all. The other mountains were still below mist level.

But we were above the mists. Sanders had built his hotel atop the tallest mountain in the chain. We were floating alone in a swirling white ocean, on a flying castle amid a sea of clouds.

Castle Cloud, in fact. That was what Sanders had named the place. It was easy to see why.

"Is it always like this?" I asked Sanders, after drinking it all in for a while.

"Every mistfall," he replied, turning toward me with a wistful smile. He was a fat man, with a jovial red face. Not the sort who should smile wistfully. But he did.

He gestured toward the east, where Wraithworld's sun rising above the mists made a crimson and orange spectacle of the dawn sky.

"The sun," he said. "As it rises, the heat drives the mists back into the valleys, forces them to surrender the mountains they've conquered during the night. The mists sink, and one by one the peaks come into view. By noon the whole range is visible for miles and miles. There's nothing like it on Earth, or anywhere else."

He smiled again, and led me over to one of the tables scattered around the balcony. "And then, at sunset, it's all reversed. You must watch mistrise tonight," he said.

We sat down, and a sleek robowaiter came rolling out to serve us as the chairs registered our presence. Sanders ignored it. "It's war, you know," he continued. "Eternal war between the sun and the mists. And the mists have the better of it. They have the valleys, and the plains, and the seacoasts. The sun has only a few mountaintops. And them only by day."

He turned to the robowaiter and ordered coffee for both of us, to keep us occupied until the others arrived. It would be fresh-brewed, of course. Sanders didn't tolerate instants or synthetics on his planet.

"You like it here," I said, while we waited for the coffee.

Sanders laughed. "What's not to like? Castle Cloud has everything. Good food, entertainment, gambling, and all the other comforts of home. Plus this planet. I've got the best of both worlds, don't I?"

"I suppose so. But most people don't think in those terms. Nobody comes to Wraithworld for the gambling, or the food."

Sanders nodded. "But we do get some hunters. Out after rockcats and plains devils. And once in a while someone will come to look at the ruins."

"Maybe," I said. "But those are your exceptions. Not your rule. Most of your guests are here for one reason."

"Sure," he admitted, grinning. "The wraiths."

"The wraiths," I echoed. "You've got beauty here, and hunting and fishing and mountaineering. But none of that brings the tourists here. It's the wraiths they come for."

The coffee arrived then, two big steaming mugs accompanied by a pitcher of thick cream. It was very strong, and very hot, and very good. After weeks of spaceship synthetic, it was an awakening.

Sanders sipped at his coffee with care, his eyes studying me over the mug. He set it down thoughtfully. "And it's the wraiths you've come for, too," he said.

I shrugged. "Of course. My readers aren't interested in scenery, no matter how spectacular. Dubowski and his men are here to find wraiths, and I'm here to cover the search."

Sanders was about to answer, but he never got the chance. A sharp, precise voice cut in suddenly. "If there are any wraiths to find," the voice said.

We turned to face the balcony entrance. Dr. Charles Dubowski, head of the Wraithworld Research Team, was standing in the doorway, squinting at the light. He had managed to shake the gaggle of research assistants who usually trailed him everywhere.

Dubowski paused for a second, then walked over to our table, pulled out a chair, and sat down. The robowaiter came rolling out again.

Sanders eyed the thin scientist with unconcealed distaste. "What makes you think the wraiths aren't there, Doctor?" he asked.

Dubowski shrugged, and smiled lightly. "I just don't feel there's enough evidence," he said. "But don't worry. I never let my feelings interfere with my work. I want the truth as much as anyone. So I'll run an impartial expedition. If your wraiths *are* out there, I'll find them."

"Or they'll find you," Sanders said. He looked grave. "And that might not be too pleasant."

Dubowski laughed. "Oh, come now, Sanders. Just because you

live in a castle doesn't mean you have to be so melodramatic."

"Don't laugh, Doctor. The wraiths have killed people before, you know."

"No proof of that," said Dubowski. "No proof at all. Just as there's no proof of the wraiths themselves. But that's why we're here. To find proof. Or disproof. But come, I'm famished." He turned to our robowaiter, who had been standing by and humming impatiently.

Dubowski and I ordered rockcat steaks, with a basket of hot, freshly baked biscuits. Sanders took advantage of the Earth supplies our ship had brought in last night, and got a massive slab of ham with a half-dozen eggs.

Rockcat has a flavor that Earth meat hasn't had in centuries. I loved it, although Dubowski left much of his steak uneaten. He was too busy talking to eat.

"You shouldn't dismiss the wraiths so lightly," Sanders said after the robowaiter had stalked off with our orders. "There is evidence. Plenty of it. Twenty-two deaths since this planet was discovered. And eyewitness accounts of wraiths by the dozens."

"True," Dubowski said. "But I wouldn't call that real evidence. Deaths? Yes. Most are simple disappearances, however. Probably people who fell off a mountain, or got eaten by a rockcat, or something. It's impossible to find the bodies in the mists. More people vanish every day on Earth, and nothing is thought of it. But here, every time someone disappears, people claim the wraiths got him. No, I'm sorry. It's not enough."

"Bodies have been found, Doctor," Sanders said quietly. "Slain horribly. And not by falls or rockcats, either."

It was my turn to cut in. "Only four bodies have been recovered that I know of," I said. "And I've backgrounded myself pretty thoroughly on the wraiths."

Sanders frowned. "All right," he admitted. "But what about those four cases? Pretty convincing evidence, if you ask me."

The food showed up about then, but Sanders continued as we ate. "The first sighting, for example. That's never been explained satisfactorily. The Gregor Expedition."

I nodded. Dave Gregor had captained the ship that had discovered Wraithworld, nearly seventy-five years earlier. He had probed through the mists with his sensors, and set his ship down on the seacoast plains. Then he sent teams out to explore.

There were two men in each team, both well-armed. But in one case, only a single man came back, and he was in hysteria. He and his partner had gotten separated in the mists, and suddenly he heard a blood-curdling scream. When he found his friend, he was quite dead. And something was standing over the body.

The survivor described the killer as manlike, eight feet tall, and somehow insubstantial. He claimed that when he fired at it, the blaster bolt went right through it. Then the creature had wavered, and vanished in the mists.

Gregor sent other teams out to search for the thing. They recovered the body, but that was all. Without special instruments, it was difficult to find the same place twice in the mists. Let alone something like the creature that had been described.

So the story was never confirmed. But nonetheless, it caused a sensation when Gregor returned to Earth. Another ship was sent to conduct a more thorough search. It found nothing. But one of its search teams disappeared without a trace.

And the legend of the mist wraiths was born, and began to grow. Other ships came to Wraithworld, and a trickle of colonists came and went, and Paul Sanders landed one day and erected the Castle Cloud so the public might safely visit the mysterious planet of the wraiths.

And there were other deaths, and other disappearances, and many people claimed to catch brief glimpses of wraiths prowling through the mists. And then someone found the ruins. Just tumbled stone blocks, now. But once, structures of some sort. The homes of the wraiths, people said.

There was evidence, I thought. And some of it was hard to deny. But Dubowski was shaking his head vigorously.

"The Gregor affair proves nothing," he said. "You know as well as I this planet has never been explored thoroughly. Especially the plains area, where Gregor's ship put down. It was probably some sort of animal that killed that man. A rare animal of some sort native to that area."

"What about the testimony of his partner?" Sanders asked.

"Hysteria, pure and simple."

"The other sightings? There have been an awful lot of them. And the witnesses weren't always hysterical."

"Proves nothing," Dubowski said, shaking his head. "Back on Earth, plenty of people still claim to have seen ghosts and flying saucers. And here, with those damned mists, mistakes and hallucinations are naturally even easier."

He jabbed at Sanders with the knife he was using to butter a biscuit. "It's these mists that foul up everything. The wraith myth would have died long ago without the mists. Up to now, no one has had the equipment or the money to conduct a really thorough investigation. But we do. And we will. We'll get the truth once and for all."

Sanders grimaced. "If you don't get yourself killed first. The wraiths may not like being investigated."

"I don't understand you, Sanders," Dubowski said. "If you're so afraid of the wraiths and so convinced that they're down there prowling about, why have you lived here so long?"

"Castle Cloud was built with safeguards," Sanders said. "The brochure we send prospective guests describes them. No one is in danger here. For one thing, the wraiths won't come out of the mists. And we're in sunlight most of the day. But it's a different story down in the valleys."

"That's superstitious nonsense. If I had to guess, I'd say these mist wraiths of yours were nothing but transplanted Earth ghosts. Phantoms of someone's imagination. But I won't guess—I'll wait until the results are in. Then we'll see. If they are real, they won't be able to hide from us."

Sanders looked over at me. "What about you? Do you agree with him?"

"I'm a journalist," I said carefully. "I'm just here to cover what happens. The wraiths are famous, and my readers are interested. So I've got no opinions. Or none that I'd care to broadcast, anyway."

Sanders lapsed into a disgruntled silence, and attacked his ham and eggs with a renewed vigor. Dubowski took over for him, and steered the conversation over to the details of the investigation he was planning. The rest of the meal was a montage of eager talk about wraith traps, and search plans, and roboprobes, and sensors. I listened carefully and took mental notes for a column on the subject.

Sanders listened carefully, too. But you could tell from his face that he was far from pleased by what he heard.

Nothing much else happened that day. Dubowski spent his time at the spacefield, built on a small plateau below the castle, and supervised the unloading of his equipment. I wrote a column on his plans for the expedition, and beamed it back to Earth. Sanders tended to his other guests, and did whatever else a hotel manager does, I guess.

I went out to the balcony again at sunset, to watch the mists rise.

It was war, as Sanders had said. At mistfall, I had seen the sun victorious in the first of the daily battles. But now the conflict was renewed. The mists began to creep back to the heights as the temperature fell. Wispy gray-white tendrils stole up silently from the valleys, and curled around the jagged mountain peaks like ghostly fingers. Then the fingers began to grow thicker and stronger, and after a while they pulled the mists up after them.

One by one the stark, wind-carved summits were swallowed up for another night. The Red Ghost, the giant to the north, was the last mountain to vanish in the lapping white ocean. And then the mists began to pour in over the balcony ledge, and close around Castle Cloud itself.

I went back inside. Sanders was standing there, just inside the doors. He had been watching me.

"You were right," I said. "It was beautiful."

He nodded. "You know, I don't think Dubowski has bothered to look yet," he said.

"Busy, I guess."

Sanders sighed. "Too damn busy. C'mon. I'll buy you a drink."

The hotel bar was quiet and dark, with the kind of mood that promotes good talk and serious drinking. The more I saw of Sanders' castle, the more I liked the man. Our tastes were in remarkable accord.

We found a table in the darkest and most secluded part of the room, and ordered drinks from a stock that included liquors from a dozen worlds. And we talked.

"You don't seem very happy to have Dubowski here," I said after the drinks came. "Why not? He's filling up your hotel."

Sanders looked up from his drink, and smiled. "True. It is the slow season. But I don't like what he's trying to do."

"So you try to scare him away?"

Sanders' smile vanished. "Was I that transparent?"

I nodded.

He sighed. "Didn't think it would work," he said. He sipped thoughtfully at his drink. "But I had to try something."

"Why?"

"Because. Because he's going to destroy this world, if I let him. By the time he and his kind get through, there won't be a mystery left in the universe."

"He's just trying to find some answers. Do the wraiths exist? What about the ruins? Who built them? Didn't you ever want to know those things, Sanders?"

He drained his drink, looked around, and caught the waiter's eye to order another. No robowaiters in here. Only human help. Sanders was particular about atmosphere.

"Of course," he said when he had his drink. "Everyone's wondered about those questions. That's why people come here to Wraithworld, to the Castle Cloud. Each guy who touches down here is secretly hoping he'll have an adventure with the wraiths, and find out all the answers personally.

"So he doesn't. So he slaps on a blaster and wanders around the mist forests for a few days, or a few weeks, and finds nothing. So what? He can come back and search again. The dream is still there, and the romance, and the mystery.

"And who knows? Maybe one trip he glimpses a wraith drifting through the mists. Or something he thinks is a wraith. And then he'll go home happy, because he's been part of a legend. He's touched a little bit of creation that hasn't had all the awe and the wonder ripped from it yet by Dubowski's sort."

He fell silent, and stared morosely into his drink. Finally, after a long pause, he continued. "Dubowski! Bah! He makes me boil. He comes here with his ship full of lackeys and his million-credit grant and all his gadgets, to hunt for wraiths. Oh, he'll get them all right. That's what frightens me. Either he'll prove they don't exist, or he'll find them, and they'll turn out to be some kind of submen or animals or something."

He emptied his glass again, savagely. "And that will ruin it. Ruin it, you hear! He'll answer all the questions with his gadgets, and there'll be nothing left for anyone else. It isn't fair."

I sat there and sipped quietly at my drink and said nothing. Sanders ordered another. A foul thought was running around in my head. Finally I had to say it aloud.

"If Dubowski answers all the questions," I said, "then there will be no reason to come here anymore. And you'll be put out of business. Are you sure that's not why you're so worried?"

Sanders glared at me, and I thought he was going to hit me for a second. But he didn't. "I thought you were different. You looked at mistfall, and understood. I thought you did, anyway. But I guess I was wrong." He jerked his head toward the door. "Get out of here," he said.

I rose. "All right," I said. "I'm sorry, Sanders. But it's my job to ask nasty questions like that."

He ignored me, and I left the table. When I reached the door, I turned and looked back across the room. Sanders was staring into his drink again, and talking loudly to himself.

"Answers," he said. He made it sound obscene. "Answers. Always they have to have answers. But the questions are so much finer. Why can't they leave them alone?"

I left him alone then. Alone with his drinks.

The next few weeks were hectic ones, for the expedition and for me. Dubowski went about things thoroughly, you had to give him that. He had planned his assault on Wraithworld with meticulous precision.

Mapping came first. Thanks to the mists, what maps there were of Wraithworld were very crude by modern standards. So Dubowski sent out a whole fleet of roboprobes, to skim above the mists and steal their secrets with sophisticated sensory devices. From the information that came pouring in, a detailed topography of the region was pieced together.

That done, Dubowski and his assistants then used the maps to carefully plot every recorded wraith sighting since the Gregor Expedition. Considerable data on the sightings had been compiled and analyzed long before we left Earth, of course. Heavy use of the matchless collection on wraiths in the Castle Cloud library filled in the gaps that remained. As expected, sightings were most common in the valleys around the hotel, the only permanent human habitation on the planet.

When the plotting was completed, Dubowski set out his wraith traps, scattering most of them in the areas where wraiths had been reported most frequently. He also put a few in distant, outlying regions, however, including the seacoast plain where Gregor's ship had made the initial contact.

The traps weren't really traps, of course. They were squat duralloy pillars, packed with most every type of sensing and recording equipment known to Earth science. To the traps, the mists were all but nonexistent. If some unfortunate wraith wandered into survey range, there would be no way it could avoid detection.

Meanwhile, the mapping roboprobes were pulled in to be overhauled and reprogrammed, and then sent out again. With the topography known in detail, the probes could be sent through the mists on low-level patrols without fear of banging into a concealed mountain. The sensing equipment carried by the probes was not the equal of that in the wraith traps, of course. But the probes had a much greater range, and could cover thousands of square miles each day.

Finally, when the wraith traps were deployed and the robo-probes were in the air, Dubowski and his men took to the mist forests themselves. Each carried a heavy backpack of sensors and detection devices. The human search teams had more mobility than the wraith traps, and more sophisticated equipment than the probes. They covered a different area each day, in painstaking detail.

I went along on a few of those trips, with a backpack of my own. It made for some interesting copy, even though we never found anything. And while on search, I fell in love with the mist forests.

The tourist literature likes to call them "the ghastly mist forests of haunted Wraithworld." But they're not ghastly. Not really. There's a strange sort of beauty there, for those who can appreciate it.

The trees are thin and very tall, with white bark and pale gray leaves. But the forests are not without color. There's a parasite, a hanging moss of some sort, that's very common, and it drips from the overhanging branches in cascades of dark green and scarlet. And there are rocks, and vines, and low bushes choked with mis-shapen purplish fruits.

But there's no sun, of course. The mists hide everything. They swirl and slide around you as you walk, caressing you with unseen hands, clutching at your feet.

Once in a while, the mists play games with you. Most of the time you walk through a thick fog, unable to see more than a few feet in any direction, your own shoes lost in the mist carpet below. Sometimes, though, the fog closes in suddenly. And then you can't see at all. I blundered into more than one tree when that happened.

At other times, though, the mists—for no apparent reason—will roll back suddenly, and leave you standing alone in a clear pocket within a cloud. That's when you can see the forest in all its grotesque beauty. It's a brief, breathtaking glimpse of never-never land. Moments like that are few and short-lived. But they stay with you.

They stay with you.

In those early weeks, I didn't have much time for walking in the forests, except when I joined a search team to get the feel of it. Mostly I was busy writing. I did a series on the history of the planet, highlighted by the stories of the most famous sightings. I did feature profiles on some of the more colorful members of the expedition. I did a piece on Sanders, and the problems he encountered and overcame in building Castle Cloud. I did science pieces on the little known about the planet's ecology. I did mood pieces about the forests and the mountains. I did speculative-thought pieces about the ruins. I wrote about rockcat hunting, and mountain climbing, and the huge and dangerous swamp lizards native to some offshore islands.

And, of course, I wrote about Dubowski and his search. On that I wrote reams.

Finally, however, the search began to settle down into dull routine, and I began to exhaust the myriad other topics Wraithworld offered. My output began to decline. I started to have time on my hands.

That's when I really began to enjoy Wraithworld. I began to take daily walks through the forests, ranging wider each day. I visited the ruins, and flew half a continent away to see the swamp lizards firsthand instead of by holo. I befriended a group of hunters passing through, and shot myself a rockcat. I accompanied some other hunters to the western seacoast, and nearly got myself killed by a plains devil.

And I began to talk to Sanders again.

Through all of this, Sanders had pretty well ignored me and Dubowski and everyone else connected with the wraith research. He spoke to us grudgingly if at all, greeted us curtly, and spent all his free time with his other guests.

At first, after the way he had talked in the bar that night, I worried about what he might do. I had visions of him murdering someone out in the mists, and trying to make it look like a wraith killing. Or maybe just sabotaging the wraith traps. But I was sure he would try something to scare off Dubowski or otherwise undermine the expedition.

Comes of watching too much holovision, I guess. Sanders did nothing of the sort. He merely sulked, glared at us in the castle corridors, and gave us less than full cooperation at all times.

After a while, though, he began to warm up again. Not toward Dubowski and his men. Just toward me.

I guess that was because of my walks in the forests. Dubowski never went out into the mists unless he had to. And then he went out reluctantly, and came back quickly. His men followed their chief's example. I was the only joker in the deck. But then, I wasn't really part of the same deck.

Sanders noticed, of course. He didn't miss much of what went on in his castle. And he began to speak to me again. Civilly. One day, finally, he even invited me for drinks again.

It was about two months into the expedition. Winter was coming to Wraithworld and Castle Cloud, and the air was getting cold and crisp. Dubowski and I were out on the dining balcony, lingering over coffee after another superb meal. Sanders sat at a nearby table, talking to some tourists.

I forget what Dubowski and I were discussing. Whatever it was, Dubowski interrupted me with a shiver at one point. "It's getting cold out here," he complained. "Why don't we move inside?" Dubowski never liked the dining balcony very much.

I sort of frowned. "It's not that bad," I said. "Besides, it's nearly sunset. One of the best parts of the day."

Dubowski shivered again, and stood up. "Suit yourself," he said. "But I'm going in. I don't feel like catching a cold just so you can watch another mistfall."

He started to walk off. But he hadn't taken three steps before Sanders was up out of his seat, howling like a wounded rockcat.

"Mistfall," he bellowed. *"Mistfall!"* He launched into a long, incoherent string of obscenities. I had never seen Sanders so angry, not even when he threw me out of the bar that first night. He stood there, literally trembling with rage, his face flushed, his fat fists clenching and unclenching at his sides.

I got up in a hurry, and got between them. Dubowski turned to me, looking baffled and scared. "Wha—" he started.

"Get inside," I interrupted. "Get up to your room. Get to the lounge. Get somewhere. Get anywhere. But get out of here before he kills you."

"But—but—what's wrong? What happened? I don't—"

"Mistfall is in the morning," I told him. "At night, at sunset, it's mistrise. Now *go."*

"That's *all?* Why should that get him so—so—"

"GO!"

Dubowski shook his head, as if to say he still didn't understand what was going on. But he went.

I turned to Sanders. "Calm down," I said. "Calm down."

He stopped trembling, but his eyes threw blaster bolts at Dubowski's back. "Mistfall," he muttered. "Two months that bastard has been here, and he doesn't know the difference between mistfall and mistrise."

"He's never bothered to watch either one," I said. "Things like that don't interest him. That's his loss, though. No reason for you to get upset about it."

He looked at me, frowning. Finally he nodded. "Yeah," he said. "Maybe you're right." He sighed. "But *mistfall!* Hell." There was a short silence, then, "I need a drink. Join me?"

I nodded.

We wound up in the same dark corner as the first night, at what must have been Sanders's favorite table. He put away three drinks before I had finished my first. Big drinks. Everything in Castle Cloud was big.

There were no arguments this time. We talked about mistfall, and the forests, and the ruins. We talked about the wraiths, and

Sanders lovingly told me the stories of the great sightings. I knew them all already, of course. But not the way Sanders told them.

At one point, I mentioned that I'd been born in Bradbury when my parents were spending a short vacation on Mars. Sanders's eyes lit up at that, and he spent the next hour or so regaling me with Earthman jokes. I'd heard them all before, too. But I was getting more than a little drunk, and somehow they all seemed hilarious.

After that night, I spent more time with Sanders than with anyone else in the hotel. I thought I knew Wraithworld pretty well by that time. But that was an empty conceit, and Sanders proved it. He showed me hidden spots in the forests that have haunted me ever since. He took me to island swamps, where the trees are of a very different sort and sway horribly without a wind. We flew to the far north, to another mountain range where the peaks are higher and sheathed in ice, and to a southern plateau where the mists pour eternally over the edge in a ghostly imitation of a waterfall.

I continued to write about Dubowski and his wraith hunt, of course. But there was little new to write about, so most of my time was spent with Sanders. I didn't worry too much about my output. My Wraithworld series had gotten excellent play on Earth and most of the colony worlds, so I thought I had it made.

Not so.

I'd been on Wraithworld just a little over three months when my syndicate beamed me. A few systems away, a civil war had broken out on a planet called New Refuge. They wanted me to cover it. No news was coming out of Wraithworld anyway, they said, since Dubowski's expedition still had over a year to run.

Much as I liked Wraithworld, I jumped at the chance. My stories had been getting a little stale, and I was running out of ideas, and the New Refuge thing sounded like it could be very big.

So I said good-bye to Sanders and Dubowski and Castle Cloud, and took a last walk through the mist forests, and booked passage on the next ship through.

The New Refuge civil war was a firecracker. I spent less than a month on the planet, but it was a dreary month. The place had been colonized by religious fanatics, but the original cult had schismed, and both sides accused the other of heresy. It was all very dingy. The planet itself had all the charm of a Martian suburb.

I moved on as quickly as I could, hopping from planet to planet, from story to story. In six months, I had worked myself back to Earth. Elections were coming up, so I got slapped onto a political beat. That was fine by me. It was a lively campaign, and there was a ton of good stories to be mined.

But throughout it all, I kept myself up on the little news that came out of Wraithworld. And finally, as I'd expected, Dubowski announced a press conference. As the syndicate's resident wraith, I got myself assigned to cover, and headed out on the fastest starship I could find.

I got there a week before the conference, ahead of everyone else. I had beamed Sanders before taking ship, and he met me at the spaceport. We adjourned to the dining balcony, and had our drinks served out there.

"Well?" I asked him, after we had traded amenities. "You know what Dubowski's going to announce?"

Sanders looked very glum. "I can guess," he said. "He called in all his damn gadgets a month ago, and he's been cross-checking findings on a computer. We've had a couple of wraith sightings since you left. Dubowski moved in hours after each sighting, and went over the areas with a fine-tooth comb. Nothing. That's what he's going to announce, I think. Nothing."

I nodded. "Is that so bad, though? Gregor found nothing."

"Not the same," Sanders said. "Gregor didn't look the way Dubowski has. People will believe him, whatever he says."

I wasn't so sure of that, and was about to say so, when Dubowski arrived. Someone must have told him I was there. He came striding out on the balcony, smiling, spied me, and came over to sit down.

Sanders glared at him, and studied his drink. Dubowski trained all of his attention on me. He seemed very pleased with himself. He asked what I'd been doing since I left, and I told him, and he said that was nice.

Finally I got to ask him about his results. "No Comment," he said. "That's what I've called the press conference for."

"C'mon," I said. "I covered you for months when everybody else was ignoring the expedition. You can give me some kind of beat. What have you got?"

He hesitated. "Well, O.K.," he said doubtfully. "But don't release it yet. You can beam it out a few hours ahead of the conference. That should be enough time for a beat."

I nodded agreement. "What do you have?"

"The wraiths," he said. "I have the wraiths, bagged neatly. They don't exist. I've got enough evidence to prove it beyond a shadow of a doubt." He smiled broadly.

"Just because you didn't find anything?" I started. "Maybe they were avoiding you. If they're sentient, they might be smart enough. Or maybe they're beyond the ability of your sensors to detect."

"Come now," Dubowski said. "You don't believe that. Our wraith traps had every kind of sensor we could come up with. If the wraiths existed, they would have registered on something. But they didn't. We had the traps planted in the areas where three of Sanders's so-called sightings took place. Nothing. Absolutely nothing. Conclusive proof that those people were seeing things. Sightings, indeed."

"What about the deaths, the vanishings?" I asked. "What about the Gregor Expedition and the other classic cases?"

His smile spread. "Couldn't disprove all the deaths, of course. But our probes and our searches turned up four skeletons." He ticked them off on his fingers. "Two were killed by a rockslide, and one had rockcat claw marks on the bones."

"The fourth?"

"Murder," he said. "The body was buried in a shallow grave, clearly by human hands. A flood of some sort had exposed it. It was down in the records as a disappearance. I'm sure all the other bodies could be found, if we searched long enough. And we'd find that all died perfectly normal deaths."

Sanders raised his eyes from his drink. They were bitter eyes. "Gregor," he said stubbornly. "Gregor and the other classics."

Dubowski's smile became a smirk. "Ah, yes. We searched that area quite thoroughly. My theory was right. We found a tribe of apes nearby. Big brutes. Like giant baboons, with dirty white fur. Not a very successful species, either. We found only one small tribe, and they were dying out. But clearly, that was what Gregor's man sighted. And exaggerated all out of proportion."

There was silence. Then Sanders spoke, but his voice was beaten. "Just one question," he said softly. "Why?"

That brought Dubowski up short, and his smile faded. "You never have understood, have you, Sanders?" he said. "It was for truth. To free this planet from ignorance and superstition."

"Free Wraithworld?" Sanders said. "Was it enslaved?"

"Yes," Dubowski answered. "Enslaved by foolish myth. By fear. Now this planet will be free, and open. We can find out the truth behind those ruins now, without murky legends about half-human wraiths to fog the facts. We can open this planet for colonization. People won't be afraid to come here, and live, and farm. We've conquered the fear."

"A colony world? Here?" Sanders looked amused. "Are you going to bring big fans to blow away the mists, or what? Colonists have come before. And left. The soil's all wrong. You can't farm here, with all these mountains. At least not on a commercial scale. There's no way you can make a profit growing things on Wraithworld.

"Besides, there are hundreds of colony worlds crying for people. Did you need another so badly? Must Wraithworld become yet another Earth?"

Sanders shook his head sadly, drained his drink, and continued. "You're the one who doesn't understand, Doctor. Don't kid yourself. You haven't freed Wraithworld. You've destroyed it. You've stolen its wraiths, and left an empty planet."

Dubowski shook his head. "I think you're wrong. They'll find plenty of good, profitable ways to exploit this planet. But even if you were correct, well, it's just too bad. Knowledge is what man is all about. People like you have tried to hold back progress since the beginning of time. But they failed, and you failed. Man needs to know."

"Maybe," Sanders said. "But is that the *only* thing man needs? I don't think so. I think he also needs mystery, and poetry, and romance. I think he needs a few unanswered questions, to make him brood and wonder."

Dubowski stood up abruptly, and frowned. "This conversation is as pointless as your philosophy, Sanders. There's no room in my universe for unanswered questions."

"Then you live in a very drab universe, Doctor."

"And you, Sanders, live in the stink of your own ignorance. Find some new superstitions if you must. But don't try to foist them off on me with your tales and legends. I've got no time for wraiths." He looked at me. "I'll see you at the press conference," he said. Then he turned and walked briskly from the balcony.

Sanders watched him depart in silence, then swiveled in his chair to look out over the mountains. "The mists are rising," he said.

Sanders was wrong about the colony, too, as it turned out. They did establish one, although it wasn't much to boast of. Some vineyards, some factories, and a few thousand people; all belonging to no more than a couple of big companies.

Commercial farming did turn out to be unprofitable, you see. With one exception—a native grape, a fat gray thing the size of a lemon. So Wraithworld has only one export, a smoky white wine with a mellow, lingering flavor.

They call it mistwine, of course. I've grown fond of it over the years. The taste reminds me of mistfall somehow, and makes me dream. But that's probably me, not the wine. Most people don't care for it much.

Still, in a very minor way, it's a profitable item. So Wraithworld is still a regular stop on the spacelanes. For freighters, at least.

The tourists are long gone, though. Sanders was right about that. Scenery they can get closer to home, and cheaper. The wraiths were why they came.

Sanders is long gone, too. He was too stubborn and too impractical to buy in on the mistwine operations when he had the chance. So he stayed behind his ramparts at Castle Cloud until the last. I don't know what happened to him afterwards, when the hotel finally went out of business.

The castle itself is still there. I saw it a few years ago, when I stopped for a day en route to a story on New Refuge. It's already crumbling, though. Too expensive to maintain. In a few years, you won't be able to tell it from those other, older ruins.

Otherwise the planet hasn't changed much. The mists still rise at sunset, and fall at dawn. The Red Ghost is still stark and beautiful in the early morning light. The forests are still there, and the rockcats still prowl.

Only the wraiths are missing.

Only the wraiths.

BEN BOVA

The Future of Science: Prometheus, Apollo, Athena

Where is science heading? Is it taking us on a one-way ride to oblivion, or leading the human spirit upward to the stars? Science fiction writers have been predicting both, for centuries.

"I have but one lamp by which my feet are guided," Patrick Henry said, "and that is the lamp of experience. I know of no way of judging of the future but by the past."

Look at the past, at the way science and technology have affected the human race. Look far back. Picture all of humanity from the earliest *Homo erectus* of a half-million years ago as a single human being. Now picture science as a genie that will grant that person the traditional three wishes of every good fable.

We have already used up one of those wishes. We are working on the second one of them now. And the future of humankind, the difference between oblivion and infinity, lies in our choice of the third wish.

Our three wishes can be given classical names: Prometheus, Apollo, and Athena.

Prometheus

Long before there was science, perhaps even before there was speech, our primitive ancestors discovered technology. Modern man thinks of technology as the stepson of scientific research, but

110

that is only a very recent reversal of a half-million-year-long situation. Technology—*toolmaking*—came first. Science—*understanding*—came a long time later.

Look at the Prometheus legend. It speaks the truth as clearly as any modern science fiction story. It speaks of the first of our three wishes.

Prometheus brought the gift of fire. He saw from his Olympian height that man was a weak, cold, hungry, miserable creature, little better than the animals of the fields. At enormous cost to himself, Prometheus stole fire from the heavens and gave it to man. With fire, man became almost godlike in his domination of all the rest of the world.

Like most myths, the legend of the fire-bringer is fantastic in detail and absolutely correct in spirit. Anthropologists who have sifted through the fossil remains of early man have drawn a picture that is much less romantic, yet startlingly close to the essence of the Prometheus legend.

The first evidence of man's use of fire dates back some half-million years. The hero of the story is hardly godlike in appearance. He is *Homo erectus,* an ancestor of ours who lived in Africa, Asia, and possibly Europe during the warm millennia between the second and third glaciations of the Ice Age. *Homo erectus* was scarcely five feet tall. His skull was rather halfway between the shape of an ape's and our own. His brain case was only two-thirds of our size. But his body was fully human: he walked erect and had human, grasping hands.

And he was dying. The titanic climate shifts of the Ice Age caused drought even in tropical Africa, his most likely home territory. Forests dwindled. Anthropologists have found many *H. erectus* skulls scratched by leopard's teeth. Our ancestors were not well equipped to protect themselves. Picture Moon Watcher and his tribe from Arthur C. Clarke's *2001.*

It was a gift from the skies that saved *Homo erectus* from oblivion. Not an extraterrestrial visitor, but a blast of lightning that set a bush afire. An especially curious and courageous member of the *erectus* clan overcame his very natural fear to reach out for the bright warm promise of the flames. No telling how many times our ancestors got nothing for their curiosity and courage except a set of burnt fingers and a yowl of pain. But eventually they learned to handle fire safely, and to use it.

With fire, humankind's technology was born.

Fire, the gift of Prometheus, satisfied our first wish, which was: Feed me, warm me, protect me.

Fire not only frightened away the night-stalking beasts and gave our ancestors a source of warmth, it helped to change the very shape of their faces and their society.

Homo erectus was the world's first cook. He used fire to cook the food that had always been eaten raw previously. Cooked food is softer and juicier than raw food. Cooking cuts down greatly on the amount of chewing that must be done. Our ancestors found that they could spend less time actually eating and have more time available for hunting or traveling or making better spearpoints.

More important, the apelike muzzle of *Homo erectus*, with its powerful jaw muscles, was no longer needed. Faces became more human. The brain case grew as the jaw shortened. No one can definitely say that these two face changes are related. But they happened at the same time. The apelike face of the early hominids changed into the present small-jawed, big-domed head of *Homo sapiens sapiens.*

Beyond that, fire was the first source of energy for any animal outside its own muscles. Fire liberated us from physical labor and unleashed forces that have made us masters of the world. Fire is the basis of all technology. Without fire we would have no metals, no steam, no electricity, no books, no cities, no agriculture, nothing that we would recognize as civilization.

The gift of Prometheus satisfied our first wish. It has fed us, kept us warm, protected us from our enemies. Too well. It has led to the development of a technology that is now itself a threat to our survival on this planet.

The price Prometheus paid for giving fire to us was to be

chained eternally to a rock and suffer daily torture. Again, the myth is truer than it sounds. The technology that we have developed over the past half-million years is gutting the Earth. Forests have been stripped away, mountains leveled, our air and water fouled with the wastes of modern industry.

For our first wish, the wish that Prometheus answered, was actually: Feed me, warm me, protect me, *regardless of the consequences.* Our leopard-stalked ancestors gave no thought to the air pollution arising from their primitive fires. And our waistcoated entrepreneurs of the Industrial Revolution did not care if their factories turned the millstream into an open sewer.

But today, when the air we breathe can kill us and the water is often unfit to drink, we care deeply about the consequences of technology.

The gift of Prometheus was a first-generation technology. It bought the survival of the human race at the price of eventual ecological danger. Now we seek a second-generation technology, one that can give us all the benefits of Prometheus's gift without the harmful by-products.

This is our second wish. We have already asked it, and if it is truly answered, it will be answered by Apollo.

The sun god. The symbol of brilliance and clarity and music and poetry. The beautiful one.

Apollo

Although our first-generation technology predated actual science by some half-million years, the second-generation technology of Apollo cannot come about without the deep understandings that only science can bring us. To go beyond the ills of first-generation technology, we must turn to science, to the quality of mind that sees beyond the immediate and makes the desire to know, to understand, the central theme of human activity.

Science is something very new in human history. As new, actually, as the founding of America. In the year 1620, when the Puritans were stepping on Plymouth Rock, Francis Bacon published the book that signaled the opening of the scientific age: *Novum Organum.*

Men had pursued a quest for knowledge for ages before that date. Ancients had mapped the heavens, tribal shamans had started the study of medicine, mystics had developed some rudimentary understandings of the human mind, philosophers had argued about causes and origins. But it was not until the first few decades of the seventeenth century that the deliberate, organized method of thinking that we now call science was created.

It was in those decades, some 350 years ago, that Galileo began settling arguments about physical phenomena by setting up experiments and measuring the results. Kepler was deducing the laws that govern planetary motion. Bacon was writing about a new method of thinking and investigating the secrets of nature: the technique of inductive reasoning, a technique that requires a careful interplay of observation, measurement, and logic.

Bacon's landmark book, *Novum Organum*, was written and titled in reaction to Aristotle's *De Organum*, written some fifteen hundred years earlier as a summarization of all that was known about the physical universe. For fifteen hundred years, Aristotle's word was the last one on any subject dealing with "natural philosophy," or what we today call the physical sciences. For fifteen hundred years it was blindly accepted that a heavy body falls faster than a light one, that the Earth is the center of the universe, that the heart is the seat of human emotion. (And when have you seen a Valentine card bearing a picture of the brain or an adrenal gland?)

For fifteen hundred years, human knowledge and understanding advanced so little that the peasant of Aristotle's day and that of Bacon's would scarcely seem different to each other. This was not due to a Dark Age that blotted out ancient knowledge and prevented progress. For this fifteen-hundred-year stasis affected not only Europe, but the Middle East, Asia, Africa, and the Americas as well.

The lack of advancement during this long millennium and a half was due, more than anything else, to the limits of the ancient method of thought. Only incremental gains in technology could be made by people who accepted ancient authority as the answer to every question, who believed that the Earth was flat and placed at the exact center of the universe, who "knew" that empirical evidence was not to be trusted because it could be a trick played upon the senses by the forces of evil.

In the 350 years since the scientific method of thought has become established, human life has changed so enormously that a peasant of Bacon's time (or a nobleman, for that matter!) would be lost and bewildered in today's society. Today the poorest American controls more energy, at the touch of a button or the turn of an ignition key, than most of the high-born nobles of all time ever commanded. We can see and hear the world's history, current news, the finest artists, whenever we choose to. We live longer, grow taller and stronger, and can blithely disregard diseases that scourged civilization, generation after generation.

This is what science-based technology has done for us. Yet this is almost trivial, compared to what the scientific method of thinking has accomplished.

For the basic theme of scientific thought is that the universe is knowable. Man is not a helpless pawn of forces beyond his own ken. Order can be brought out of chaos. Albert Einstein said it best: "The eternal mystery of the world is its comprehensibility."

Faced, then, with a first-generation technology that threatens to strangle us in its effluvia, we have already turned to science for the basis of a second-generation technology. We have turned to Apollo.

We recognize that it is Apollo's symbol—the dazzling sun—that will be the key to our second-generation technology. The touchstone of all our history has been our ability to command constantly richer sources of energy. *Homo erectus*'s burning bush gave way to fires fueled by coal, oil, natural gas—the fossils of antediluvian creatures. Today we take energy from the fission of uranium atoms.

Tomorrow our energy will come from the sun. Either we will tap the sunlight streaming down on us and convert it into the forms of energy that we need, such as electricity or heat, or we will create miniature suns here on Earth and draw energy directly from them. This is thermonuclear fusion, the energy of the H-bomb. In thermonuclear fusion, the nuclei of light atoms such as hydrogen isotopes are forced together to create heavier nuclei and give off energy. This is the energy source of the sun itself, and the stars. It promises clean, inexpensive, inexhaustible energy for all the rest of human history.

The fuel for fusion is deuterium, the isotope of hydrogen that is in "heavy water." For every six thousand atoms of ordinary hydrogen in the world's oceans, there is one atom of deuterium. The fusion process is energetic enough so that the deuterium in one cubic meter of water (about 225 gallons) can yield 450,000 kilowatt-hours of energy. That means that a single cubic kilometer of seawater has the energy equivalent of all the known oil reserves on Earth. And that is using only one six-thousandth of the hydrogen in the water.

Fusion power will be cheap and abundant enough to be the driving force of our second-generation technology. The gift of Apollo can provide all our energy needs for millions of years into the future.

There will eventually be no further need for fossil fuels or even fissionables. Which in turn means there will be no need to gut our world for coal, oil, gas, uranium. No oil wells. No black lung disease. No problems of disposing of highly radioactive wastes.

The waste products of the fusion process are clean, inert helium and highly energetic neutrons. The neutrons could be a radiation danger if they escape the fusion reactor, but they are far too valuable to let loose, for energetic neutrons are the philosopher's stone of the modern alchemists. They can transform the atoms of one element into atoms of another.

Instead of changing lead into gold, however, the neutrons will be used to transmute light metals such as lithium into the hydrogen isotopes that fuel the fusion reactors. They can also transmute the radioactive wastes of fission power plants into safely inert substances.

The energy from fusion can also be used to make the ultimate recycling system. Fusion "torches" will be able to vaporize anything. An automobile, for example, could be flashed into a cloud of its component atoms—iron, carbon, chromium, oxygen, etc. Using apparatus that already exists today, it is possible to separate these elements and collect them, in ultrapure form, for reuse. With effective and efficient recycling, the need for fresh raw materials will go down drastically. The mining and lumbering industries will dwindle; the scars on the face of the Earth will begin to heal.

Fusion energy will produce abundant electricity without significant pollution, and with thousands of times less radiation hazard than modern power plants. With cheap and abundant energy there need be no such thing as a "have-not" nation. Seawater can be desalted and piped a thousand kilometers inland, if necessary. The energy to do it will be cheap enough. All forms of transportation—from automobiles to spacecraft—will either use fusion power directly or the electricity derived from fusion.

The gift of Apollo, then, can mark as great a turning point in human history as the gift of Prometheus. Like the taming of fire, the taming of fusion will so change our way of life that our descendants a scarce century from now will be hard put to imagine how we could have lived without this ultimate energy source.

Apollo is a significant name for humankind's second wish for another reason, too. Apollo was the title given to humanity's most ambitious exploration program. In the name of the sun-god we reached the moon. Not very consistent nomenclature or mythology, perhaps, but extremely significant for the future of science and the human race.

For to truly fulfill our second wish, we must and will expand the habitat of the human race into space.

We live on a finite planet. We are already beginning to see the consequences of overpopulation and overconsumption of this planet's natural resources. Sooner or later, we must begin to draw our resources from other worlds.

We have already "imported" some minerals from the moon. The cost for a few hundred pounds of rocks was astronomically high: more than $20 billion. Clearly, more efficient modes of transportation must be found, and scientists and engineers are at work on them now.

It is interesting to realize that the actual cost of the energy it takes to send an average-sized man to the moon and back—if you bought the energy from your local electric utility—is less than $200. There is much room for improvement in our space transportation systems.

Improvements are coming. Engineers are now building the Space Shuttle, which will be a reusable "bus" for shuttling cargo and people into orbit. Fusion energy itself will someday propel spacecraft. Scientists are working on very high-powered lasers that could boost spacecraft into orbit. And the eventual payoff of the esoteric investigations into subatomic physics might well be an insight into the basic forces of nature, an insight that may someday give us some control over gravity.

There is an entire solar system of natural resources waiting for us, once we have achieved economical means of operating in deep space. Many science fiction stories have speculated on the possibilities of "mining" the asteroids, that belt of stone and metal fragments in orbit between Mars and Jupiter.

There are thousands upon thousands of asteroids out there. A single 10-kilometer chunk of the nickel-iron variety (which is common) would contain approximately 20 million million tons of high-grade iron. That's 2×10^{13} tons. Considering that world steel production in 1973 was a bit less than a thousand million tons (10^9), this one asteroid could satisfy our need for steel for about ten thousand years!

The resources are there. And eventually much of our industrial operations will themselves move into space: into orbit around

Earth initially, and then farther out, to the areas where the resources are.

There are excellent reasons for doing so. Industrial operations have traditionally been sited as close as possible to the source of raw material. This is why Pittsburgh is near the Pennsylvania coal fields, and not far from the iron-ore deposits further west. It is cheaper to transport finished manufactured products than haul bulky raw materials.

The very nature of space offers advantages for many industrial processes. The high vacuum, low gravity, and virtually free solar energy of the space environment will be irresistible attractions to designers of future industrial operations. Also, the problems of handling waste products and pollution emissions will be easier in space than on Earth.

The pressures of social history will push industry off-planet. We cannot afford to cover the Earth with factories. Yet the alternative is a cessation of economic growth—as long as industrial operations are limited to our finite planet.

Although studies such as the MIT/Club of Rome's "Limits to Growth" have urged a stabilized society, human nature usually wants to have its cake and eat it, too. It should be possible to maintain economic growth by expanding off-planet, and thereby avoid the catastrophic effects of polluting our world to death.

What about the ultimate pollution: overpopulation? Will our expansion into space simply allow the human race to continue its population explosion until civilization collapses under the sheer groaning weight of human flesh?

Many science fiction stories have depicted a rigidly stabilized future society, where vocation, recreation, and even procreation are strictly controlled by the state. Given modern techniques of behavior modification and genetic manipulation, this might someday be possible. Indeed, this is the world that "The Limits to Growth" inevitably leads to.

There is an alternative. In all of human history, the only sure technique for leveling off an expanding population has been to increase the people's standard of living. War, famine, pestilence inevitably lead to a higher birthrate. Modern science has reduced the death rate to the point where even a moderately rising birthrate is a threat to society.

If economic growth can be maintained or even accelerated by expanding the economy into space—and this growth is shared by all people everywhere on Earth—we may have the means for leveling off the population explosion without the repressions that most science fiction writers are haunted by.

Eventually, people will go into space to live. There will be no large-scale migrations—not for a century, at least. But within a few decades, we may see self-sufficient communities in orbit around the Earth, on the moon, and eventually farther out in space.

For the first time since the settling of the Americas, humankind will have an opportunity to develop new social codes. In the strange and harsh environments we will encounter in space, we will perforce evolve new ways of life. Old manners and customs will wither; new ones will arise.

Scientists such as astronomer Carl Sagan look forward to these "experimental communities." They point out that social evolution on Earth is stultified by the success of Western technological civilization. Nearly every human society on this planet lives in a Westernized culture. Variety among human cultures is being homogenized away. The new environment of space offers an opportunity to produce new types of societies, new ways of life that might teach those who remain on Earth how to live better, more fully, more humanly.

Which brings us to the last of humankind's three wishes, the most important one of all, the wish for the gift of Athena.

Athena

The gray-eyed goddess of civilization and wisdom. The warrior-goddess who was born with shield and spear in her hands, but who evolved from Homer's time to Pericles' into a goddess of counsel, of arts and industries, the protectress of cities, the patron deity of Athens.

It is to Athena that we must turn if we are to succeed in our long struggle against the darkness. For human history can be viewed as an attempt to countervene the inevitable chaos of entropy. We succeed as individuals, as a society, as a species, when we are able to bring order out of confusion, understanding out of mystery. Athena, whose symbol is the owl, represents the wisdom and self-knowledge that we so desperately need.

Knowledge we have. And we are acquiring more, so rapidly that people suffer "future shock" from their inability to digest the swift changes flowing across our lives. Wisdom is what we need; the gift of Athena. Self-understanding.

Human beings are understanding-seeking creatures. But when we seek understanding from authorities—in ivied towers of learning, or marbled halls of government, or dark caves of mysticism —we fall short of our goal. Proclamations from authorities are not understanding. When we as individuals give up our quest for understanding and allow others to think and decide for us, we allow the inevitable darkness to gather closer. The brilliant Aegean sunlight is what we seek, and we must turn to Athena's gift of wisdom to find it.

Science will be the crucial factor in finding Athena's gift. As a mode of thinking, a technique for learning and understanding, it is central to our search for self-knowledge.

Our first two wishes were largely focused outside ourselves. They were aimed at manipulating the world outside our skins. Our third and final wish concerns the universe within us: our bodies, our brains, our minds. Until now, scientific research has been mainly concerned with the physical world around us. Physics, chemistry, astronomy, engineering—all deal with the universe that we lay hands on. Even biology and sociology have dealt mainly with matters external to the individual human being. Medical research has been confined to chemistry, mysticism, and sharper surgical tools, until very recently.

But starting with psychology, the major thrust of scientific research has been slowly turning over the past century or so toward the universe inside our flesh.

Molecular biology is delving into the basic mechanics of what makes us what we are: the chemistry of genetic inheritance. Ethnology and psychology are probing the fundamentals of why we behave the way we do: the essence of learning and behavior. Neurophysiology is examining the basic structure and workings of the brain itself: the electrochemistry of memory and thought.

Many view this research with horror. From Mary Wollstonecraft Shelley's vision of Frankenstein, generations of writers and readers have feared scientists' attempts to tamper with the human mind and body. "There are some things that man was not meant to know," has become not only a cliché, but a rallying cry for the fearful and the ignorant.

Genetic manipulation could someday create an elite of geniuses who rule a race of zombies. Behavior modification techniques can turn every jailbird into a model prisoner, and make prisoners of us all. Psychosurgery is performed on the poor, the uninformed, the helpless.

Yet molecular biology may erase the scourge of cancer and genetic diseases, bringing the human race to a pinnacle of physical perfection. Behavior modification techniques will someday unravel the tangled engrams of hopeless psychotics and restore them to the light of healthy adulthood. Brain research could bring quantum leaps in our abilities to understand and learn.

Human societies have developed in such a way that new ideas and new capabilities are acquired by the rulers long before the ruled ever hear of them. All societies are ruled by elites. But the eventual effect of new knowledge is to destroy the elite, to spread the new capabilities among all the people. Far from fearing new knowledge, or shunning it, we must seek it out and embrace it wholeheartedly. For only out of the new knowledge that scientists are acquiring will we derive the understanding that we need to survive as individuals and as a species.

The gift of Athena is what we must have. And it must be shared by all of us, not merely an elite at the top of society. The gift of Prometheus gave us mastery of this world. The gift of Apollo is bringing us powers so vast that we can turn this planet into a paradise or a barren lifeless wasteland.

Only the wisdom of Athena can control the powers of modern science and technology. Only when all the people know what is possible will it be possible to know what to do. As long as an elite controls the power of science and technology, the masses will be manipulated. And such manipulation will inevitably lead to collapse and destruction.

We stand poised on the brink of godhood. The knowledge and wisdom that modern scientific research offers can help us to take the next evolutionary step, and transform ourselves into a race of intelligent beings who truly understand themselves and the universe around them. It is possible, by our own efforts, to climb as far above our present condition as we today are above primitive little *Homo erectus.*

The anthropologist Carleton Coon painted the prospect twenty years ago, in his book, *The Story of Man:*

A half-million years of experience in outwitting beasts on mountains and plains, in heat and cold, in light and darkness, gave our ancestors the equipment that we still desperately need if we are to slay the dragon that roams the earth today, marry the princess of outer space, and live happily ever after in the deer-filled glades of a world in which everyone is young and beautiful forever.

We have the means within our grasp. The gift of Athena, like our first two gifts, actually comes from no one but ourselves.

VONDA N. MCINTYRE

Of Mist, and Grass, and Sand

"Wherever nature is revered as self-moving, and is inherently divine, the serpent is revered as symbolic of its divine life . . . where the serpent is cursed, all nature is devaluated and its power of life regarded as nothing in itself . . ." (*Creative Mythology* by Joseph Campbell). In two stories in this volume the serpent appears, and is not cursed. This one finished first, the other second, in the voting for the Nebula awards. Within us, modern, civilized humankind, there is something that recognizes and responds to the ancient symbols. Something that answers, yes, I am still here.

The little boy was frightened. Gently, Snake touched his hot forehead. Behind her, three adults stood close together, watching, suspicious, afraid to show their concern with more than narrow lines around their eyes. They feared Snake as much as they feared their only child's death. In the dimness of the tent, the flickering lamplights gave no reassurance.

The child watched with eyes so dark the pupils were not visible, so dull that Snake herself feared for his life. She stroked his hair. It was long and very pale, a striking color against his dark skin, dry and irregular for several inches near the scalp. Had Snake been with these people months ago, she would have known the child was growing ill.

"Bring my case, please," Snake said.

The child's parents started at her soft voice. Perhaps they had expected the screech of a bright jay, or the hissing of a shining serpent. This was the first time Snake had spoken in their presence. She had only watched, when the three of them had come to observe her from a distance and whisper about her occupation and her youth; she had only listened, and then nodded, when finally they came to ask her help. Perhaps they had thought she was mute.

The fair-haired younger man lifted her leather case from the felt

floor. He held the satchel away from his body, leaning to hand it
to her, breathing shallowly with nostrils flared against the faint
smell of musk in the dry desert air. Snake had almost accustomed
herself to the kind of uneasiness he showed; she had already seen
it often.

When Snake reached out, the young man jerked back and
dropped the case. Snake lunged and barely caught it, set it gently
down, and glanced at him with reproach. His husband and his wife
came forward and touched him to ease his fear. "He was bitten
once," the dark and handsome woman said. "He almost died." Her
tone was not of apology, but of justification.

"I'm sorry," the younger man said. "It's—" He gestured toward
her; he was trembling, and trying visibly to control the reactions
of his fear. Snake glanced down to her shoulder, where she had
been unconsciously aware of the slight weight and movement. A
tiny serpent, thin as the finger of a baby, slid himself around
behind her neck to show his narrow head below her short black
curls. He probed the air with his trident tongue, in a leisurely
manner, out, up and down, in, to savor the taste of the smells.

"It's only Grass," Snake said. "He cannot harm you."

If he were bigger, he might frighten; his color was pale green,
but the scales around his mouth were red, as if he had just feasted
as a mammal eats, by tearing. He was, in fact, much neater.

The child whimpered. He cut off the sound of pain; perhaps he
had been told that Snake, too, would be offended by crying. She
only felt sorry that his people refused themselves such a simple
way of easing fear. She turned from the adults, regretting their
terror of her, but unwilling to spend the time it would take to
convince them their reactions were unjustified. "It's all right," she
said to the little boy. "Grass is smooth, and dry, and soft, and if I
left him to guard you, even death could not reach your bedside."
Grass poured himself into her narrow, dirty hand, and she extended him toward the child. "Gently." He reached out and
touched the sleek scales with one fingertip. Snake could sense the
effort of even such a simple motion, yet the boy almost smiled.

"What are you called?"

He looked quickly toward his parents, and finally they nodded. "Stavin," he whispered. He had no strength or breath for speaking.

"I am Snake, Stavin, and in a little while, in the morning, I must hurt you. You may feel a quick pain, and your body will ache for several days, but you will be better afterward."

He stared at her solemnly. Snake saw that though he understood and feared what she might do, he was less afraid than if she had lied to him. The pain must have increased greatly as his illness became more apparent, but it seemed that others had only reassured him, and hoped the disease would disappear or kill him quickly.

Snake put Grass on the boy's pillow and pulled her case nearer. The lock opened at her touch. The adults still could only fear her; they had had neither time nor reason to discover any trust. The wife was old enough that they might never have another child, and Snake could tell by their eyes, their covert touching, their concern, that they loved this one very much. They must, to come to Snake in this country.

It was night, and cooling. Sluggish, Sand slid out of the case, moving his head, moving his tongue, smelling, tasting, detecting the warmth of bodies.

"Is that—?" The older husband's voice was low, and wise, but terrified, and Sand sensed the fear. He drew back into striking position, and sounded his rattle softly. Snake spoke to him and extended her arm. The pit viper relaxed and flowed around and around her slender wrist to form black and tan bracelets. "No," she said. "Your child is too ill for Sand to help. I know it is hard, but please try to be calm. This is a fearful thing for you, but it is all I can do."

She had to annoy Mist to make her come out. Snake rapped on the bag, and finally poked her twice. Snake felt the vibration of sliding scales, and suddenly the albino cobra flung herself into the tent. She moved quickly, yet there seemed to be no end to her.

She reared back and up. Her breath rushed out in a hiss. Her head rose well over a meter above the floor. She flared her wide hood. Behind her, the adults gasped, as if physically assaulted by the gaze of the tan spectacle design on the back of Mist's hood. Snake ignored the people and spoke to the great cobra in a singsong voice. "Ah, thou. Furious creature. Lie down; 'tis time for thee to earn thy piglet. Speak to this child, and touch him. He is called Stavin." Slowly, Mist relaxed her hood, and allowed Snake to touch her. Snake grasped her firmly behind the head, and held her so she looked at Stavin. The cobra's silver eyes picked up the yellow of the lamplight. "Stavin," Snake said, "Mist will only meet you now. I promise that this time she will touch you gently."

Still, Stavin shivered when Mist touched his thin chest. Snake did not release the serpent's head, but allowed her body to slide against the boy's. The cobra was four times longer than Stavin was tall. She curved herself in stark white loops across Stavin's swollen abdomen, extending herself, forcing her head toward the boy's face, straining against Snake's hands. Mist met Stavin's frightened stare with the gaze of lidless eyes. Snake allowed her a little closer.

Mist flicked out her tongue to taste the child.

The younger husband made a small, cut-off, frightened sound. Stavin flinched at it, and Mist drew back, opening her mouth, exposing her fangs, audibly thrusting her breath through her throat. Snake sat back on her heels, letting out her own breath. Sometimes, in other places, the kinfolk could stay while she worked. "You must leave," she said gently. "It's dangerous to frighten Mist."

"I won't—"

"I'm sorry. You must wait outside."

Perhaps the younger husband, perhaps even the wife, would have made the indefensible objections and asked the answerable questions, but the older man turned them and took their hands and led them away.

"I need a small animal," Snake said as the man lifted the tent flap. "It must have fur, and it must be alive."

"One will be found," he said, and the three parents went into the glowing night. Snake could hear their footsteps in the sand outside.

Snake supported Mist in her lap, and soothed her. The cobra wrapped herself around Snake's narrow waist, taking in her warmth. Hunger made her even more nervous than usual, and she was hungry, as was Snake. Coming across the black sand desert, they had found sufficient water, but Snake's traps were unsuccessful. The season was summer, the weather was hot, and many of the furry tidbits Sand and Mist preferred were estivating. When the serpents missed their regular meal, Snake began a fast as well.

She saw with regret that Stavin was more frightened now. "I am sorry to send your parents away," she said. "They can come back soon."

His eyes glistened, but he held back the tears. "They said to do what you told me."

"I would have you cry, if you are able," Snake said. "It isn't such a terrible thing." But Stavin seemed not to understand, and Snake did not press him; she knew that his people taught themselves to resist a difficult land by refusing to cry, refusing to mourn, refusing to laugh. They denied themselves grief, and allowed themselves little joy, but they survived.

Mist had calmed to sullenness. Snake unwrapped her from her waist and placed her on the pallet next to Stavin. As the cobra moved, Snake guided her head, feeling the tension of the striking muscles. "She will touch you with her tongue," she told Stavin. "It might tickle, but it will not hurt. She smells with it, as you do with your nose."

"With her tongue?"

Snake nodded, smiling, and Mist flicked out her tongue to caress Stavin's cheek. Stavin did not flinch; he watched, his child's delight in knowledge briefly overcoming pain. He lay perfectly still as Mist's long tongue brushed his cheeks, his eyes, his mouth. "She tastes the sickness," Snake said. Mist stopped fighting the restraint of her grasp, and drew back her head. Snake sat on her heels and released the cobra, who spiraled up her arm and laid herself across her shoulders.

"Go to sleep, Stavin," Snake said. "Try to trust me, and try not to fear the morning."

Stavin gazed at her for a few seconds, searching for truth in Snake's pale eyes. "Will Grass watch?"

The question startled her, or, rather, the acceptance behind the question. She brushed his hair from his forehead and smiled a smile that was tears just beneath the surface. "Of course." She picked Grass up. "Thou wilt watch this child, and guard him." The snake lay quiet in her hand, and his eyes glittered black. She laid him gently on Stavin's pillow.

"Now sleep."

Stavin closed his eyes, and the life seemed to flow out of him. The alteration was so great that Snake reached out to touch him, then saw that he was breathing, slowly, shallowly. She tucked a blanket around him and stood up. The abrupt change in position dizzied her; she staggered and caught herself. Across her shoulders, Mist tensed.

Snake's eyes stung and her vision was oversharp, fever-clear. The sound she imagined she heard swooped in closer. She steadied herself against hunger and exhaustion, bent slowly, and picked up the leather case. Mist touched her cheek with the tip of her tongue.

She pushed aside the tent flap and felt relief that it was still night. She could stand the heat, but the brightness of the sun curled through her, burning. The moon must be full; though the clouds obscured everything, they diffused the light so the sky appeared gray from horizon to horizon. Beyond the tents, groups of formless shadows projected from the ground. Here, near the edge of the desert, enough water existed so clumps and patches of bush grew, providing shelter and sustenance for all manner of creatures. The black sand, which sparkled and blinded in the sunlight, at night was like a layer of soft soot. Snake stepped out of the tent, and the illusion of softness disappeared; her boots slid crunching into the sharp hard grains.

Stavin's family waited, sitting close together between the dark tents that clustered in a patch of sand from which the bushes had been ripped and burned. They looked at her silently, hoping with their eyes, showing no expression in their faces. A woman somewhat younger than Stavin's mother sat with them. She was dressed, as they were, in a long loose robe, but she wore the only adornment Snake had seen among these people: a leader's circle, hanging around her neck on a leather thong. She and the older husband were marked close kin by their similarities: sharp-cut planes of face, high cheekbones, his hair white and hers graying early from deep black, their eyes the dark brown best suited for survival in the sun. On the ground by their feet a small black animal jerked sporadically against a net, and infrequently gave a shrill weak cry.

"Stavin is asleep," Snake said. "Do not disturb him, but go to him if he wakes."

The wife and young husband rose and went inside, but the older man stopped before her. "Can you help him?"

"I hope we may. The tumor is advanced, but it seems solid." Her own voice sounded removed, slightly hollow, as if she were lying. "Mist will be ready in the morning." She still felt the need to give him reassurance, but she could think of none.

"My sister wished to speak with you," he said, and left them alone, without introduction, without elevating himself by saying that the tall woman was the leader of this group. Snake glanced back, but the tent flap fell shut. She was feeling her exhaustion more deeply, and across her shoulders Mist was, for the first time, a weight she thought heavy.

"Are you all right?"

Snake turned. The woman moved toward her with a natural elegance made slightly awkward by advanced pregnancy. Snake had to look up to meet her gaze. She had small fine lines at the corners of her eyes, as if she laughed, sometimes, in secret. She smiled, but with concern. "You seem very tired. Shall I have someone make you a bed?"

"Not now," Snake said, "not yet. I won't sleep until afterward."

The leader searched her face, and Snake felt a kinship with her, in their shared responsibility.

"I understand, I think. Is there anything we can give you? Do you need aid with your preparations?"

Snake found herself having to deal with the questions as if they were complex problems. She turned them in her tired mind, examined them, dissected them, and finally grasped their meanings. "My pony needs food and water—"

"It is taken care of."

"And I need someone to help me with Mist. Someone strong. But it's more important that they are not afraid."

The leader nodded. "I would help you," she said, and smiled again, a little. "But I am a bit clumsy of late. I will find someone."

"Thank you."

Somber again, the older woman inclined her head and moved slowly toward a small group of tents. Snake watched her go, admiring her grace. She felt small and young and grubby in comparison.

Sand began to unwrap himself from her wrist. Feeling the anticipatory slide of scales on her skin, she caught him before he could drop to the ground. Sand lifted the upper half of his body from her hands. He flicked out his tongue, peering toward the little animal, feeling its body heat, smelling its fear. "I know thou art hungry," Snake said, "but that creature is not for thee." She put Sand in the case, lifted Mist from her shoulder, and let her coil herself in her dark compartment.

The small animal shrieked and struggled again when Snake's diffuse shadow passed over it. She bent and picked it up. The rapid series of terrified cries slowed and diminished and finally stopped as she stroked it. Finally it lay still, breathing hard, exhausted, staring up at her with yellow eyes. It had long hind legs and wide pointed ears, and its nose twitched at the serpent smell. Its soft black fur was marked off in skewed squares by the cords of the net.

"I am sorry to take your life," Snake told it. "But there will be no more fear, and I will not hurt you." She closed her hand gently around it, and, stroking it, grasped its spine at the base of its skull. She pulled, once, quickly. It seemed to struggle, briefly, but it was already dead. It convulsed; its legs drew up against its body, and its toes curled and quivered. It seemed to stare up at her, even now. She freed its body from the net.

Snake chose a small vial from her belt pouch, pried open the animal's clenched jaws, and let a single drop of the vial's cloudy preparation fall into its mouth. Quickly she opened the satchel again, and called Mist out. She came slowly, slipping over the edge, hood closed, sliding in the sharp-grained sand. Her milky scales caught the thin light. She smelled the animal, flowed to it, touched it with her tongue. For a moment Snake was afraid she would refuse dead meat, but the body was still warm, still twitching reflexively, and she was very hungry. "A tidbit for thee," Snake said. "To whet thy appetite." Mist nosed it, reared back, and struck, sinking her short fixed fangs into the tiny body, biting again, pumping out her store of poison. She released it, took a better grip, and began to work her jaws around it; it would hardly distend her throat. When Mist lay quiet, digesting the small meal, Snake sat beside her and held her, waiting.

She heard footsteps in the coarse sand.

"I'm sent to help you."

He was a young man, despite a scatter of white in his dark hair. He was taller than Snake, and not unattractive. His eyes were dark, and the sharp planes of his face were further hardened because his hair was pulled straight back and tied. His expression was neutral.

"Are you afraid?"

"I will do as you tell me."

Though his body was obscured by his robe, his long fine hands showed strength.

"Then hold her body, and don't let her surprise you." Mist was beginning to twitch from the effects of the drugs Snake had put in the small animal's body. The cobra's eyes stared, unseeing.

"If it bites—"

"Hold, quickly!"

The young man reached, but he had hesitated too long. Mist writhed, lashing out, striking him in the face with her tail. He staggered back, at least as surprised as hurt. Snake kept a close grip behind Mist's jaws, and struggled to catch the rest of her as well. Mist was no constrictor, but she was smooth and strong and fast. Thrashing, she forced out her breath in a long hiss. She would have bitten anything she could reach. As Snake fought with her, she managed to squeeze the poison glands and force out the last drops of venom. They hung from Mist's fangs for a moment, catching light as jewels would; the force of the serpent's convulsions flung them away into the darkness. Snake struggled with the cobra, speaking softly, aided for once by the sand, on which Mist could get no purchase. Snake felt the young man behind her, grabbing for Mist's body and tail. The seizure stopped abruptly, and Mist lay limp in their hands.

"I am sorry—"

"Hold her," Snake said. "We have the night to go."

During Mist's second convulsion, the young man held her firmly and was of some real help. Afterward, Snake answered his interrupted question. "If she were making poison and she bit you, you would probably die. Even now her bite would make you ill. But unless you do something foolish, if she manages to bite, she will bite me."

"You would benefit my cousin little, if you were dead or dying."

"You misunderstand. Mist cannot kill me." She held out her hand, so he could see the white scars of slashes and punctures. He stared at them, and looked into her eyes for a long moment, then looked away.

The bright spot in the clouds from which the light radiated moved westward in the sky; they held the cobra like a child. Snake found herself half-dozing, but Mist moved her head, dully attempting to evade restraint, and Snake woke herself abruptly. "I must not sleep," she said to the young man. "Talk to me. What are you called?"

As Stavin had, the young man hesitated. He seemed afraid of her, or of something. "My people," he said, "think it unwise to speak our names to strangers."

"If you consider me a witch you should not have asked my aid. I know no magic, and I claim none. I can't learn all the customs of all the people on this earth, so I keep my own. My custom is to address those I work with by name."

"It's not a superstition," he said. "Not as you might think. We're not afraid of being bewitched."

Snake waited, watching him, trying to decipher his expression in the dim light.

"Our families know our names, and we exchange names with those we would marry."

Snake considered that custom, and thought it would fit badly on her. "No one else? Ever?"

"Well . . . a friend might know one's name."

"Ah," Snake said. "I see. I am still a stranger, and perhaps an enemy."

"A *friend* would know my name," the young man said again. "I would not offend you, but now you misunderstand. An acquaintance is not a friend. We value friendship highly."

"In this land one should be able to tell quickly if a person is worth calling 'friend.' "

"We make friends seldom. Friendship is a commitment."

"It sounds like something to be feared."

He considered that possibility. "Perhaps it's the betrayal of friendship we fear. That is a very painful thing."

"Has anyone ever betrayed you?"

He glanced at her sharply, as if she had exceeded the limits of propriety. "No," he said, and his voice was as hard as his face. "No friend. I have no one I call friend."

His reaction startled Snake. "That's very sad," she said, and grew silent, trying to comprehend the deep stresses that could close people off so far, comparing her loneliness of necessity and theirs of choice. "Call me Snake," she said finally, "if you can bring yourself to pronounce it. Speaking my name binds you to nothing."

The young man seemed about to speak; perhaps he thought again that he had offended her, perhaps he felt he should further defend his customs. But Mist began to twist in their hands, and they had to hold her to keep her from injuring herself. The cobra was slender for her length, but powerful, and the convulsions she went through were more severe than any she had ever had before. She thrashed in Snake's grasp, and almost pulled away. She tried to spread her hood, but Snake held her too tightly. She opened her mouth and hissed, but no poison dripped from her fangs.

She wrapped her tail around the young man's waist. He began to pull her and turn, to extricate himself from her coils.

"She's not a constrictor," Snake said. "She won't hurt you. Leave her—"

But it was too late; Mist relaxed suddenly and the young man lost his balance. Mist whipped herself away and lashed figures in the sand. Snake wrestled with her alone while the young man tried to hold her, but she curled herself around Snake and used the grip for leverage. She started to pull herself from Snake's hands. Snake threw them both backward into the sand; Mist rose above her, openmouthed, furious, hissing. The young man lunged and grabbed her just beneath her hood. Mist struck at him, but Snake, somehow, held her back. Together they deprived Mist of her hold, and regained control of her. Snake struggled up, but Mist suddenly went quite still and lay almost rigid between them. They were both sweating; the young man was pale under his tan, and even Snake was trembling.

"We have a little while to rest," Snake said. She glanced at him and noticed the dark line on his cheek where, earlier, Mist's tail had slashed him. She reached up and touched it. "You'll have a bruise, no more," she said. "It will not scar."

"If it were true that serpents sting with their tails, you would be restraining both the fangs and the stinger, and I'd be of little use."

"Tonight I'd need someone to keep me awake, whether or not he helped me with Mist." Fighting the cobra had produced adrenaline, but now it ebbed, and her exhaustion and hunger were returning, stronger.

"Snake . . ."

"Yes?"

He smiled, quickly, half-embarrassed. "I was trying the pronunciation."

"Good enough."

"How long did it take you to cross the desert?"

"Not very long. Too long. Six days."

"How did you live?"

"There is water. We traveled at night, except yesterday, when I could find no shade."

"You carried all your food?"

She shrugged. "A little." And wished he would not speak of food.

"What's on the other side?"

"More sand, more bush, a little more water. A few groups of people, traders, the station I grew up and took my training in. And farther on, a mountain with a city inside."

"I would like to see a city. Someday."

"The desert can be crossed."

He said nothing, but Snake's memories of leaving home were recent enough that she could imagine his thoughts.

The next set of convulsions came, much sooner than Snake had expected. By their severity, she gauged something of the stage of Stavin's illness, and wished it were morning. If she were to lose him, she would have it done, and grieve, and try to forget. The cobra would have battered herself to death against the sand if Snake and the young man had not been holding her. She suddenly went completely rigid, with her mouth clamped shut and her forked tongue dangling.

She stopped breathing.

"Hold her," Snake said. "Hold her head. Quickly, take her, and if she gets away, run. Take her! She won't strike at you now, she could only slash you by accident."

He hesitated only a moment, then grasped Mist behind the head. Snake ran, slipping in the deep sand, from the edge of the circle of tents to a place where bushes still grew. She broke off dry thorny branches that tore her scarred hands. Peripherally she noticed a mass of horned vipers, so ugly they seemed deformed, nesting beneath the clump of dessicated vegetation; they hissed at her: she ignored them. She found a narrow hollow stem and carried it back. Her hands bled from deep scratches.

Kneeling by Mist's head, she forced open the cobra's mouth and pushed the tube deep into her throat, through the air passage at the base of Mist's tongue. She bent close, took the tube in her mouth, and breathed gently into Mist's lungs.

She noticed: the young man's hands, holding the cobra as she had asked; his breathing, first a sharp gasp of surprise, then ragged; the sand scraping her elbows where she leaned; the cloying smell of the fluid seeping from Mist's fangs; her own dizziness, she thought from exhaustion, which she forced away by necessity and will.

Snake breathed, and breathed again, paused, and repeated, until Mist caught the rhythm and continued it unaided.

Snake sat back on her heels. "I think she'll be all right," she said. "I hope she will." She brushed the back of her hand across her forehead. The touch sparked pain: she jerked her hand down and agony slid along her bones, up her arm, across her shoulder, through her chest, enveloping her heart. Her balance turned on its edge. She fell, tried to catch herself but moved too slowly, fought nausea and vertigo and almost succeeded, until the pull of the earth seemed to slip away in pain and she was lost in darkness with nothing to take a bearing by.

She felt sand where it had scraped her cheek and her palms, but it was soft. "Snake, can I let go?" She thought the question must be for someone else, while at the same time she knew there was no one else to answer it, no one else to reply to her name. She felt hands on her, and they were gentle; she wanted to respond to them, but she was too tired. She needed sleep more, so she pushed them away. But they held her head and put dry leather to her lips and poured water into her throat. She coughed and choked and spat it out.

She pushed herself up on one elbow. As her sight cleared, she realized she was shaking. She felt as she had the first time she was snake-bit, before her immunities had completely developed. The young man knelt over her, his water flask in his hand. Mist, beyond him, crawled toward the darkness. Snake forgot the throbbing pain. "Mist!"

The young man flinched and turned, frightened; the serpent reared up, her head nearly at Snake's standing eye level, her hood spread, swaying, watching, angry, ready to strike. She formed a wavering white line against black. Snake forced herself to rise, feeling as though she were fumbling with the control of some unfamiliar body. She almost fell again, but held herself steady. "Thou must not go to hunt now," she said. "There is work for thee to do." She held out her right hand, to the side, a decoy, to draw Mist if she struck. Her hand was heavy with pain. Snake feared, not being bitten, but the loss of the contents of Mist's poison sacs. "Come here," she said. "Come here, and stay thy anger." She noticed blood flowing down between her fingers, and the fear she felt for Stavin was intensified. "Didst thou bite me, creature?" But the pain was wrong: poison would numb her, and the new serum only sting . . .

"No," the young man whispered, from behind her.

Mist struck. The reflexes of long training took over. Snake's right hand jerked away, her left grabbed Mist as she brought her head back. The cobra writhed a moment, and relaxed. "Devious beast," Snake said. "For shame." She turned, and let Mist crawl up her arm and over her shoulder, where she lay like the outline of an invisible cape and dragged her tail like the edge of a train.

"She did not bite me?"

"No," the young man said. His contained voice was touched
with awe. "You should be dying. You should be curled around the
agony, and your arm swollen purple. When you came back—" He
gestured toward her hand. "It must have been a bush viper."

Snake remembered the coil of reptiles beneath the branches,
and touched the blood on her hand. She wiped it away, revealing
the double puncture of a snakebite among the scratches of the
thorns. The wound was slightly swollen. "It needs cleaning," she
said. "I shame myself by falling to it." The pain of it washed in
gentle waves up her arm, burning no longer. She stood looking at
the young man, looking around her, watching the landscape shift
and change as her tired eyes tried to cope with the low light of
setting moon and false dawn. "You held Mist well, and bravely,"
she said to the young man. "Thank you."

He lowered his gaze, almost bowing to her. He rose, and approached her. Snake put her hand gently on Mist's neck so she
would not be alarmed.

"I would be honored," the young man said, "if you would call
me Arevin."

"I would be pleased to."

Snake knelt down and held the winding white loops as Mist
crawled slowly into her compartment. In a little while, when Mist
had stabilized, by dawn, they could go to Stavin.

The tip of Mist's white tail slid out of sight. Snake closed the case
and would have risen, but she could not stand. She had not yet
quite shaken off the effects of the new venom. The flesh around
the wound was red and tender, but the hemorrhaging would not
spread. She stayed where she was, slumped, staring at her hand,
creeping slowly in her mind toward what she needed to do, this
time for herself.

"Let me help you. Please."

He touched her shoulder and helped her stand. "I'm sorry," she
said. "I'm so in need of rest . . ."

"Let me wash your hand," Arevin said. "And then you can sleep.
Tell me when to waken you—"

"No. I can't sleep yet." She pulled together the skeins of her nerves, collected herself, straightened, tossed the damp curls of her short hair off her forehead. "I'm all right now. Have you any water?"

Arevin loosened his outer robe. Beneath it he wore a loincloth and a leather belt that carried several leather flasks and pouches. The color of his skin was slightly lighter than the sun-darkened brown of his face. He brought out his water flask, closed his robe around his lean body, and reached for Snake's hand.

"No, Arevin. If the poison gets in any small scratch you might have, it could infect."

She sat down and sluiced lukewarm water over her hand. The water dripped pink to the ground and disappeared, leaving not even a damp spot visible. The wound bled a little more, but now it only ached. The poison was almost inactivated.

"I don't understand," Arevin said, "how it is that you're unhurt. My younger sister was bitten by a bush viper." He could not speak as uncaringly as he might have wished. "We could do nothing to save her—nothing we had would even lessen her pain."

Snake gave him his flask and rubbed salve from a vial in her belt pouch across the closing punctures. "It's a part of our preparation," she said. "We work with many kinds of serpents, so we must be immune to as many as possible." She shrugged. "The process is tedious and somewhat painful." She clenched her fist; the film held, and she was steady. She leaned toward Arevin and touched his abraded cheek again. "Yes . . ." She spread a thin layer of the salve across it. "That will help it heal."

"If you cannot sleep," Arevin said, "can you at least rest?"

"Yes," she said. "For a little while."

Snake sat next to Arevin, leaning against him, and they watched the sun turn the clouds to gold and flame and amber. The simple physical contact with another human being gave Snake pleasure, though she found it unsatisfying. Another time, another place, she might do something more, but not here, not now.

When the lower edge of the sun's bright smear rose above the horizon, Snake rose and teased Mist out of the case. She came slowly, weakly, and crawled across Snake's shoulders. Snake picked up the satchel, and she and Arevin walked together back to the small group of tents.

Stavin's parents waited, watching for her, just outside the entrance of their tent. They stood in a tight, defensive, silent group. For a moment Snake thought they had decided to send her away. Then, with regret and fear like hot iron in her mouth, she asked if Stavin had died. They shook their heads, and allowed her to enter.

Stavin lay as she had left him, still asleep. The adults followed her with their stares, and she could smell fear. Mist flicked out her tongue, growing nervous from the implied danger.

"I know you would stay," Snake said. "I know you would help, if you could, but there is nothing to be done by any person but me. Please go back outside."

They glanced at each other, and at Arevin, and she thought for a moment that they would refuse. Snake wanted to fall into the silence and sleep. "Come, cousins," Arevin said. "We are in her hands." He opened the tent flap and motioned them out. Snake thanked him with nothing more than a glance, and he might almost have smiled. She turned toward Stavin, and knelt beside him. "Stavin—" She touched his forehead; it was very hot. She noticed that her hand was less steady than before. The slight touch awakened the child. "It's time," Snake said.

He blinked, coming out of some child's dream, seeing her, slowly recognizing her. He did not look frightened. For that Snake was glad; for some other reason she could not identify she was uneasy.

"Will it hurt?"

"Does it hurt now?"

He hesitated, looked away, looked back. "Yes."

"It might hurt a little more. I hope not. Are you ready?"

"Can Grass stay?"

"Of course," she said.

And realized what was wrong.

"I'll come back in a moment." Her voice changed so much, she had pulled it so tight, that she could not help but frighten him. She left the tent, walking slowly, calmly, restraining herself. Outside, the parents told her by their faces what they feared.

"Where is Grass?" Arevin, his back to her, started at her tone. The younger husband made a small grieving sound, and could look at her no longer.

"We were afraid," the older husband said. "We thought it would bite the child."

"I thought it would. It was I. It crawled over his face, I could see its fangs—" The wife put her hands on the younger husband's shoulders, and he said no more.

"Where is he?" She wanted to scream; she did not.

They brought her a small open box. Snake took it, and looked inside.

Grass lay cut almost in two, his entrails oozing from his body, half turned over, and as she watched, shaking, he writhed once, and flicked his tongue out once, and in. Snake made some sound, too low in her throat to be a cry. She hoped his motions were only reflex, but she picked him up as gently as she could. She leaned down and touched her lips to the smooth green scales behind his head. She bit him quickly, sharply, at the base of the skull. His blood flowed cool and salty in her mouth. If he were not dead, she had killed him instantly.

She looked at the parents, and at Arevin; they were all pale, but she had no sympathy for their fear, and cared nothing for shared grief. "Such a small creature," she said. "Such a small creature, who could only give pleasure and dreams." She watched them for a moment more, then turned toward the tent again.

"Wait—" She heard the older husband move up close behind her. He touched her shoulder; she shrugged away his hand. "We will give you anything you want," he said, "but leave the child alone."

She spun on him in a fury. "Should I kill Stavin for your stupid-

ity?" He seemed about to try to hold her back. She jammed her
shoulder hard into his stomach, and flung herself past the tent flap.
Inside, she kicked over the satchel. Abruptly awakened, and angry, Sand crawled out and coiled himself. When the younger husband and the wife tried to enter, Sand hissed and rattled with a
violence Snake had never heard him use before. She did not even
bother to look behind her. She ducked her head and wiped her
tears on her sleeve before Stavin could see them. She knelt beside
him.

"What's the matter?" He could not help but hear the voices
outside the tent, and the running.

"Nothing, Stavin," Snake said. "Did you know we came across
the desert?"

"No," he said, with wonder.

"It was very hot, and none of us had anything to eat. Grass is
hunting now. He was very hungry. Will you forgive him and let
me begin? I will be here all the time."

He seemed so tired; he was disappointed, but he had no strength
for arguing. "All right." His voice rustled like sand slipping
through the fingers.

Snake lifted Mist from her shoulders, and pulled the blanket
from Stavin's small body. The tumor pressed up beneath his rib-
cage, distorting his form, squeezing his vital organs, sucking nour-
ishment from him for its own growth. Holding Mist's head, Snake
let her flow across him, touching and tasting him. She had to
restrain the cobra to keep her from striking; the excitement had
agitated her. When Sand used his rattle, she flinched. Snake spoke
to her softly, soothing her; trained and bred-in responses began to
return, overcoming the natural instincts. Mist paused when her
tongue flicked the skin above the tumor, and Snake released her.

The cobra reared, and struck, and bit as cobras bite, sinking her
fangs their short length once, releasing, instantly biting again for
a better purchase, holding on, chewing at her prey. Stavin cried
out, but he did not move against Snake's restraining hands.

Mist expended the contents of her venom sacs into the child, and released him. She reared up, peered around, folded her hood, and slid across the mats in a perfectly straight line toward her dark, close compartment.

"It is all finished, Stavin."

"Will I die now?"

"No," Snake said. "Not now. Not for many years, I hope." She took a vial of powder from her belt pouch. "Open your mouth." He complied, and she sprinkled the powder across his tongue. "That will help the ache." She spread a pad of cloth across the series of shallow puncture wounds, without wiping off the blood.

She turned from him.

"Snake? Are you going away?"

"I will not leave without saying good-bye. I promise."

The child lay back, closed his eyes, and let the drug take him.

Sand coiled quiescently on the dark matting. Snake called him. He moved toward her, and suffered himself to be replaced in the satchel. Snake closed it, and lifted it, and it still felt empty. She heard noises outside the tent. Stavin's parents and the people who had come to help them pulled open the tent flap and peered inside, thrusting sticks in even before they looked.

Snake set down her leather case. "It's done."

They entered. Arevin was with them, too; only he was empty-handed. "Snake—" He spoke through grief, pity, confusion, and Snake could not tell what he believed. He looked back. Stavin's mother was just behind him. He took her by the shoulder. "He would have died without her. Whatever has happened now, he would have died."

The woman shook his hand away. "He might have lived. It might have gone away. We—" She could not speak for hiding tears.

Snake felt the people moving, surrounding her. Arevin took one step toward her and stopped, and she could see he wanted her to defend herself. "Can any of you cry?" she said. "Can any of you cry for me and my despair, or for them and their guilt, or for small things and their pain?" She felt tears slip down her cheeks.

They did not understand her; they were offended by her crying. They stood back, still afraid of her, but gathering themselves. She no longer needed the pose of calmness she had used to deceive the child. "Ah, you fools." Her voice sounded brittle. "Stavin—"

Light from the entrance struck them. "Let me pass." The people in front of Snake moved aside for their leader. She stopped in front of Snake, ignoring the satchel her foot almost touched. "Will Stavin live?" Her voice was quiet, calm, gentle.

"I cannot be certain," Snake said, "but I feel that he will."

"Leave us." The people understood Snake's words before they did their leader's; they looked around and lowered their weapons, and finally, one by one, they moved out of the tent. Arevin remained. Snake felt the strength that came from danger seeping from her. Her knees collapsed. She bent over the satchel with her face in her hands. The older woman knelt in front of her, before Snake could notice or prevent her. "Thank you," she said. "Thank you. I am so sorry . . ." She put her arms around Snake, and drew her toward her, and Arevin knelt beside them, and he embraced Snake, too. Snake began to tremble again, and they held her while she cried.

Later she slept, exhausted, alone in the tent with Stavin, holding his hand. They had given her food, and small animals for Sand and Mist, and supplies for her journey, and sufficient water for her to bathe, though that must have strained their resources. About that, Snake no longer cared.

When she awakened, she felt the tumor, and found that it had begun to dissolve and shrivel, dying, as Mist's changed poison affected it. Snake felt little joy. She smoothed Stavin's pale hair back from his face. "I would not lie to you again, little one," she said, "but I must leave soon. I cannot stay here." She wanted another three days' sleep, to finish fighting off the effects of the bush viper's poison, but she would sleep somewhere else. "Sta—vin?"

He half woke, slowly. "It doesn't hurt any more," he said.

"I am glad."

"Thank you . . ."

"Good-bye, Stavin. Will you remember later on that you woke up, and that I did stay to say good-bye?"

"Good-bye," he said, drifting off again. "Good-bye, Snake. Good-bye, Grass." He closed his eyes, and Snake picked up the satchel and left the tent. Dusk cast long indistinct shadows; the camp was quiet. She found her tiger-striped pony, tethered with food and water. New, full water-skins lay on the ground next to the saddle. The tiger pony whickered at her when she approached. She scratched his striped ears, saddled him, and strapped the case on his back. Leading him, she started west, the way she had come.

"Snake—"

She took a breath, and turned back to Arevin. He faced the sun, and it turned his skin ruddy and his robe scarlet. His streaked hair flowed loose to his shoulders, gentling his face. "You will not stay?"

"I cannot."

"I had hoped . . ."

"If things were different, I might have stayed."

"They were frightened. Can't you forgive them?"

"I can't face their guilt. What they did was my fault. I said he could not hurt them, but they saw his fangs and they didn't know his bite only gave dreams and eased dying. They couldn't know; I didn't understand them until too late."

"You said it yourself, you can't know all the customs and all the fears."

"I'm crippled," she said. "Without Grass, if I cannot heal a person, I cannot help at all. I must go home. Perhaps my teachers will forgive me my stupidity, but I am afraid to face them. They seldom give the name I bear, but they gave it to me, and they'll be disappointed."

"Let me come with you."

She wanted to; she hesitated, and cursed herself for that weakness. "They may cast me out, and you would be cast out, too. Stay here, Arevin."

"It wouldn't matter."

"It would. After a while, we would hate each other. I don't know you, and you don't know me. We need calmness, and quiet, and time to understand each other."

He came toward her, and put his arms around her, and they stood together for a moment. When he raised his head, he was crying. "Please come back," he said. "Whatever happens, please come back."

"I will try," Snake said. "Next spring, when the winds stop, look for me. And the spring after that, if I do not come, forget me. Wherever I am, if I live, I will forget you."

"I will look for you," Arevin said, and he would promise no more.

Snake picked up the pony's lead, and started across the desert.

HARLAN ELLISON

The Deathbird

Beginnings and ends, ends and beginnings. How they tantalize us! This story, only ten thousand words, comprises not only the beginning and the end of this world, but also, perhaps even more relevant, the middle. The end is written in the beginning, and the middle is as inescapable as growing old. A tour de force that scans billions of years, and manages to focus on minute details with excruciating exactness, this is "The Deathbird."

1

This is a test. Take notes. This will count as ¾ of your final grade. Hints: remember, in chess, kings cancel each other out and cannot occupy adjacent squares, are therefore all-powerful and totally powerless, cannot affect one another, produce stalemate. Hinduism is a polytheistic religion; the sect of Atman worships the divine spark of life within Man; in effect saying, "Thou art God." Provisos of equal time are not served by one viewpoint having media access to two hundred million people in prime time while opposing viewpoints are provided with a soapbox on the corner. Not everyone tells the truth. Operational note: these sections may be taken out of numerical sequence: rearrange to suit yourself for optimum clarity. Turn over your test papers and begin.

2

Uncounted layers of rock pressed down on the magma pool. White-hot with the bubbling ferocity of the molten nickel-iron core, the pool spat and shuddered, yet did not pit or char or smoke or damage in the slightest the smooth and reflective surfaces of the strange crypt.

Nathan Stack lay in the crypt—silent, sleeping.

A shadow passed through rock. Through shale, through coal, through marble, through mica schist, through quartzite; through miles-thick deposits of phosphates, through diatomaceous earth, through feldspars, through diorite; through faults and folds, through anticlines and monoclines, through dips and synclines; through hellfire; and came to the ceiling of the great cavern and passed through; and saw the magma pool and dropped down; and came to the crypt. The shadow.

A triangular face with a single eye peered into the crypt, saw Stack, and laid four-fingered hands on the crypt's cool surface. Nathan Stack woke at the touch, and the crypt became transparent; he woke though the touch had not been upon his body. His soul felt the shadowy pressure and he opened his eyes to see the leaping brilliance of the worldcore around him, to see the shadow with its single eye staring in at him.

The serpentine shadow enfolded the crypt; its darkness flowed upward again, through the Earth's mantle, toward the crust, toward the surface of the cinder, the broken toy that was the Earth.

When they reached the surface, the shadow bore the crypt to a place where the poison winds did not reach, and caused it to open.

Nathan Stack tried to move, and moved only with difficulty. Memories rushed through his head of other lives, many other lives, as many other men; then the memories slowed and melted into a background tone that could be ignored.

The shadow thing reached down a hand and touched Stack's naked flesh. Gently, but firmly, the thing helped him to stand, and gave him garments, and a neck-pouch that contained a short knife and a warming-stone and other things. He offered his hand, and Stack took it, and after two hundred and fifty thousand years sleeping in the crypt, Nathan Stack stepped out on the face of the sick planet Earth.

Then the thing bent low against the poison winds and began walking away. Nathan Stack, having no other choice, bent forward and followed the shadow creature.

3

A messenger had been sent for Dira and he had come as quickly as the meditations would permit. When he reached the Summit, he found the fathers waiting, and they took him gently into their cove, where they immersed themselves and began to speak.

"We've lost the arbitration," the coil-father said. "It will be necessary for us to go and leave it to him."

Dira could not believe it. "But didn't they listen to our arguments, to our logic?"

The fang-father shook his head sadly and touched Dira's shoulder. "There were . . . accommodations to be made. It was their time. So we must leave."

The coil-father said, "We've decided you will remain. One was permitted, in caretakership. Will you accept our commission?"

It was a very great honor, but Dira began to feel the loneliness even as they told him they would leave. Yet he accepted. Wondering why they had selected *him,* of all their people. There were reasons, there were always reasons, but he could not ask. And so he accepted the honor, with all its attendant sadness, and remained behind when they left.

The limits of his caretakership were harsh, for they insured he could not defend himself against whatever slurs or legends would be spread, nor could he take action unless it became clear the trust was being breached by the other—who now held possession. And he had no threat save the Deathbird. A final threat that could be used only when final measures were needed: and therefore too late.

But he was patient. The most patient of all his people.

Thousands of years later, when he saw how it was destined to go, when there was no doubt left how it would end, he understood *that* was the reason he had been chosen to stay behind.

But it did not help the loneliness.

Nor could it save the Earth. Only Stack could do that.

4

1 Now the serpent was more subtil than any beast of the field which the LORD God had made. And he said unto the woman, Yea hath God said, Ye shall not eat of every tree of the garden?

2 And the woman said unto the serpent, We may eat of the fruit of the trees of the garden:

3 But of the fruit of the tree which is in the midst of the garden, God hath said, Ye shall not eat of it, neither shall ye touch it, lest ye die.

4 And the serpent said unto the woman, Ye shall not surely die:

5 (Omitted)

6 And when the woman saw that the tree was good for food, and that it was pleasant to the eyes, and a tree to be desired to make one wise, she took of the fruit thereof, and did eat, and gave also unto her husband with her; and he did eat.

7 (Omitted)

8 (Omitted)

9 And the LORD God called unto Adam, and said unto him, Where art thou?

10 (Omitted)

11 And he said, Who told thee that thou wast naked? Hast thou eaten of the tree, whereof I commanded thee that thou shouldest not eat?

12 And the man said, The woman whom thou gavest to be with me, she gave me of the tree, and I did eat.

13 And the LORD God said unto the woman, What is this that thou hast done? And the woman said, The serpent beguiled me, and I did eat.

14 And the LORD God said unto the serpent, Because thou hast done this, thou art cursed above all cattle, and above every beast of the field; upon thy belly shalt thou go, and dust shalt thou eat all the days of thy life:

15 And I will put enmity between thee and the woman, and

*between thy seed and her seed; it shall bruise thy head, and thou
shalt bruise his heel.*

GENESIS, *Chap. III*

TOPICS FOR DISCUSSION
(Give 5 points per right answer)

1. Melville's *Moby Dick* begins, "Call me Ishmael." We say it
is told in the *first* person. In what person is Genesis told? From
whose viewpoint?

2. Who is the "good guy" in this story? Who is the "bad guy"?
Can you make a strong case for reversal of the roles?

3. Traditionally, the apple is considered to be the fruit the serpent offered to Eve. But apples are not endemic to the Near East.
Select one of the following, more logical substitutes, and discuss
how myths come into being and are corrupted over long periods
of time: olive, fig, date, pomegranate.

4. Why is the word LORD always in capitals and the name God
always capitalized? Shouldn't the serpent's name be capitalized, as
well? If no, why?

5. If God created everything (see *Genesis*, Chap. I), why did he
create problems for himself by creating a serpent who would lead
his creations astray? Why did God create a tree he did not want
Adam and Eve to know about, and then go out of his way to warn
them against it?

6. Compare and contrast Michelangelo's Sistine Chapel ceiling
panel of the *Expulsion from Paradise* with Bosch's *Garden of
Earthly Delights.*

7. Was Adam being a gentleman when he placed blame on Eve?
Who was Quisling? Discuss "narking" as a character flaw.

8. God grew angry when he found out he had been defied. If
God is omnipotent and omniscient, didn't he know? Why couldn't
he find Adam and Eve when they hid?

9. If God had not wanted Adam and Eve to taste the fruit of the
forbidden tree, why didn't he warn the serpent? Could God have

prevented the serpent from tempting Adam and Eve? If yes, why
didn't he? If no, discuss the possibility the serpent was as powerful
as God.

10. Using examples from two different media journals, demonstrate the concept of "slanted news."

5

The poison winds howled and tore at the powder covering the
land. Nothing lived there. The winds, green and deadly, dived out
of the sky and raked the carcass of the Earth, seeking, seeking:
anything moving, anything still living. But there was nothing.
Powder. Talc. Pumice.

And the onyx spire of the mountain toward which Nathan Stack
and the shadow thing had moved, all that first day. When night fell
they dug a pit in the tundra and the shadow thing coated it with
a substance thick as glue that had been in Stack's neck-pouch.
Stack had slept the night fitfully, clutching the warming-stone to
his chest and breathing through a filter tube from the pouch.

Once he had awakened, at the sound of great batlike creatures
flying overhead; he had seen them swooping low, coming in flat
trajectories across the wasteland toward his pit in the earth. But
they seemed unaware that he—and the shadow thing—lay in the
hole. They defecated thin, phosphorescent stringers that fell glowing through the night and were lost on the plains; then the creatures swooped upward and were whirled away on the winds. Stack
resumed sleeping with difficulty.

In the morning, frosted with an icy light that gave everything
a blue tinge, the shadow thing scrabbled its way out of the choking
powder and crawled along the ground, then lay flat, fingers claw-
ing for purchase in the whiskaway surface. Behind it, from the
powder, Stack bore toward the surface, reached up a hand and
trembled for help.

The shadow creature slid across the ground, fighting the winds
that had grown stronger in the night, back to the soft place that

had been their pit, to the hand thrust up through the powder. It grasped the hand, and Stack's fingers tightened convulsively. Then the crawling shadow exerted pressure and pulled the man from the treacherous pumice.

Together they lay against the earth, fighting to see, fighting to draw breath without filling their lungs with suffocating death.

"Why is it like this . . . what *happened?*" Stack screamed against the wind. The shadow creature did not answer, but it looked at Stack for a long moment and then, with very careful movements, raised its hand, held it up before Stack's eyes and slowly, making claws of the fingers, closed the four fingers into a cage, into a fist, into a painfully tight ball that said more eloquently than words: *destruction.*

Then they began to crawl toward the mountain.

6

The onyx spire of the mountain rose out of hell and struggled toward the shredded sky. It was monstrous arrogance. Nothing should have tried that climb out of desolation. But the black mountain had tried, and succeeded.

It was like an old man. Seamed, ancient, dirt caked in striated lines, autumnal, lonely; black and desolate, piled strength upon strength. It would *not* give in to gravity and pressure and death. It struggled for the sky. Ferociously alone, it was the only feature that broke the desolate line of the horizon.

In another twenty-five million years the mountain might be worn as smooth and featureless as a tiny onyx offering to the deity night. But though the powder plains swirled and the poison winds drove the pumice against the flanks of the pinnacle, thus far their scouring had only served to soften the edges of the mountain's profile, as though divine intervention had protected the spire.

Lights moved near the summit.

7

Stack learned the nature of the phosphorescent stringers defecated onto the plain the night before by the batlike creatures. They were spores that became, in the wan light of day, strange bleeder plants.

All around them as they crawled through the dawn, the little live things sensed their warmth and began thrusting shoots up through the talc. As the fading red ember of the dying sun climbed painfully into the sky, the bleeding plants were already reaching maturity.

Stack cried out as one of the vine tentacles fastened around his ankle, holding him. A second looped itself around his neck.

Thin films of berry-black blood coated the vines, leaving rings on Stack's flesh. The rings burned terribly.

The shadow creature slid on its belly and pulled itself back to the man. Its triangular head came close to Stack's neck, and it bit into the vine. Thick black blood spurted as the vine parted, and the shadow creature rasped its razor-edged teeth back and forth till Stack was able to breathe again. With a violent movement Stack folded himself down and around, pulling the short knife from the neck-pouch. He sawed through the vine tightening inexorably around his ankle. It screamed as it was severed, in the same voice Stack had heard from the skies the night before. The severed vine writhed away, withdrawing into the talc.

Stack and the shadow thing crawled forward once again, low, flat, holding onto the dying earth: toward the mountain. High in the bloody sky, the Deathbird circled.

8

On their own world, they had lived in luminous, oily-walled caverns for millions of years, evolving and spreading their race through the universe. When they had had enough of empire-building, they turned inward, and much of their time was spent in the intricate construction of songs of wisdom, and the designing of fine worlds for many races.

There were other races that designed, however. And when there was a conflict over jurisdiction, an arbitration was called, adjudicated by a race whose *raison d'être* was impartiality and cleverness unraveling knotted threads of claim and counter-claim. Their racial honor, in fact, depended on the flawless application of these qualities. Through the centuries they had refined their talents in more and more sophisticated arenas of arbitration until the time came when they were the final authority. The litigants were compelled to abide by the judgments, not merely because the decisions were always wise and creatively fair, but because the judges' race would, if its decisions were questioned as suspect, destroy itself. In the holiest place on their world they had erected a religious machine. It could be activated to emit a tone that would shatter their crystal carapaces. They were a race of exquisite cricket-like creatures, no larger than the thumb of a man. They were treasured throughout the civilized worlds, and their loss would have been catastrophic. Their honor and their value was never questioned. All races abided by their decisions.

So Dira's people gave over jurisdiction to that certain world, and went away, leaving Dira with only the Deathbird, a special caretakership the adjudicators had creatively woven into their judgment.

There is recorded one last meeting between Dira and those who had given him his commission. There were readings that could not be ignored—had, in fact, been urgently brought to the attention of the fathers of Dira's race by the adjudicators—and the Great Coiled One came to Dira at the last possible moment to tell him of the mad thing into whose hands this world had been given, to tell Dira of what the mad thing could do.

The Great Coiled One—whose rings were loops of wisdom acquired through centuries of gentleness and perception and immersed meditations that had brought forth lovely designs for many worlds—he who was the holiest of Dira's race, honored Dira by coming to *him*, rather than commanding Dira to appear.

We have only one gift to leave them, he said. *Wisdom. This mad one will come, and he will lie to them, and he will tell them: created he them. And we will be gone, and there will be nothing between them and the mad one but you. Only you can give them the wisdom to defeat him in their own good time.* Then the Great Coiled One stroked the skin of Dira with ritual affection, and Dira was deeply moved and could not reply. Then he was left alone.

The mad one came, and interposed himself, and Dira gave them wisdom, and time passed. His name became other than Dira, it became Snake, and the new name was despised: but Dira could see the Great Coiled One had been correct in his readings. So Dira made his selection. A man, one of them, and gifted him with the spark.

All of this is recorded somewhere. It is history.

9

The man was not Jesus of Nazareth. He may have been Simon. Not Genghis Khan, but perhaps a foot soldier in his horde. Not Aristotle, but possibly one who sat and listened to Socrates in the agora. Neither the shambler who discovered the wheel nor the link who first ceased painting himself blue and applied the colors to the walls of the cave. But one near them, somewhere near at hand. The man was not Richard *Coeur de Lion*, Rembrandt, Richelieu, Rasputin, Robert Fulton or the Mahdi. Just a man. With the spark.

10

Once, Dira came to the man. Very early on. The spark was there, but the light needed to be converted to energy. So Dira came to the man, and did what had to be done before the mad one knew of it, and when he discovered that Dira, the Snake, had made contact, he quickly made explanations.

This legend has come down to us as the fable of *Faust.*

TRUE or FALSE?

11

Light converted to energy, thus:

In the fortieth year of his five hundredth incarnation, all-unknowing of the eons of which he had been part, the man found himself wandering in a terrible dry place under a thin, flat burning disc of sun. He was a Berber tribesman who had never considered shadows save to relish them when they provided shade. The shadow came to him, sweeping down across the sands like the *khamsin* of Egypt, the *simoom* of Asia Minor, the *harmattan*, all of which he had known in his various lives, none of which he remembered. The shadow came over him like the *sirocco.*

The shadow stole the breath from his lungs and the man's eyes rolled up in his head. He fell to the ground and the shadow took him down and down, through the sands, into the Earth.

Mother Earth.

She lived, this world of trees and rivers and rocks with deep stone thoughts. She breathed, had feelings, dreamed dreams, gave birth, laughed and grew contemplative for millennia. This great creature swimming in the sea of space.

What a wonder, thought the man, for he had never understood that the Earth was his mother, before this. He had never understood, before this, that the Earth had a life of its own, at once a part of mankind and quite separate from mankind. A mother with a life of her own.

Dira, Snake, shadow . . . took the man down and let the spark of light change itself to energy as the man became one with the Earth. His flesh melted and became quiet, cool soil. His eyes glowed with the light that shines in the darkest centers of the planet and he saw the way the mother cared for her young: the worms, the roots of plants, the rivers that cascaded for miles over great cliffs in enormous caverns, the bark of trees. He was taken once more to the bosom of that great Earth mother, and understood the joy of her life.

Remember this, Dira said to the man.

What a wonder, the man thought . . .

. . . and was returned to the sands of the desert, with no remembrance of having slept with, loved, enjoyed the body of his natural mother.

12

They camped at the base of the mountain, in a greenglass cave; not deep but angled sharply so the blown pumice could not reach them. They put Nathan Stack's stone in a fault in the cave's floor, and the heat spread quickly, warming them. The shadow thing with its triangular head sank back in shadow and closed its eye and sent its hunting instinct out for food. A shriek came back on the wind.

Much later, when Nathan Stack had eaten, when he was reasonably content and well-fed, he stared into the shadows and spoke to the creature sitting there.

"How long was I down there . . . how long was the sleep?"

The shadow thing spoke in whispers. *A quarter of a million years.*

Stack did not reply. The figure was beyond belief. The shadow creature seemed to understand.

In the life of a world no time at all.

Nathan Stack was a man who could make accommodations. He smiled quickly and said, "I must have been tired."

The shadow did not respond.

"I don't understand very much of this. It's pretty damned frightening. To die, then to wake up . . . here. Like this."

You did not die. You were taken, put down there. By the end you will understand everything, I promise you.

"Who put me down there?"

I did. I came and found you when the time was right, and I put you down there.

"Am I still Nathan Stack?"

If you wish.

"But am I Nathan Stack?"

You always were. You had many other names, many other bodies, but the spark was always yours. Stack seemed about to speak, and the shadow creature added, *You were always on your way to being who you are.*

"But what *am* I? Am I still Nathan Stack, dammit?"

If you wish.

"Listen: you don't seem too sure about that. You came and got me, I mean I woke up and there you were; now who should know better than you what my name is?"

You have had many names in many times. Nathan Stack is merely the one you remember. You had a very different name long ago, at the start, when I first came to you.

Stack was afraid of the answer, but he asked, "What was my name then?"

Ish-lilith. Husband of Lilith. Do you remember her?

Stack thought, tried to open himself to the past, but it was as unfathomable as the quarter of a million years through which he had slept in the crypt.

"No. But there were other women, in other times."

Many. There was one who replaced Lilith.

"I don't remember."

Her name . . . does not matter. But when the mad one took her from you and replaced her with the other . . . then I knew it would end like this. The Deathbird.

"I don't mean to be stupid, but I haven't the faintest idea what you're talking about."

Before it ends, you will understand everything.

"You said that before." Stack paused, stared at the shadow creature for a long time only moments long, then, "What was your name?"

Before I met you my name was Dira.

He said it in his native tongue. Stack could not pronounce it.

"Before you met me. What is it now?"

Snake.

Something slithered past the mouth of the cave. It did not stop, but it called out with the voice of moist mud sucking down into a quagmire.

"Why did you put *me* down there? Why did you come to me in the first place? What spark? Why can't I remember these other lives or who I was? What do you want from me?"

You should sleep. It will be a long climb. And cold.

"I slept for two hundred and fifty thousand years, I'm hardly tired," Stack said. "Why did you pick me?"

Later. Now sleep. Sleep has other uses.

Darkness deepened around Snake, seeped out around the cave, and Nathan Stack lay down near the warming-stone, and the darkness took him.

13

SUPPLEMENTARY READING

This is an essay by a writer. It is clearly an appeal to the emotions. As you read it ask yourself how it applies to the subject under discussion. What is the writer trying to say? Does he succeed in making his point? Does this essay cast light on the point of the subject under discussion? After you have read this essay, using the reverse side of your test paper, write your own essay (500 words or less) on the loss of a loved one. If you have never lost a loved one, fake it.

AHBHU

Yesterday my dog died. For eleven years Ahbhu was my closest friend. He was responsible for my writing a story about a boy and his dog that many people have read. He was not a pet, he was a person. It was impossible to anthropomorphize him, he wouldn't stand for it. But he was so much his own kind of creature, he had such a strongly formed personality, he was so determined to share his life with only those *he* chose, that it was also impossible to think of him as simply a dog. Apart from those canine characteristics into which he was locked by his species, he comported himself like one of a kind.

We met when I came to him at the West Los Angeles Animal Shelter. I'd wanted a dog because I was lonely and I'd remembered when I was a little boy how my dog had been a friend when I had no other friends. One summer I went away to camp and when I returned I found a rotten old neighbor lady from up the street had had my dog picked up and gassed while my father was at work. I crept into the woman's back yard that night and found a rug hanging on the clothesline. The rug beater was hanging from a post. I stole it and buried it.

At the Animal Shelter there was a man in line ahead of me. He had brought in a puppy only a week or so old. A Puli, a Hungarian sheep dog; it was a sad-looking little thing. He had too many in the litter and had brought in this one to either be taken by someone else, or to be put to sleep. They took the dog inside and the man behind the counter called my turn. I told him I wanted a dog and he took me back inside to walk down the line of cages.

In one of the cages the little Puli that had just been brought in was being assaulted by three larger dogs who had been earlier tenants. He was a little thing, and he was on the bottom, getting the stuffing knocked out of him. But he was struggling mightily. The runt of the litter.

"Get him out of there!" I yelled. "I'll take him, I'll take him, get him out of there!"

He cost two dollars. It was the best two bucks I ever spent.

Driving home with him, he was lying on the other side of the front seat, staring at me. I had had a vague idea what I'd name a pet, but as I stared at him, and he stared back at me, I suddenly was put in mind of the scene in Alexander Korda's 1939 film *The Thief of Bagdad*, where the evil vizier, played by Conrad Veidt, had changed Ahbhu, the little thief, played by Sabu, into a dog. The film had superimposed the human over the canine face for a moment so there was an extraordinary look of intelligence in the face of the dog. The little Puli was looking at me with that same expression. "Ahbhu," I said.

He didn't react to the name, but then he couldn't have cared less. But that was his name, from that time on.

No one who ever came into my house was unaffected by him. When he sensed someone with good vibrations, he was right there, lying at their feet. He loved to be scratched, and despite years of admonitions he refused to stop begging for scraps at table, because he found most of the people who had come to dinner at my house were patsies unable to escape his woebegone Jackie-Coogan-as-the-Kid look.

But he was a certain barometer of bums, as well. On any number of occasions when I found someone I liked, and Ahbhu would have nothing to do with him or her, it always turned out the person was a wrongo. I took to noting his attitude toward newcomers, and I must admit it influenced my own reactions. I was always wary of someone Ahbhu shunned.

Women with whom I had had unsatisfactory affairs would nonetheless return to the house from time to time—to visit the dog. He had an intimate circle of friends, many of whom had nothing to do with me, and numbering among their company some of the most beautiful actresses in Hollywood. One exquisite lady used to send her driver to pick him up for Sunday afternoon romps at the beach.

I never asked him what happened on those occasions. He didn't talk.

Last year he started going downhill, though I didn't realize it because he maintained the manner of a puppy almost to the end. But he began sleeping too much, and he couldn't hold down his food—not even the Hungarian meals prepared for him by the Magyars who lived up the street. And it became apparent to me something was wrong with him when he got scared during the big Los Angeles earthquake last year. Ahbhu wasn't afraid of anything. He attacked the Pacific Ocean and walked tall around vicious cats. But the quake terrified him and he jumped up in my bed and threw his forelegs around my neck. I was very nearly the only victim of the earthquake to die from animal strangulation.

He was in and out of the veterinarian's shop all through the early part of this year, and the idiot always said it was his diet.

Then one Sunday when he was out in the backyard, I found him lying at the foot of the porch stairs, covered with mud, vomiting so heavily all he could bring up was bile. He was matted with his own refuse and he was trying desperately to dig his nose into the earth for coolness. He was barely breathing. I took him to a different vet.

At first they thought it was just old age . . . that they could pull him through. But finally they took X-rays and saw the cancer had taken hold in his stomach and liver.

I put off the day as much as I could. Somehow I just couldn't conceive of a world that didn't have him in it. But yesterday I went to the vet's office and signed the euthanasia papers.

"I'd like to spend a little time with him, before," I said.

They brought him in and put him on the stainless steel examination table. He had grown so thin. He'd always had a pot-belly and it was gone. The muscles in his hind legs were weak, flaccid. He came to me and put his head into the hollow of my armpit. He was trembling violently. I lifted his head and he looked at me with that comic face I'd always thought made him look like Lawrence Talbot, the Wolf Man. He knew. Sharp as hell right up to the end, hey old friend? He knew, and he was scared. He trembled all the way down to his spiderweb legs. This bouncing ball of hair that, when lying on a dark carpet, could be taken for a sheepskin rug, with no way to tell at which end head and which end tail. So thin. Shaking, knowing what was going to happen to him. But still a puppy.

I cried and my eyes closed as my nose swelled with the crying, and he buried his head in my arms because we hadn't done much crying at one another. I was ashamed of myself not to be taking it as well as he was.

"I *got* to, pup, because you're in pain and you can't eat. I *got* to." But he didn't want to know that.

The vet came in, then. He was a nice guy and he asked me if I wanted to go away and just let it be done.

Then Ahbhu came up out of there and *looked* at me.

There is a scene in Kazan's *Viva Zapata* where a close friend of Zapata's, Brando's, has been condemned for conspiring with the *Federales*. A friend that had been with Zapata since the mountains, since the *revolucion* had begun. And they come to the hut to take him to the firing squad, and Brando starts out, and his friend stops him with a hand on his arm, and he says to him with great friendship, "Emiliano, do it yourself."

Ahbhu looked at me and I know he was just a dog, but if he could have spoken with human tongue he could not have said more eloquently than he did with a look, *don't leave me with strangers.*

So I held him as they laid him down and the vet slipped the lanyard up around his right foreleg and drew it tight to bulge the vein, and I held his head and he turned it away from me as the needle went in. It was impossible to tell the moment he passed over from life to death. He simply laid his head on my hand, his eyes fluttered shut and he was gone.

I wrapped him in a sheet with the help of the vet, and I drove home with Ahbhu on the seat beside me, just the way we had come home eleven years before. I took him out in the backyard and began digging his grave. I dug for hours, crying and mumbling to myself, talking to him in the sheet. It was a very neat, rectangular grave with smooth sides and all the loose dirt scooped out by hand.

I laid him down in the hole and he was so tiny in there for a dog who had seemed to be so big in life, so furry, so funny. And I covered him over and when the hole was packed full of dirt I replaced the neat divot of grass I'd scalped off at the start. And that was all.

But I couldn't send him to strangers.

THE END

QUESTIONS FOR DISCUSSION

1. Is there any significance to the reversal of the word *god* being *dog?* If so, what?
2. Does the writer try to impart human qualities to a non-human creature? Why? Discuss anthropomorphism in the light of the phrase, "Thou art God."
3. Discuss the love the writer shows in this essay. Compare and contrast it with other forms of love: the love of a man for a woman, a mother for a child, a son for a mother, a botanist for plants, an ecologist for the Earth.

14

In his sleep, Nathan Stack talked.
"Why did you pick me? Why me . . ."

15

Like the Earth, the Mother was in pain.

The great house was very quiet. The doctor had left, and the relatives had gone into town for dinner. He sat by the side of her bed and stared down at her. She looked gray and old and crumpled; her skin was a soft ashy hue of moth-dust. He was crying softly.

He felt her hand on his knee, and looked up to see her staring at him. "You weren't supposed to catch me," he said.

"I'd be disappointed if I hadn't," she said. Her voice was very thin, very smooth.

"How is it?"

"It hurts. Ben didn't dope me too well."

He bit his lower lip. The doctor had used massive doses, but the pain was more massive. She gave little starts as tremors of sudden agony hit her. Impacts. He watched the life leaking out of her eyes.

"How is your sister taking it?"

He shrugged. "You know Charlene. She's sorry, but it's all pretty intellectual to her."

His mother let a tiny ripple of a smile move her lips. "It's a terrible thing to say, Nathan, but your sister isn't the most likeable woman in the world. I'm glad you're here." She paused, thinking, then added, "It's just possible your father and I missed something from the gene pool. Charlene isn't whole."

"Can I get you something? A drink of water?"

"No. I'm fine."

He looked at the ampoule of narcotic pain killer. The syringe lay mechanical and still on a clean towel beside it. He felt her eyes on him. She knew what he was thinking. He looked away.

"I would kill for a cigarette," she said.

He laughed. At sixty-five, both legs gone, what remained of her left side paralyzed, the cancer spreading like deadly jelly toward her heart, she was still the matriarch. "You can't have a cigarette, so forget it."

"Then why don't you use that hypo and let me out of here."

"Shut up, Mother."

"Oh, for Christ's sake, Nathan. It's hours if I'm lucky. Months if I'm not. We've had this conversation before. You know I always win."

"Did I ever tell you you were a bitchy old lady?"

"Many times, but I love you anyhow."

He got up and walked to the wall. He could not walk through it, so he went around the inside of the room.

"You can't get away from it."

"Mother, Jesus! Please!"

"All right. Let's talk about the business."

"I could care less about the business right now."

"Then what should we talk about? The lofty uses to which an old lady can put her last moments?"

"You know, you're really ghoulish. I think you're enjoying this in some sick way."

"What other way is there to enjoy it."

"An adventure."

"The biggest. A pity your father never had the chance to savor it."

"I hardly think he'd have savored the feeling of being stamped to death in a hydraulic press."

Then he thought about it, because that little smile was on her lips again. "Okay, he probably would have. The two of you were so unreal, you'd have sat there and discussed it and analyzed the pulp."

"And you're our son."

He was, and he was. And he could not deny it, nor had he ever. He was hard and gentle and wild just like them, and he remembered the days in the jungle beyond Brasilia, and the hunt in the Cayman Trench, and the other days working in the mills alongside his father, and he knew when his moment came he would savor death as she did.

"Tell me something. I've always wanted to know. Did Dad kill Tom Golden?"

"Use the needle and I'll tell you."

"I'm a Stack. I don't bribe."

"I'm a Stack, and I know what a killing curiosity you've got. Use the needle and I'll tell you."

He walked widdershins around the room. She watched him, eyes bright as the mill vats.

"You old bitch."

"Shame, Nathan. You know you're not the son of a bitch. Which is more than your sister can say. Did I ever tell you she wasn't your father's child?"

"No, but I knew."

"You'd have liked her father. He was Swedish. Your father liked him."

"Is that why Dad broke both his arms?"

"Probably. But I never heard the Swede complain. One night in bed with me in those days was worth a couple of broken arms. Use the needle."

Finally, while the family was between the entree and the dessert, he filled the syringe and injected her. Her eyes widened as the stuff smacked her heart, and just before she died she rallied all her strength and said, "A deal's a deal. Your father didn't kill Tom Golden, I did. You're a hell of a man, Nathan, and you fought us the way we wanted, and we both loved you more than you could know. Except, dammit, you cunning s.o.b., you do know, don't you?"

"I know," he said, and she died; and he cried; and that was the extent of the poetry in it.

16

He knows we are coming.

They were climbing the northern face of the onyx mountain. Snake had coated Nathan Stack's feet with the thick glue and, though it was hardly a country walk, he was able to keep a foothold and pull himself up. Now they had paused to rest on a spiral ledge, and Snake had spoken for the first time of what waited for them where they were going.

"He?"

Snake did not answer. Stack slumped against the wall of the ledge. At the lower slopes of the mountain they had encountered slug-like creatures that had tried to attach themselves to Stack's flesh, but when Snake had driven them off they had returned to sucking the rocks. They had not come near the shadow creature. Further up, Stack could see the lights that flickered at the summit; he had felt fear that crawled up from his stomach. A short time before they had come to this ledge they had stumbled past a cave in the mountain where the bat creatures slept. They had gone mad at the presence of the man and the Snake and the sounds they had made sent waves of nausea through Stack. Snake had helped him and they had gotten past. Now they had stopped and Snake would not answer Stack's questions.

We must keep climbing.

"Because he knows we're here." There was a sarcastic rise in Stack's voice.

Snake started moving. Stack closed his eyes. Snake stopped and came back to him. Stack looked up at the one-eyed shadow.

"Not another step."

There is no reason why you should not know.

"Except, friend, I have the feeling you aren't going to tell me anything."

It is not yet time for you to know.

"Look: just because I haven't asked, doesn't mean I don't want to know. You've told me things I shouldn't be able to handle . . . all kinds of crazy things . . . I'm as old as, as . . . I don't know *how* old, but I get the feeling you've been trying to tell me I'm Adam . . ."

That is so.

". . . uh." He stopped rattling and stared back at the shadow creature. Then, very softly, accepting even more than he had thought possible, he said, "Snake." He was silent again. After a time he asked, "Give me another dream and let me know the rest of it?"

You must be patient. The one who lives at the top knows we are coming but I have been able to keep him from perceiving your danger to him only because you do not know yourself.

"Tell me this, then: does he *want* us to come up . . . the one on the top?"

He allows it. Because he doesn't know.

Stack nodded, resigned to following Snake's lead. He got to his feet and performed an elaborate butler's motion, after you, Snake.

And Snake turned, his flat hands sticking to the wall of the ledge, and they climbed higher, spiraling upward toward the summit.

The Deathbird swooped, then rose toward the Moon. There was still time.

17

Dira came to Nathan Stack near sunset, appearing in the board room of the industrial consortium Stack had built from the family empire.

Stack sat in the pneumatic chair that dominated the conversation pit where top-level decisions were made. He was alone. The others had left hours before and the room was dim with only the barest glow of light from hidden banks that shone through the soft walls.

The shadow creature passed through the walls—and at his passage they became rose quartz, then returned to what they had been. He stood staring at Nathan Stack, and for long moments the man was unaware of any other presence in the room.

You have to go now, Snake said.

Stack looked up, his eyes widened in horror, and through his mind flitted the unmistakable image of Satan, fanged mouth smiling, horns gleaming with scintillas of light as though seen through crosstar filters, rope tail with its spade-shaped pointed tip thrashing, large cloven hoofs leaving burning imprints in the carpet, eyes as deep as pools of oil, the pitchfork, the satin-lined cape, the hairy legs of a goat, talons. He tried to scream but the sound dammed up in his throat.

No, Snake said, *that is not so. Come with me, and you will understand.*

There was a tone of sadness in the voice. As though Satan had been sorely wronged. Stack shook his head violently.

There was no time for argument. The moment had come, and Dira could not hesitate. He gestured and Nathan Stack rose from the pneumatic chair, leaving behind something that looked like Nathan Stack asleep, and he walked to Dira and Snake took him by the hand and they passed through rose quartz and went away from there.

Down and down Snake took him.

The Mother was in pain. She had been sick for eons, but it had reached the point where Snake knew it would be terminal, and the Mother knew it, too. But she would hide her child, she would intercede in her own behalf and hide him away deep in her bosom where no one, not even the mad one, could find him.

Dira took Stack to Hell.

It was a fine place.

Warm and safe and far from the probing of mad ones.

And the sickness raged on unchecked. Nations crumbled, the oceans boiled and then grew cold and filmed over with scum, the air became thick with dust and killing vapors, flesh ran like oil, the skies grew dark, the sun blurred and became dull. The Earth moaned.

The plants suffered and consumed themselves, beasts became crippled and went mad, trees burst into flame and from their ashes rose glass shapes that shattered in the wind. The Earth was dying; a long, slow, painful death.

In the center of the Earth, in the fine place, Nathan Stack slept.

Don't leave me with strangers.

Overhead, far away against the stars, the Deathbird circled and circled, waiting for the word.

18

When they reached the highest peak, Nathan Stack looked across through the terrible burning cold and the ferocious grittiness of the demon wind and saw the sanctuary of always, the cathedral of forever, the pillar of remembrance, the haven of perfection, the pyramid of blessings, the toyshop of creation, the vault of deliverance, the monument of longing, the receptacle of thoughts, the maze of wonder, the catafalque of despair, the podium of pronouncements and the kiln of last attempts.

On a slope that rose to a star pinnacle, he saw the home of the one who dwelled here—lights flashing and flickering, lights that could be seen far off across the deserted face of the planet—and he began to suspect the name of the resident.

Suddenly everything went red for Nathan Stack. As though a filter had been dropped over his eyes, the black sky, the flickering lights, the rocks that formed the great plateau on which they stood, even Snake became red, and with the color came pain. Terrible pain that burned through every channel of Stack's body, as though his blood had been set afire. He screamed and fell to his knees, the pain crackling through his brain, following every nerve and blood vessel and ganglion and neural track. His skull flamed.

Fight him, Snake said. *Fight him!*

I can't, screamed silently through Stack's mind, the pain too great even to speak. Fire licked and leaped and he felt the delicate tissues of thought shriveling. He tried to focus his thoughts on ice. He clutched for salvation at ice, chunks of ice, mountains of ice, swimming icebergs of ice half-buried in frozen water, even as his soul smoked and smoldered. *Ice!* He thought of millions of particles of hail rushing, falling, thundering against the firestorm eating his mind, and there was a spit of steam, a flame that went out, a corner that grew cool . . . and he took his stand in that corner, thinking ice, thinking blocks and chunks and monuments of ice, edging them out to widen the circle of coolness and safety. Then the flames began to retreat, to slide back down the channels, and he sent ice after them, snuffing them, burying them in ice and chill waters.

When he opened his eyes, he was still on his knees, but he could think again, and the red surfaces had become normal again.

He will try again. You must be ready.

"Tell me *everything!* I can't go through this without knowing, I need help!"

You can help yourself. You have the strength. I gave you the spark.

. . . and the second derangement struck!

The air turned shaverasse and he held dripping chunks of unclean rova in his jowls, the taste making him weak with nausea. His pods withered and drew up into his shell and as the bones cracked he howled with strings of pain that came so fast they were almost one. He tried to scuttle away, but his eyes magnified the shatter of light that beat against him. Facets of his eyes cracked and the juice began to bubble out. The pain was unbelievable.

Fight him!

Stack rolled onto his back, sending out cilia to touch the earth, and for an instant he realized he was seeing through the eyes of another creature, another form of life he could not even describe. But he was under an open sky and that produced fear, he was surrounded by air that had become deadly and *that* produced fear, he was going blind and *that* produced fear, he was . . . he was a *man* . . . he fought back against the feeling of being some other thing . . . he was a *man* and he would not feel fear, he would stand.

He rolled over, withdrew his cilia, and struggled to lower his pods. Broken bones grated and pain thundered through his body. He forced himself to ignore it, and finally the pods were down and he was breathing and he felt his head reeling . . .

And when he opened his eyes he was Nathan Stack again.

. . . and the third derangement struck:

Hopelessness.

Out of unending misery he came back to be Stack.

. . . and the fourth derangement struck:

Madness.

Out of raging lunacy he fought his way to be Stack.

. . . and the fifth derangement, and the sixth, and the seventh, and the plagues, and the whirlwinds, and the pools of evil, and the reduction in size and accompanying fall forever through sub-microscopic hells, and the things that fed on him from inside, and the twentieth, and the fortieth, and the sound of his voice screaming for release, and the voice of Snake always beside him, whispering *Fight him!*

Finally it stopped.

Quickly, now.

Snake took Stack by the hand and half-dragging him they raced to the great palace of light and glass on the slope, shining brightly under the star pinnacle, and they passed under an arch of shining metal into the ascension hall. The portal sealed behind them.

There were tremors in the walls. The inlaid floors of jewels began to rumble and tremble. Bits of high and faraway ceilings began to drop. Quaking, the palace gave one hideous shudder and collapsed around them.

Now, Snake said. *Now you will know everything!*

And everything forgot to fall. Frozen in mid-air, the wreckage of the palace hung suspended above them. Even the air ceased to swirl. Time stood still. The movement of the Earth was halted. Everything held utterly immobile as Nathan Stack was permitted to understand all.

19

MULTIPLE CHOICE
(Counts for 1/2 your final grade)

1. **God is:**

   A. An invisible spirit with a long beard.
   B. A small dog dead in a hole.
   C. Everyman.
   D. The Wizard of Oz.

2. **Nietzsche wrote "God is dead." By this did he mean:**

   A. Life is pointless.
   B. Belief in supreme deities has waned.
   C. There never was a God to begin with.
   D. Thou art God.

3. **Ecology is another name for:**

   A. Mother love.
   B. Enlightened self-interest.

   C. A good health salad with Granola.
   D. God.

4. Which of these phrases most typifies the profoundest love:

   A. Don't leave me with strangers.
   B. I love you.
   C. God is love.
   D. Use the needle.

5. Which of these powers do we usually associate with God:

   A. Power.
   B. Love.
   C. Humanity.
   D. Docility.

20

None of the above.

Starlight shone in the eyes of the Deathbird and its passage through the night cast a shadow on the Moon.

21

Nathan Stack raised his hands and around them the air was still as the palace fell crashing. They were untouched. *Now you know all there is to know,* Snake said, sinking to one knee as though worshiping. There was no one there to worship but Nathan Stack.

"Was he always mad?"

From the first.

"Then those who gave our world to him were mad, and your race was mad to allow it."

Snake had no answer.

"Perhaps it was supposed to be like this," Stack said.

He reached down and lifted Snake to his feet, and he touched the shadow creature's head. "Friend," he said.

Snake's race was incapable of tears. He said, *I have waited longer than you can know for that word.*

"I'm sorry it comes at the end."

Perhaps it was supposed to be like this.

Then there was a swirling of air, a scintillance in the ruined palace, and the owner of the mountain, the owner of the ruined Earth came to them in a burning bush.

AGAIN, SNAKE? AGAIN YOU ANNOY ME?

The time for toys is ended.

NATHAN STACK YOU BRING TO STOP ME? *I* SAY WHEN THE TIME IS ENDED. *I* SAY, AS I'VE ALWAYS SAID.

Then, to Nathan Stack:

GO AWAY. FIND A PLACE TO HIDE UNTIL I COME FOR YOU.

Stack ignored the burning bush. He waved his hand and the cone of safety in which they stood vanished. "Let's find him, first, then I know what to do."

The Deathbird sharpened its talons on the night wind and sailed down through emptiness toward the cinder of the Earth.

22

Nathan Stack had once contracted pneumonia. He had lain on the operating table as the surgeon made the small incision in the chest wall. Had he not been stubborn, had he not continued working around the clock while the pneumonic infection developed into empyema, he would never have had to go under the knife, even for an operation as safe as a thoractomy. But he was a Stack, and so he lay on the operating table as the rubber tube was inserted into the chest cavity to drain off the pus in the pleural cavity, and heard someone speak his name.

NATHAN STACK.

He heard it, from far off, across an Arctic vastness; heard it echoing over and over, down an endless corridor; as the knife sliced.

NATHAN STACK.

He remembered Lilith, with hair the color of dark wine. He remembered taking hours to die beneath a rock slide as his hunting companions in the pack ripped apart the remains of the bear and ignored his grunted moans for help. He remembered the impact of the crossbow bolt as it ripped through his hauberk and split his chest and he died at Agincourt. He remembered the icy water of the Ohio as it closed over his head and the flatboat disappearing without his mates noticing his loss. He remembered the mustard gas that ate his lungs and trying to crawl toward a farmhouse near Verdun. He remembered looking directly into the flash of the bomb and feeling the flesh of his face melt away. He remembered Snake coming to him in the board room and husking him like corn from his body. He remembered sleeping in the molten core of the Earth for a quarter of a million years.

Across the dead centuries he heard his mother pleading with him to set her free, to end her pain. *Use the needle.* Her voice mingled with the voice of the Earth crying out in endless pain at her flesh that had been ripped away, at her rivers turned to arteries of dust, at her rolling hills and green fields slagged to greenglass and ashes. The voices of his mother and the mother that was Earth became one, and mingled to become Snake's voice telling him he was the one man in the world—the last man in the world—who could end the terminal case the Earth had become.

Use the needle. Put the suffering Earth out of its misery. *It belongs to you now.*

Nathan Stack was secure in the power he contained. A power that far outstripped that of gods or Snakes or mad creators who stuck pins in their creations, who broke their toys.

YOU CAN'T. I WON'T LET YOU.

Nathan Stack walked around the burning bush crackling impotently in rage. He looked at it almost pityingly, remembering the Wizard of Oz with his great and ominous disembodied head floating in mist and lightning, and the poor little man behind the curtain turning the dials to create the effects. Stack walked around the effect, knowing he had more power than this sad, poor thing that had held his race in thrall since before Lilith had been taken from him.

He went in search of the mad one who capitalized his name.

23

Zarathustra descended alone from the mountains, encountering no one. But when he came into the forest, all at once there stood before him an old man who had left his holy cottage to look for roots in the woods. And thus spoke the old man to Zarathustra.

"No stranger to me is this wanderer: many years ago he passed this way. Zarathustra he was called, but he has changed. At that time you carried your ashes to the mountains; would you now carry your fire into the valleys? Do you not fear to be punished as an arsonist?

"Zarathustra has changed, Zarathustra has become a child, Zarathustra is an awakened one; what do you now want among the sleepers? You lived in your solitude as in the sea, and the sea carried you. Alas, would you now climb ashore? Alas, would you again drag your own body?"

Zarathustra answered: "I love man."

"Why," asked the saint, "did I go into the forest and the desert? Was it not because I loved man all-too-much? Now I love God; man I love not. Man is for me too imperfect a thing. Love of man would kill me."

"And what is the saint doing in the forest?" asked Zarathustra.

The saint answered: "I make songs and sing them; and when I make songs, I laugh, cry, and hum: thus I praise God. With singing, crying, laughing, and humming, I praise the god who is my god. But what do you bring us as a gift?"

When Zarathustra had heard these words he bade the saint farewell and said: "What could I have to give you? But let me go quickly lest I take something from you!" And thus they separated, the old one and the man, laughing as two boys laugh.

But when Zarathustra was alone he spoke thus to his heart:

"Could it be possible? This old saint in the forest had not yet heard anything of this, that *God is dead!*"

24

Stack found the mad one wandering in the forest of final moments. He was an old, tired man, and Stack knew with a wave of his hand he could end it for this god in a moment. But what was the reason for it? It was even too late for revenge. It had been too late from the start. So he let the old one go his way, wandering in the forest mumbling to himself, I WON'T LET YOU DO IT, in the voice of a cranky child; mumbling pathetically, OH, PLEASE, I DON'T WANT TO GO TO BED YET. I'M NOT YET DONE PLAYING.

And Stack came back to Snake, who had served his function and protected Stack until Stack had learned that he was more powerful than the God he'd worshipped all through the history of men. He came back to Snake and their hands touched and the bond of friendship was sealed at last, at the end.

Then they worked together and Nathan Stack used the needle with a wave of his hands, and the Earth could not sigh with relief as its endless pain was ended . . . but it did sigh, and it settled in upon itself, and the molten core went out, and the winds died, and from high above them Stack heard the fulfillment of Snake's final act; he heard the descent of the Deathbird.

"What was your name?" Stack asked his friend.

Dira.

And the Deathbird settled down across the tired shape of the Earth, and it spread its wings wide, and brought them over and down, and enfolded the Earth as a mother enfolds her weary child. Dira settled down on the amethyst floor of the dark-shrouded palace, and closed his single eye with gratitude. To sleep at last, at the end.

All this, as Nathan Stack stood watching. He was the last, at the end, and because he had come to own—if even for a few moments

—that which could have been his from the start, had he but known, he did not sleep but stood and watched. Knowing at last, at the end, that he had loved and done no wrong.

25

The Deathbird closed its wings over the Earth until at last, at the end, there was only the great bird crouched over the dead cinder. Then the Deathbird raised its head to the star-filled sky and repeated the sigh of loss the Earth had felt at the end. Then its eyes closed, it tucked its head carefully under its wing, and all was night.

Far away, the stars waited for the cry of the Deathbird to reach them so final moments could be observed at last, at the end, for the race of men.

26

THIS IS FOR MARK TWAIN

NORMAN SPINRAD

A Thing of Beauty

"I once showed some native hunters, who were as keen-sighted as hawks, magazine pictures in which any of our children would have instantly recognized human figures. But my hunters turned the pictures round and round until one of them, tracing the outlines with his finger, finally exclaimed: 'These are white men.' It was hailed by all as a great discovery" (C. G. Jung, *Modern Man in Search of a Soul*). We can make no greater mistake than to believe what we see is what is seen by everyone else.

"There's a gentleman by the name of Mr. Shiburo Ito to see you," my intercom said. "He is interested in the purchase of an historic artifact of some significance."

While I waited for him to enter my private office, I had computer central display his specs on the screen discreetly built into the back of my desk. My Mr. Ito was none other than Ito of Ito Freight Boosters of Osaka; there was no need to purchase a readout from Dun & Bradstreet's private banks. If Shiburo Ito of Ito Boosters wrote a check for anything short of the national debt, it could be relied upon not to bounce.

The slight, balding man who glided into my office wore a red silk kimono with a richly brocaded black obi, Mendocino needlepoint by the look of it. No doubt back in the miasmic smog of Osaka, he bonged the peons with the latest skins from Savile Row. Everything about him was *just so;* he purchased confidently on that razor edge between class and ostentation that only the Japanese can handle with such grace, and then only when they have millions of hard yen to back them up. Mr. Ito would be no sucker. He would want whatever he wanted for precise reasons all his own, and would not be budgeable from the center of his desires. The typical heavyweight Japanese businessman, a prime example of the breed that's pushed us out of the center of the international arena.

Mr. Ito bowed almost imperceptibly as he handed me his card. I countered by merely bobbing my head in his direction and remaining seated. These face and posture games may seem ridiculous, but you can't do business with the Japanese without playing them.

As he took a seat before me, Ito drew a black cylinder from the sleeve of his kimono and ceremoniously placed it on the desk before me.

"I have been given to understand that you are a connoisseur of Filmore posters of the early-to-mid-1960s period, Mr. Harris," he said. "The repute of your collection has penetrated even to the environs of Osaka and Kyoto, where I make my habitation. Please permit me to make this minor addition. The thought that a contribution of mine may repose in such illustrious surroundings will afford me much pleasure and place me forever in your debt."

My hands trembled as I unwrapped the poster. With his financial resources, Ito's polite little gift could be almost anything but disappointing. My daddy loved to brag about the old expense account days when American businessmen ran things, but you had to admit that the fringe benefits of business Japanese style had plenty to recommend them.

But when I got the gift open, it took a real effort not to lose points by whistling out loud. For what I was holding was nothing less than a mint example of the very first Grateful Dead poster in subtle black and gray, a super-rare item, not available for any amount of sheer purchasing power. I dared not inquire as to how Mr. Ito had acquired it. We simply shared a long, silent moment contemplating the poster, its beauty and historicity transcending whatever questionable events might have transpired to bring us together in its presence.

How could I not like Mr. Ito now? Who can say that the Japanese occupy their present international position by economic might alone?

"I hope I may be afforded the opportunity to please your sensibilities as you have pleased mine, Mr. Ito," I finally said. That was the way to phrase it; you didn't thank them for a gift like this, and you brought them around to business as obliquely as possible.

Ito suddenly became obviously embarrassed, even furtive. "Forgive me my boldness, Mr. Harris, but I have hopes that you may be able to assist me in resolving a domestic matter of some delicacy."

"A domestic matter?"

"Just so. I realize that this is an embarrassing intrusion, but you are obviously a man of refinement and infinite discretion, so if you will forgive my forwardness . . ."

His composure seemed to totally evaporate, as if he was going to ask me to pimp for some disgusting perversion he had. I had the feeling that the power had suddenly taken a quantum jump in my direction, that a large financial opportunity was about to present itself.

"Please feel free, Mr. Ito . . ."

Ito smiled nervously. "My wife comes from a family of extreme artistic attainment," he said. "In fact, both her parents have attained the exalted status of National Cultural Treasurers, a distinction of which they never tire of reminding me. While I have achieved a large measure of financial success in the freight-booster enterprise, they regard me as *nikulturi*, a mere merchant, severely lacking in aesthetic refinement as compared to their own illustrious selves. You understand the situation, Mr. Harris?"

I nodded as sympathetically as I could. These Japs certainly have a genius for making life difficult for themselves! Here was a major Japanese industrialist shrinking into low posture at the very thought of his sponging in-laws, whom he could probably buy and sell out of petty cash. At the same time, he was obviously out to cream the sons of bitches in some crazy way that would only make sense to a Japanese. Seems to me the Japanese are better at running the world than they are at running their lives.

"Mr. Harris, I wish to acquire a major American artifact for the gardens of my Kyoto estate. Frankly, it must be of sufficient magni-

tude so as to remind the parents of my wife of my success in the
material realm every time they should chance to gaze upon it, and
I shall display it in a manner which will assure that they gaze upon
it often. But of course, it must be of sufficient beauty and historicity
so as to prove to them that my taste is no less elevated than their
own. Thus shall I gain respect in their eyes and reestablish tranquility in my household. I have been given to understand that you
are a valued counselor in such matters, and I am eager to inspect
whatever such objects you may deem appropriate."

So that was it! He wanted to buy something big enough to bong
the minds of his artsy-fartsy relatives, but he really didn't trust his
own taste; he wanted me to show him something he would want
to see. And he was swimming like a goldfish in a sea of yen! I could
hardly believe my good luck. How much could I take him for?

"Ah . . . what size artifact did you have in mind, Mr. Ito?" I asked
as casually as I could.

"I wish to acquire a major piece of American monumental archi-
tecture so that I may convert the gardens of my estate into a shrine
to its beauty and historicity. Therefore, a piece of classical propor-
tions is required. Of course, it must be worthy of enshrinement,
otherwise an embarrassing loss of esteem will surely ensue."

"Of course."

This was not going to be just another Howard Johnson or gas
station sale; even something like an old Hilton or the Cooperstown
Baseball Hall of Fame I unloaded last year was thinking too small.
In his own way, Ito was telling me that price was no object, the
sky was the limit. This was the dream of a lifetime! A sucker with
a bottomless bank account placing himself trustingly in my tender
hands!

"Should it please you, Mr. Ito," I said, "we can inspect several
possibilities here in New York immediately. My jumper is on the
roof."

"Most gracious of you to interrupt your most busy schedule on
my behalf, Mr. Harris. I would be delighted."

I lifted the jumper off the roof, floated her to a thousand feet, then took a Mach 1.5 jump south over the decayed concrete jungles at the tip of Manhattan. The curve brought us back to float about a mile north of Bedloe's Island. I took her down to three hundred and brought her in toward the Statue of Liberty at a slow drift, losing altitude imperceptibly as we crept up on the Headless Lady, so that by the time we were just off shore, we were right down on the deck. It was a nice touch to make the goods look more impressive—manipulating the perspectives so that the huge, green, headless statue, with its patina of firebomb soot, seemed to rise up out of the bay like a ruined colossus as we floated toward it.

Mr. Ito betrayed no sign of emotion. He stared straight ahead out the bubble without so much as a word or a flicker of gesture.

"As you are no doubt aware, this is the famous Statue of Liberty," I said. "Like most such artifacts, it is available to any buyer who will display it with proper dignity. Of course, I would have no trouble convincing the Bureau of National Antiquities that your intentions are exemplary in this regard."

I set the autopilot to circle the island at fifty yards offshore so that Ito could get a fully rounded view, and see how well the statue would look from any angle, how eminently suitable it was for enshrinement. But he still sat there with less expression on his face than the average C-grade servitor.

"You can see that nothing has been touched since the Insurrectionists blew the statue's head off," I said, trying to drum up his interest with a pitch. "Thus, the statue has picked up yet another level of historical significance to enhance its already formidable venerability. Originally a gift from France, it has historical significance as an emblem of kinship between the American and French revolutions. Situated as it is in the mouth of New York harbor, it became a symbol of America itself to generations of immigrants. And the damage the Insurrectionists did only serves as a reminder of how lucky we were to come through that mess as lightly as we did. Also, it adds a certain melancholy atmosphere, don't you think? Emotion, intrinsic beauty, and historicity combined in one elegant piece of monumental statuary. And the asking price is a good deal less than you might suppose."

Mr. Ito seemed embarrassed when he finally spoke. "I trust you will forgive my saying so, Mr. Harris, since the emotion is engendered by the highest regard for the noble past of your great nation, but I find this particular artifact somewhat depressing."

"How so, Mr. Ito?"

The jumper completed a circle of the Statue of Liberty and began another as Mr. Ito lowered his eyes and stared at the oily waters of the bay as he answered.

"The symbolism of this broken statue is quite saddening, representing as it does a decline from your nation's past greatness. For me to enshrine such an artifact in Kyoto would be an ignoble act, an insult to the memory of your nation's greatness. It would be a statement of overweening pride."

Can you beat that? *He* was offended because he felt that displaying the statue in Japan would be insulting the United States, and therefore I was implying he was *nikulturi* by offering it to him. When all that the damned thing was to any American was one more piece of old junk left over from the glorious days that the Japanese, who were nuts for such rubbish, might be persuaded to pay through the nose for the dubious privilege of carting away. These Japs could drive you crazy—who else could you offend by suggesting they do something that they thought would offend you but you thought was just fine in the first place?

"I hope I haven't offended you, Mr. Ito," I blurted out. I could have bitten my tongue off the moment I said it, because it was exactly the wrong thing to say. I *had* offended him, and it was only a further offense to put him in a position where politeness demanded that he deny it.

"I'm sure that could not have been further from your intention, Mr. Harris," Ito said with convincing sincerity. "A pang of sadness at the perishability of greatness, nothing more. In fact as such, the experience might be said to be healthful to the soul. But making such an artifact a permanent part of one's surroundings would be more than I could bear."

Were these his true feelings or just smooth Japanese politeness? Who could tell what these people really felt? Sometimes I think they don't even know what they feel themselves. But at any rate, I had to show him something that would change his mood, and fast. Hm-m-m . . .

"Tell me, Mr. Ito, are you fond of baseball?"

His eyes lit up like satellite beacons and the heavy mood evaporated in the warm, almost childish, glow of his sudden smile. "Ah, yes!" he said. "I retain a box at Osaka Stadium, though I must confess I secretly retain a partiality for the Giants. How strange it is that this profound game has so declined in the country of its origin."

"Perhaps. But that very fact has placed something on the market which I'm sure you'll find most congenial. Shall we go?"

"By all means," Mr. Ito said. "I find our present environs somewhat overbearing."

I floated the jumper to five hundred feet and programmed a Mach 2.5 jump curve to the north that quickly put the great hunk of moldering, dirty copper far behind. It's amazing how much sickening emotion the Japanese are able to attach to almost any piece of old junk. *Our* old junk at that, as if Japan didn't have enough useless old clutter of its own. But I certainly shouldn't complain about it; it makes me a pretty good living. Everyone knows the old saying about a fool and his money.

The jumper's trajectory put us at float over the confluence of the Harlem and East rivers at a thousand feet. Without dropping any lower, I whipped the jumper northeast over the Bronx at three hundred miles per hour. This area had been covered by tenements before the Insurrection, and had been thoroughly razed by firebombs, high explosives, and napalm. No one had ever found an economic reason for clearing away the miles of rubble, and now the scarred earth and ruined buildings were covered with tall grass, poison sumac, tangled scrub growth, and scattered thickets of trees which might merge to form a forest in another generation or two. Because of the crazy, jagged, overgrown topography, this land was utterly useless, and no one lived here except some pathetic remnants of old hippie tribes that kept to themselves and weren't worth hunting down. Their occasional huts and patchwork tents were the only signs of human habitation in the area. This was *really* depressing territory, and I wanted to get Mr. Ito over it high and fast.

Fortunately, we didn't have far to go, and in a couple of minutes, I had the jumper floating at five hundred feet over our objective, the only really intact structure in the area. Mr. Ito's stone face lit up with such boyish pleasure that I knew I had it made; I had figured right when I figured he couldn't resist something like this.

"So!" he cried in delight. "Yankee Stadium!"

The ancient ballpark had come through the Insurrection with nothing worse than some atmospheric blacking and cratering of its concrete exterior walls. Everything around it had been pretty well demolished except for a short section of old elevated subway line, which still stood beside it, a soft rusty-red skeleton covered with vines and moss. The surrounding ruins were thoroughly overgrown, huge piles of rubble, truncated buildings, rusted-out tanks, forming tangled man-made jungled foothills around the high point of the stadium, which itself had creepers and vines growing all over it, partially blending it into the wild, overgrown landscape around it.

The Bureau of National Antiquities had circled the stadium with a high, electrified, barbed-wire fence to keep out the hippies who roamed the badlands. A lone guard armed with a Japanese-made slicer patrolled the fence in endless circles at fifteen feet on a one-man skimmer. I brought the jumper down to fifty feet and orbited the stadium five times, giving the enthralled Ito a good, long, contemplative look at how lovely it would look as the centerpiece of his gardens instead of hidden away in these crummy ruins.

The guard waved to us each time our paths crossed—it must be a lonely, boring job out here with nothing but old junk and crazy wandering hippies for company.

"May we go inside?" Ito said in absolutely reverent tones. Man, was he hooked! He glowed like a little kid about to inherit a candy store.

"Certainly, Mr. Ito," I said, taking the jumper out of its circling pattern and floating it gently up over the lip of the old ballpark, putting it on hover at roof-level over what had once been short center field. Very slowly, I brought the jumper down toward the tangle of tall grass, shrubbery, and occasional stunted trees that covered what had once been the playing field.

It was like descending into some immense, ruined, roofless cathedral. As we dropped, the cavernous triple-decked grandstands—rotten wooden seats rich with moss and fungi, great overhanging rafters concealing flocks of chattering birds in their deep glowering shadows—rose to encircle the jumper in a weird, lost grandeur.

By the time we touched down, Ito seemed to be floating in his seat with rapture. "So beautiful!" he sighed. "Such a sense of history and venerability. Ah, Mr. Harris, what noble deeds were done in this Yankee Stadium in bygone days! May we set foot on this historic playing field?"

"Of course, Mr. Ito." It was beautiful. I didn't have to say a word; he was doing a better job of selling the moldy, useless heap of junk to himself than I ever could.

We got out of the jumper and tramped around through the tangled vegetation while scruffy pigeons wheeled overhead and the immensity of the empty stadium gave the place an illusion of mystical significance, as if it were some Greek ruin or Stonehenge, instead of just a ruined old baseball park. The grandstands seemed choked with ghosts; the echoes of great events that never were, filled the deeply shadowed cavernous spaces.

Mr. Ito, it turned out, knew more about Yankee Stadium than

I did, or ever wanted to. He led me around at a measured, reverent pace, boring my ass off with a kind of historical grand tour.

"Here Al Gionfriddo made his famous World Series catch of a potential home run by the great DiMaggio," he said, as we reached the high, crumbling black wall that ran around the bleachers. Faded numerals said "405." We followed this curving, overgrown wall around to the 467 sign in left center field. Here there were three stone markers jutting up out of the old playing field like so many tombstones, and five copper plaques on the wall behind them, so green with decay as to be illegible. They really must've taken this stuff seriously in the old days, as seriously as the Japanese take it now.

"Memorials to the great heroes of the New York Yankees," Ito said. "The legendary Ruth, Gehrig, DiMaggio, Mantle . . . Over this very spot, Mickey Mantle drove a ball into the bleachers, a feat which had been regarded as impossible for nearly half a century. Ah . . ."

And so on. Ito tramped all through the underbrush of the playing field and seemed to have a piece of trivia of vast historical significance to himself for almost every square foot of Yankee Stadium. At this spot, Babe Ruth had achieved his sixtieth home run; here Roger Maris had finally surpassed that feat, over there Mantle had almost driven a ball over the high roof of the venerable stadium. It was staggering how much of this trivia he knew, and how much importance it all had in his eyes. The tour seemed to go on forever. I would've gone crazy with boredom if it wasn't so wonderfully obvious how thoroughly sold he was on the place. While Ito conducted his love affair with Yankee Stadium, I passed the time by counting yen in my head. I figured I could probably get ten million out of him, which meant that my commission would be a cool million. Thinking about that much money about to drop into my hands was enough to keep me smiling for the two hours that Ito babbled on about home runs, no-hitters, and triple-plays.

It was late afternoon by the time he had finally saturated himself and allowed me to lead him back to the jumper. I felt it was time to talk business, while he was still under the spell of the stadium, and his resistance was at low ebb.

"It pleasures me greatly to observe the depths of your feeling for this beautiful and venerable stadium, Mr. Ito," I said. "I stand ready to facilitate the speedy transfer of title at your convenience."

Ito started as if suddenly roused from some pleasant dream. He cast his eyes downward, and bowed almost imperceptibly.

"Alas," he said sadly, "while it would pleasure me beyond all reason to enshrine the noble Yankee Stadium upon my grounds, such a self-indulgence would only exacerbate my domestic difficulties. The parents of my wife ignorantly consider the noble sport of baseball an imported American barbarity. My wife unfortunately shares in this opinion and frequently berates me for my enthusiasm for the game. Should I purchase the Yankee Stadium, I would become a laughing stock in my own household, and my life would become quite unbearable."

Can you beat that? The arrogant little son of a bitch wasted two hours of my time dragging around this stupid heap of junk babbling all that garbage and driving me half crazy, and he knew he wasn't going to buy it all the time! I felt like knocking his low-posture teeth down his unworthy throat. But I thought of all those yen I still had a fighting chance at and made the proper response: a rueful little smile of sympathy, a shared sigh of wistful regret, a murmured, "Alas."

"However," Ito added brightly, "the memory of this visit is something I shall treasure always. I am deeply in your debt for granting me this experience, Mr. Harris. For this alone, the trip from Kyoto has been made more than worthwhile."

Now that really made my day.

I was in real trouble, I was very close to blowing the biggest deal I've ever had a shot at. I'd shown Ito the two best items in my territory, and if he didn't find what he wanted in the Northeast, there were plenty of first-rank pieces still left in the rest of the country—top stuff like the St. Louis Gateway Arch, the Disneyland Matterhorn, the Salt Lake City Mormon Tabernacle—and plenty of other brokers to collect that big fat commission.

I figured I had only one more good try before Ito started thinking of looking elsewhere: the United Nations building complex. The U.N. had fallen into a complicated legal limbo. The United Nations had retained title to the buildings when they moved their headquarters out of New York, but when the U.N. folded, New York State, New York City, and the Federal Government had all laid claim to them, along with the U.N.'s foreign creditors. The Bureau of National Antiquities didn't have clear title, but they did administer the estate for the Federal Government. If I could palm the damned thing off on Ito, the Bureau of National Junk would be only too happy to take his check and let everyone else try to pry the money out of them. And once he moved it to Kyoto, the Japanese Government would not be about to let anyone repossess something that one of their heavyweight citizens had shelled out hard yen for.

So I jumped her at Mach 1.7 to a hover at three hundred feet over the greasy waters of the East River due east of the U.N. complex at 42nd Street. At this time of day and from this angle, the U.N. buildings presented what I hoped was a romantic Japanese-style vista. The Secretariat was a giant glass tombstone dramatically silhouetted by the late afternoon sun as it loomed massively before us out of the perpetual gray haze hanging over Manhattan; beside it, the low sweeping curve of the General Assembly gave the grouping a balanced calligraphic outline. The total effect seemed similar to that of one of those ancient Japanese Torii gates rising out of the foggy sunset, only done on a far grander scale.

The Insurrection had left the U.N. untouched—the rebels had had some crazy attachment for it—and from the river, you couldn't see much of the grubby open air market that had been allowed to spring up in the plaza, or the honky-tonk bars along

First Avenue. Fortunately, the Bureau of National Antiquities made a big point of keeping the buildings themselves in good shape, figuring that the Federal Government's claim would be weakened if anyone could yell that the Bureau was letting them fall apart.

I floated her slowly in off the river, keeping at the three-hundred-foot level, and started my pitch. "Before you, Mr. Ito, are the United Nations buildings, melancholy symbol of one of the noblest dreams of man, now unfortunately empty and abandoned, a monument to the tragedy of the U.N.'s unfortunate demise."

Flashes of sunlight, reflected off the river, then onto the hundreds of windows that formed the face of the Secretariat, scintillated intermittently across the glass monolith as I set the jumper to circling the building. When we came around to the western face, the great glass facade was a curtain of orange fire.

"The Secretariat could be set in your gardens so as to catch both the sunrise and sunset, Mr. Ito," I pointed out. "It's considered one of the finest examples of Twentieth-Century Utilitarian in the world, and you'll note that it's in excellent repair."

Ito said nothing. His eyes did not so much as flicker. Even the muscles of his face seemed unnaturally wooden. The jumper passed behind the Secretariat again, which eclipsed both the sun and its giant reflection; below us was the sweeping gray concrete roof of the General Assembly.

"And of course, the historic significance of the U.N. buildings is beyond measure, if somewhat tragic—"

Abruptly, Mr. Ito interrupted, in a cold, clipped voice. "Please forgive my crudity in interjecting a political opinion into this situation, Mr. Harris, but I believe such frankness will save you much wasted time and effort and myself considerable discomfort."

All at once, he was Shiburo Ito of Ito Freight Boosters of Osaka, a mover and shaper of the economy of the most powerful nation on Earth, and he was letting me know it. "I fully respect your sentimental esteem for the late United Nations, but it is a sentiment I do not share. I remind you that the United Nations was born as an alliance of the nations which humiliated Japan in a most unfortunate war, and expired as a shrill and contentious assembly of pauperized beggar-states united only in the dishonorable determination to extract international alms from more progressive, advanced, self-sustaining, and virtuous states, chief among them Japan. I must therefore regretfully point out that the sight of these buildings fills me with nothing but disgust, though they may have a certain intrinsic beauty as abstract objects."

His face had become a shiny mask and he seemed a million miles away. He had come as close to outright anger as I had ever heard one of these heavyweight Japs get; he must be really steaming inside. Damn it, how was I supposed to know that the U.N. had all those awful political meanings for him? As far as I've ever heard, the U.N. hasn't meant anything to anyone for years, except an idealistic, sappy idea that got taken over by Third Worlders and went broke. Just my rotten luck to run into one of the few people in the world who were still fighting that one!

"You are no doubt fatigued, Mr. Harris," Ito said coldly. "I shall trouble you no longer. It would be best to return to your office now. Should you have further objects to show me, we can arrange another appointment at some mutually convenient time."

What could I say to that? I had offended him deeply, and besides I couldn't think of anything else to show him. I took the jumper to five hundred and headed downtown over the river at a slow hundred miles per hour, hoping against hope that I'd somehow think of something to salvage this blown million-yen deal with before we reached my office and I lost this giant goldfish forever.

As we headed downtown, Ito stared impassively out the bubble at the bleak ranks of high-rise apartment buildings that lined the Manhattan shore below us, not deigning to speak or take further notice of my miserable existence. The deep orange light streaming in through the bubble turned his round face into a rising sun, straight off the Japanese flag. It seemed appropriate. The crazy bastard was just like his country: a politically touchy, politely arrogant economic overlord, with infinitely refined aesthetic sensibilities inexplicably combined with a pack-rat lust for the silliest of our old junk. One minute Ito seemed so superior in every way, and the next he was a stupid, childish sucker. I've been doing business with the Japanese for years, and I still don't really understand them. The best I can do is guess around the edges of whatever their inner reality actually is, and hope I hit what works. And this time out, with a million yen or more dangled in front of me, I had guessed wrong three times and now I was dragging my tail home with a dissatisfied customer whose very posture seemed designed to let me know that I was a crass, second-rate boob, and that he was one of the lords of creation!

"Mr. Harris! Mr. Harris! Over there! That magnificent structure!" Ito was suddenly almost shouting; his eyes were bright with excitement, and he was actually smiling.

He was pointing due south along the East River. The Manhattan bank was choked with the ugliest public housing projects imaginable, and the Brooklyn shore was worse: one of those huge, sprawling, so-called industrial parks, low windowless buildings, geodesic warehouses, wharves, a few freight-booster launching pads. Only one structure stood out, there was only one thing Ito could've meant: the structure linking the housing project on the Manhattan side with the industrial park on the Brooklyn shore.

Mr. Ito was pointing at the Brooklyn Bridge.

"The . . . ah . . . bridge, Mr. Ito?" I managed to say with a straight face. As far as I knew, the Brooklyn Bridge had only one claim to historicity: it was the butt of a series of jokes so ancient that they weren't funny anymore. The Brooklyn Bridge was what old comic con men traditionally sold to sucker tourists, greenhorns or hicks they used to call them, along with phony uranium stocks and gold-painted bricks.

So I couldn't resist the line: "You want to buy the Brooklyn Bridge, Mr. Ito?" It was so beautiful; he had put me through such hassles, and had finally gotten so damned high and mighty with me, and now I was in effect calling him an idiot to his face and he didn't know it.

In fact, he nodded eagerly in answer like a straight man out of some old joke and said, "I do believe so. Is it for sale?"

I slowed the jumper to forty, brought her down to a hundred feet, and swallowed my giggles as we approached the crumbling old monstrosity. Two massive and squat stone towers supported the rusty cables from which the bed of the bridge was suspended. The jumper had made the bridge useless years ago; no one had bothered to maintain it and no one had bothered to tear it down. Where the big blocks of dark gray stone met the water, they were encrusted with putrid-looking green slime. Above the waterline, the towers were whitened with about a century's worth of guano.

It was hard to believe that Ito was serious. The bridge was a filthy, decayed, reeking old monstrosity. In short, it was just what Ito deserved to be sold.

"Why, yes, Mr. Ito," I said, "I think I might be able to sell you the Brooklyn Bridge."

I put the jumper on hover about a hundred feet from one of the filthy old stone towers. Where the stones weren't caked with seagull guano, they were covered with about an inch of black soot. The roadbed was cracked and pitted and thickly paved with garbage, old shells, and more guano; the bridge must've been a seagull rookery for decades. I was mighty glad that the jumper was airtight; the stink must've been terrific.

"Excellent!" Mr. Ito exclaimed. "Quite lovely, is it not? I am determined to be the man to purchase the Brooklyn Bridge, Mr. Harris."

"I can think of no one more worthy of that honor than your esteemed self, Mr. Ito," I said with total sincerity.

About four months after the last section of the Brooklyn Bridge was boosted to Kyoto, I received two packages from Mr. Shiburo Ito. One was a mailing envelope containing a minicassette and a holo slide; the other was a heavy package about the size of a shoebox wrapped in blue rice paper.

Feeling a lot more mellow toward the memory of Ito these days, with a million of his yen in my bank account, I dropped the mini into my playback and was hardly surprised to hear his voice.

"Salutations, Mr. Harris, and once again my profoundest thanks for expediting the transfer of the Brooklyn Bridge to my estate. It has now been permanently enshrined and affords us all much aesthetic enjoyment and has enhanced the tranquility of my household immeasurably. I am enclosing a holo of the shrine for your pleasure. I have also sent you a small token of my appreciation which I hope you will take in the spirit in which it is given. Sayonara."

My curiosity aroused, I got right up and put the holo slide in my wall viewer. Before me was a heavily wooded mountain which rose into twin peaks of austere, dark-gray rock. A tall waterfall plunged gracefully down the long gorge between the two pinnacles to a shallow lake at the foot of the mountain, where it smashed onto a table of flat rock, generating perpetual billows of soft mist which turned the landscape into something straight out of a Chinese painting. Spanning the gorge between the two peaks like a spiderweb directly over the great falls, its stone towers anchored to islands of rock on the very lip of the precipice, was the Brooklyn Bridge, its ponderous bulk rendered slim and graceful by the massive scale of the landscape. The stone had been cleaned and glistened with moisture, the cables and roadbed were overgrown with lush green ivy. The holo had been taken just as the sun was setting between the towers of the bridge, outlining it in rich orange fire, turning the rising mists coppery, and sparkling in brilliant sheets off the falling water.

It was very beautiful.

It was quite a while before I tore myself away from the scene, remembering Mr. Ito's other package.

Beneath the blue paper wrapping was a single gold-painted brick. I gaped. I laughed. I looked again.

The object looked superficially like an old brick covered with gold paint. But it wasn't. It was a solid brick of soft, pure gold, a replica of the original item, in perfect detail.

I knew that Mr. Ito was trying to tell me something, but I still can't quite make out what.

JAMES TIPTREE, JR.

Love Is the Plan
the Plan Is Death

"Why do mankind flatter themselves that they alone are gifted with a spiritual and immortal principle? . . . I am persuaded that if a peacock could speak he would boast of his soul, and would affirm that it inhabited his magnificent tail," (Voltaire). "My first act of free will is to believe in free will," said William James. Illusions, a Skinnerian might reply. The perfect joy, the perfect love will ensue only if one accepts and embraces one's destiny. I choose—because I must. This is a story of joy and love and destiny.

Remembering—

Do you hear, my little red? Hold me softly. The cold grows.

I remember:

—I am hugely black and hopeful, I bounce on six legs along the mountains in the new warm! . . . *Sing the changer, Sing the stranger! Will the changes change forever?* . . . All my hums have words now. Another change!

Eagerly I bound on sunward following the tiny thrill in the air. The forests have been shrinking again. Then I see. It is me! Me-Myself, MOGGADEET—I have grown bigger more in the winter cold! I astonish myself, Moggadeet-the-small!

Excitement, enticement shrilling from the sun-side of the world. I come! . . . The sun is changing again, too. *Sun is walking in the night! Sun is walking back to Summer in the warming of the light!* . . . Warm is MeMoggadeet Myself. Forget the bad-time winter.

Memory quakes me.

The Old One.

I stop, pluck up a tree. So much I wanted to ask the Old One. No time. Cold. Tree goes end over end downcliff, I watch the fatclimbers tumble out. Not hungry.

The Old One warned me of the cold—I didn't believe him. I

move on, grieving . . . *Old One told you, The cold, the cold will hold you. Chill cold! Kill cold. In the cold I killed you.*

But it's warm now, all different. I'm Moggadeet again.

I bound over a hill and see my brother Frim.

At first I don't know him. A big black old one! I think. And in the warm, we can speak!

I surge toward him bashing trees. The big black is crouched over a ravine, peering down. Black back has shiny ripples like—It IS Frim! Frim-I-hunted-for, Frim-run-away! But he's so big now! Giant Frim! *A stranger, a changer—*

"Frim!"

He doesn't hear me; all his eye-turrets are under the trees. His end is sticking up oddlike, all atremble. What's he hunting?

"Frim! It's me, Moggadeet!"

But he only quivers his legs; I see his spurs pushing out. What a fool, Frim! I remind myself how timid he is, I try to move gently. When I get closer I'm astonished again. I'm bigger than he is now! *Changes!* I can see right over his shoulder into the ravine.

Hot yellow-green in there. A little glade all lit with sun. I bend my eyes to see what Frim is after and all astonishments blow up the world.

I see you.

I saw you.

I will always see you. Dancing in the green fire, my tiny red star! So bright! So small! So perfect! So fierce! I knew you—Oh yes I knew you in that first instant, my dawnberry, my scarlet minikin. *Red!* A tiny baby red one, smaller than my smallest eye. And so brave!

The Old One said it. Red is the color of love.

I see you swat at a hopper twice your size, my eyes bulge as you leap after it and go rolling, shrilling *Lililee! Lilileee-ee!* in baby wrath. Oh my mighty hunter, you don't know someone is looking right into your tender little love-fur! Oh yes! Palest pink it is, just brushed with rose. My jaws spurt, the world flashes and reels.

And then Frim, poor fool, feels me behind him and rears up.

But what a Frim! His throat-sacs are ballooning purple-black, his plates are engorged like the Mother of the storm-clouds! Glittering, rattling his spurs! His tail booms! "It's mine!" he bellows—I can hardly understand him. He jumps straight at me!

"Stop, Frim, stop!" I cry, dodging away bewildered. It's warm —how can Frim be wild, kill-wild?

"Brother Frim!" I call gently, soothingly. But something is badly wrong! My voice is bellowing too! Yes, in the warm and I want only to calm him, I am full of love—but the kill-roar is rushing through me, I too am swelling, rattling, booming! Invincible! To crush—to rend—

Oh, I am shamed.

I came to myself in the wreckage of Frim, Frim-pieces everywhere, myself is sodden with Frim. But I did not eat him! I did not! Should I take joy in that? Did I defy the Plan? But my throat was closed. Not because it was Frim but because of darling you. *You!* Where are you? The glade is empty! Oh fearful fear, I have frightened you, you are run away! I forget Frim. I forget everything but you my heartmeat, my precious tiny red.

I smash trees, I uproot rocks, I tear the ravine open! Oh, where are you hiding? Suddenly I have a new fear: Has my wild search harmed you? I force myself calm. I begin questing, circling, ever wider over the trees, moving cloud-silent, thrusting my eyes and ears down into every glade. A new humming fills my throat. *Oooo, Oo-oo, Rum-a-looly-loo,* I moan. Hunting, hunting for you.

Once I glimpse a black bigness far away and I am suddenly up at my full height, roaring. Attack the black! Was it another brother? I would slay him, but the stranger is already vanishing. I roar again. No—*it roars me,* the new power of black. Yet deep inside, Myself-Moggadeet is watching, fearing. Attack the black— even in the warm? Is there no safety, are we truly like the fat-climbers? But at the same time it feels—Oh, right! Oh, good! Sweet is the Plan. I give myself up to seeking you, my new song longing *Oo-loo* and *Looly rum-a-loo-oo-loo.*

And you answered! You!

So tiny you, hidden under a leaf! Shrilling *Li! Li! Lililee!* Trilling, thrilling—half-mocking, already imperious. Oh, how I whirl, crash, try to look under all my feet, stop frozen in horror of squashing the *Lilili! Lee!* Rocking, longing, moaning Moggadeet.

And you came out, you did.

My adorable firemite, threatening ME!

When I see your littlest hunting claws upraised my whole gut melts, it floods me. I am all tender jelly. *Tender!* Oh, tender-fierce like a Mother, I think! Isn't that how a Mother feels? My jaws are sluicing juice that isn't hunger-juice—I am choking, with fear of frighting you or bruising your tininess—I ache to grip and knead you, to eat you in one gulp, in a thousand nibbles—

Oh the power of *red*—the Old One said it! Now I feel my special hands, my tender hands I always carry hidden—now they come swelling out, come pushing toward my head! What? What?

My secret hands begin to knead and roll the stuff that's dripping from my jaws.

Ah, that arouses, you, too, my redling, doesn't it?

Yes, yes, I feel—torment—I feel your shy excitement! How your body remembers even now our love-dawn, our very first moments of Moggadeet-Leely. Before I knew You-Yourself, before you knew Me. It began then, my heartlet, our love-knowing began in that very first instant when your Moggadeet stared down at you like a monster bursting. I saw how new you were, how helpless!

Yes, even while I loomed over you marvelling—even while my secret hands drew and spun your fate—even then it came to me in pity that long ago, last year when I was a child, I saw other little red ones among my brothers, before our Mother drove them away. I was only a foolish baby then; I didn't understand. I thought they'd grown strange and silly in their redness and Mother did well to turn them out. Oh stupid Moggadeet!

But now I saw *you*, my flamelet—I understood! You were only that day cast out by your Mother. Never had you felt the terrors of a night alone in the world; you couldn't imagine that such a monster as Frim was hunting you. Oh my ruby nestling, my baby red! Never, I vowed it, never would I leave you—and have I not kept that vow? Never! I, Moggadeet, *I would be your Mother.* Great is the Plan, but I was greater!

All I learned of hunting in my lonely year, to drift like the air, to leap, to grip so delicately—all these learnings became for you! Not to bruise the smallest portion of your bright body. Oh, yes! I captured you whole in all your tiny perfection, though you sizzled and spat and fought me like the sunspark you are. And then—

And then—

I began to—Oh, terror! Delight-shame! How can I speak such a beautiful secret?—the Plan took me as a Mother guides her child and with my special hands I began to—

I began to bind you up!

Oh yes! Oh yes! My special hands that had no use, now all unfurled and engorged and alive, never stopping the working in the strong juice of my jaws—they began to *bind* you, passing over and around and beneath you, every moment piercing me with fear and joy. I wound among your darling little limbs, into your inmost delicate recesses, gently swathing and soothing you, winding and binding until you became a shining jewel. Mine!

—But you responded. I know that now. We know! Oh yes, in your fierce struggles, shyly you helped me, always at the end each strand fell sweetly into place ... *Winding you, binding you, loving Leelyloo! ...* How our bodies moved in our first weaving song! I feel it even now, I melt with excitement! How I wove the silk about you, tying each tiny limb, making you perfectly helpless. How fearlessly you gazed up at me, your terrifying captor! You! You were never frightened, as I'm not frightened now. Isn't it strange, my loveling? This sweetness that floods our bodies when we yield to the Plan. Great is the Plan! Fear it, fight it—but hold the sweetness yet.

Sweetly began our lovetime, when first I became your new true Mother, never to cast you out. How I fed you and caressed and tended and fondled you! What a responsibility it is to be a Mother. Anxiously I carried you furled in my secret arms, savagely I drove off all intruders, even the harmless banlings in the grass, in fear every moment that you were stifled or crushed!

And all the warm nights long, how I cared for your helpless little body, carefully releasing each infant limb, flexing and stretching it, cleaning every scarlet morsel of you with my giant tongue, nibbling your baby claws with my terrible teeth, revelling in your baby hum, pretending to devour you while you shrieked with glee, *Li! Lilili! Love-lili, Leelylee!* But the greatest joy of all—

We spoke!

We spoke together, we two! We communed, we shared, we poured ourselves one into the other. Love, how we stammered and stumbled at the first, you in your strange Mother-tongue and I in mine! How we blended our singing wordlessly and then with words, until more and more we came to see with each other's eyes, to hear, to taste, to feel the world of each other, until I became Leelyloo and you became Moggadeet, until finally we became together a new thing, Moggadeet-Leely, Lilliloo-Mogga, Lili-Mog-galooly-deet!

Oh love, are we the first? Have others loved with their whole selves? Oh sad thinking, that lovers before us have left no trace. Remember us! Will you remember, my adored, though Moggadeet has spoiled everything and the cold grows? If only I could hear you speak once more, my red, my innocent one. You are remembering, your body tells me you remember even now. Softly, hold me softly yet. Hear your Moggadeet!

You told me how it was being you, yourself, tiny-redling-Lilliloo. Of your Mother, your dreams, your baby joys and fears. And I told you mine, and all my learnings in the world since the day when my own Mother—

Hear me, my heartmate! Time runs away.

—On the last day of my childhood my Mother called us all under her.

"Sons! S-son-n-nss!" Why did her dear voice creak so?

My brothers came in slowly, fearfully from the summer green. But I, small Moggadeet, I climb eagerly up under the great arch of her body, seeking the golden Mother-fur. Right into her warm cave I come, where her Mother-eyes are glowing, the cave that sheltered us so strongly all our lives, as I shelter you, my dawn-flower.

I long to touch her, to hear her speak and sing to us again. Her Mother-fur troubles me, it is tattered and drab. Shyly I press against one of her huge food-glands. It feels dry, but a glow sparks deep in her Mother-eye.

"Mother," I whisper. "It's me, Moggadeet!"

"SONNNNNS!" Her voice rumbles through her armor. My big brothers huddle by her legs, peering back at the sunlight. They look so funny, shedding, half gold, half black.

"I'm afraid!" whimpers my brother Frim nearby. Like me Frim still has his gold baby fur. Mother is speaking again but her voice booms so I can hardly understand.

"WINNN-TER! WINTER, I SAY! AFTER THE WARM COMES THE COLD WINTER. THE COLD WINTER BEFORE THE WARM COMES AGAIN, COMES . . ."

Frim whimpers louder, I cuff him. What's wrong, why is her loving voice so hoarse and strange now? She always hummed us so tenderly, we nestled in her warm Mother-fur sucking the lovely Mother-juices, rocking to her steady walking-song. *Ee-mooly-mooly, Ee-mooly-mooly,* while far below the earth rolled by. Oh, yes, and how we held our breaths and squealed when she began her mighty hunting-hum! *Tann! Tann! Dir! Dir! Dir Hataan! HA-TONN!* How we clung in the thrilling climax when she plunged upon her prey and we heard the crunching, the tearing, the gurgling in her body that meant soon her food-glands would be richly full.

Suddenly I see a black streak down below—a big brother is running away! Mother's booming voice breaks off. Her great body tenses, her plates clash. Mother roars!

Running, screaming down below! I burrow up into her fur, am flung about as she leaps.

"OUT! GO OUT!" she bellows. Her terrible hunting-limbs crash down, she roars without words, shuddering, jolting. When I dare to peek out I see the others all have fled. All except one! A black body is lying under Mother's claws. It's my brother Sesso —yes! But Mother is tearing him, is eating him! I watch in horror —Sesso she cared for so proudly, so tenderly! I sob, bury my head in her fur. But the beautiful fur is coming loose in my hands, her golden Mother-fur is dying! I cling desperately, trying not to hear the crunches, the gulps and gurgling. The world is ending, all is terrible, terrible.

And yet, my fireberry, even then I almost understood. Great is the Plan!

Presently Mother stops feeding and begins to move. The rocky ground jolts by far below. Her stride is not smooth but jerks me, even her deep hum is strange. *On! On! Alone! Ever alone. And on!* The rumbling ceases. Silence. Mother is resting.

"Mother!" I whisper. "Mother, it's Moggadeet. I'm here!"

Her stomach plates contract, a belch reverberates in her vaults. "Go," she groans. "Go. Too late. Mother no more."

"I don't want to leave you. Why must I go? Mother!" I wail, "Speak to me!" I keen my baby hum, *Deet! Deet! Tikki-takka! Deet!* hoping Mother will answer, crooning deep, *Brum! Brrumm! Brumaloo-brum!* Now I see one huge Mother-eye glow faintly but she only makes a grating sound.

"Too late. No more . . . The winter, I say. I did speak . . . Before the winter, go. Go."

"Tell me about Outside, Mother," I plead.

Another groan or cough nearly shakes me from my perch. But when she speaks again her voice sounds gentler.

"Talk?" she grumbles, "Talk, talk, talk. You are a strange son. Talk, like your Father."

"What's that, Mother? What's a Father?"

She belches again. "Always talk. The winters grow, he said. Oh, yes. Tell them the winters grow. So I did. Late. Winter, I spoke you. Cold!" Her voice booms. "No more! Too late." Outside I hear her armor rattle and clank.

"Mother, speak to me!"

"Go. Go-o-o!"

Her belly-plates clash around me. I jump for another nest of fur but it comes loose in my grip. Wailing, I save myself by hanging to one of her great walking limbs. It is rigid, thrumming like rock.

"GO!" She roars.

Her Mother-eyes are shrivelling, dead! I panic, scramble down, everything is vibrating, resonating around me. Mother is holding back a storm of rage!

I leap for the ground, I rush diving into a crevice, I wiggle and burrow under the fearful bellowing and clanging that rains on me from above. Into the rocks I go with the hunting claws of Mother crashing behind me.

Oh my redling, my little tenderling! Never have you known such a night. Those dreadful hours hiding from the monster that had been my loving Mother!

I saw her once more, yes. When dawn came I clambered up a ledge and peered through the mist. It was warm then, the mists were warm. I knew what Mothers looked like; we had glimpses of huge horned dark shapes before our own Mother hooted us under her. Oh yes, and then would come Mother's earth-shaking challenge and the strange Mother's answering roar, and we'd cling tight, feeling her surge of kill-fury, buffeted, deafened, battered while our Mother charged and struck. And once while our Mother fed I peeped out and saw a strange baby squealing in the remnants on the ground below.

But now it was my own dear Mother I saw lurching away through the mists, that great rusty-grey hulk so horned and bossed that only her hunting-eyes showed above her armor, swivelling mindlessly, questing for anything that moved. She crashed her way across the mountains and as she went she thrummed a new harsh song. *Cold! Cold! Ice and Lone. Ice! And cold! And end.* I never saw her again.

When the sun rose I saw that the gold fur was peeling from my shiny black. All by itself my hunting-limb flashed out and knocked a hopper right into my jaws.

You see, my berry, how much larger and stronger I was than you when Mother sent us away? That also is the Plan. For you were not yet born! I had to live on while the warm turned to cold and while the winter passed to warm again before you would be waiting. I had to grow and learn. To *learn*, my Lilliloo! That is important. Only we black ones have a time to learn—the Old One said it.

Such small learnings at first! To drink the flat water-stuff without choking, to catch the shiny flying things that bite and to watch the storm-clouds and the moving of the sun. And the nights, and the soft things that moved on the trees. And the bushes that kept shrinking, shrinking—only it was me, Moggadeet, growing larger! Oh yes! And the day when I could knock down a fatclimber from its vine!

But all these learnings were easy—the Plan in my body guided me. It guides me now, Lililoo, even now it would give me peace and joy if I yielded to it. But I will not! I will remember to the end, I will speak to the end!

I will speak the big learnings. How I saw—though I was so busy catching and eating more, more, always more—I saw all things were changing, changing. *Changers!* The bushes changed their buds to berries, the fatclimbers changed their colors, even the sun changed, and the hills. And I saw all things were together with others of their kind but only me, Moggadeet. I was alone. Oh, so alone!

I went marching through the valleys in my shiny new black, humming my new song *Turra-tarra! Tarra Tan!* Once I glimpsed my brother Frim and I called him, but he ran like the wind. Away, alone! And when I went to the next valley I found the trees all mashed down. And in the distance I saw a black one like me—only many times as big! Huge! Almost as big as a Mother, sleek and glossy-new. I would have called but he reared up and saw me and roared so terribly that I too fled like the wind to empty mountains. Alone.

And so I learned, my redling, how we are alone even though my heart was full of love. And I wandered, puzzling and eating ever more and more. I saw the Trails; they meant nothing to me then. But I began to learn the important thing.

The cold.

You know it, my little red. How in the warm days I am me, Myself-Moggadeet. Ever-growing, ever-learning. In the warm we think, we speak. We love! We make our own Plan, Oh, did we not, my lovemate?

But in the cold, in the night—for the nights were growing colder—in the cold night I was—what?—Not Moggadeet. Not Moggadeet-thinking. Not Me-Myself. Only Something-that-lives, acts without thought. Helpless-Moggadeet. In the cold is only the Plan. I almost thought it.

And then one day the night-chill lingered and lingered and the sun was hidden in the mists. And I found myself going up the Trails.

The Trails are a part of the Plan too, my redling.

The Trails are of winter. There we must go all of us, we blacks. When the cold grows stronger the Plan calls us upward, upward, we begin to drift up the Trails, up along the ridges to the cold, the night-side of the mountains. Up beyond the forests where the trees grow scant and turn to stony deadwood.

So the Plan drew me and I followed, only half-aware. Sometimes I came into warmer sunlight where I could stop and feed and try to think, but the cold fogs rose again and I went on, on and up. I began to catch sight of others like me far along the mountain-flank, moving steadily up. They didn't rear or roar when they saw me. I didn't call to them. Each one alone we climbed on toward the Caves, unthinking, blind. And so I would have gone too.

But then the great thing happened.

—Oh no, my Lililoo! Not the *greatest*. The greatest of all is you, will always be you. My precious sunmite, my red lovebaby! Don't be angry, no, no, my sharing one. Hold me softly. I must say our big learning. Hear your Moggadeet, hear and remember!

In the sun's last warm I found him, the Old One. A terrible sight! So maimed and damaged, parts rotting and gone. I stared, thinking him dead. Suddenly his head rolled feebly and a croak came out.

"Young . . . one?" An eye opened in his festering head, a flyer pecked at it. "Young one . . . wait!"

And I understood him! Oh, with love—

No, no, my redling! Gently! Gently hear your Moggadeet. We *spoke,* the Old One and I! Old to young, we shared. I think it cannot happen.

"No old ones," he creaked. "Never to speak . . . we blacks. Never. It is not . . . the Plan. Only me . . . I wait . . ."

"Plan," I ask, half-knowing. "What is the Plan?"

"A beauty," he whispers. "In the warm, a beauty in the air . . . I followed . . . but another black one saw me and we fought . . . and I was damaged, but still the Plan made me follow until I was crushed and torn and dead . . . But I lived! And the Plan let me go and I crawled here . . . to wait . . . to share . . . but—"

His head sags. Quickly I snatch a flyer from the air and push it to his torn jaws.

"Old One! What is the Plan?"

He swallows painfully, his one eye holding mine.

"In us," he says thickly, stronger now. "In us, moving us in all things necessary for the life. You have seen. When the baby is golden the Mother cherishes it all winter long. But when it turns red or black she drives it away. Was it not so?"

"Yes, but—"

"That's the Plan! Always the Plan. Gold is the color of Mother-care but black is the color of rage. Attack the black! Black is to kill. Even a Mother, even her own baby, she cannot defy the Plan. Hear me, young one!"

"I hear. I have seen," I answer. "But what is red?"

"Red!" He groans. "Red is the color of love."

"No!" I say, stupid Moggadeet! "I know love. Love is gold."

The Old One's eyes turns from me. "Love," he sighs. "When the beauty comes in the air, you will see . . ." He falls silent. I fear he's dying. What can I do? We stay silent there together in the last misty sunwarm. Dimly on the slopes I can see other black ones like myself drifting steadily upward on their own Trails among the stone-tree heaps, into the icy mists.

"Old One! Where do we go?"

"You go to the Caves of Winter. That is the Plan."

"Winter, yes. The cold. Mother told us. And after the cold winter comes the warm. I remember. The winter will pass, won't it? Why did she say, the winters grow? Teach me, Old One. What is a Father?"

"Fa-ther? A word I don't know. But wait—" His mangled head turns to me. *The winters grow?* Your mother said this? Oh cold! Oh, lonely," he groans. "A big learning she gave you. This learning I fear to think."

His eye rolls, glaring. I am frightened inside.

"Look around, young one. These stony deadwoods. Dead shells of trees that grow in the warm valleys. Why are they here? The cold has killed them. No living tree grows here now. Think, young one!"

I look, and true! It is a warm forest killed to stone.

"Once it was warm here. Once it was like the valleys. But the cold has grown stronger. The winter grows. Do you see? *And the warm grows less and less.*"

"But the warm is life! The warm is Me-Myself!"

"Yes. In the warm we think, we learn. In the cold is only the Plan. In the cold we are blind . . . Waiting here, I thought, was there a time when it was warm here once? Did we come here, we blacks, in the warm to speak, to share? Oh young one, a fearful thinking. Does our time of learning grow shorter, shorter? Where will it end? Will the winters grow until we can learn nothing but only live blindly in the Plan, like the silly fatclimbers who sing but do not speak?"

His words fill me with cold fear. Such a terrible learning! I feel anger.

"No! We will not! We must—we must hold the warm!"

"Hold the warm?" He twists painfully to stare at me. "Hold the warm . . . A great thinking. Yes. But how? How? Soon it will be too cold to think, even here!"

"The warm will come again," I tell him. "Then we must learn a way to hold it, you and I!"

His head lolls.

"No . . . When the warm comes I will not be here . . . and you will be too busy for thinking, young one."

"I will help you! I will carry you to the Caves!"

"In the Caves," he gasps, "In each Cave there are two black ones like yourself. One is living, waiting mindless for the winter to pass . . . And while he waits, he eats. He eats the other, that is how he lives. That is the Plan. As you will eat me, my youngling."

"No!" I cry in horror. "I will never harm you!"

"When the cold comes you will see," he whispers. "Great is the Plan!"

"No! You are wrong! I will break the Plan," I shout. A cold wind is blowing from the summit; the sun dies.

"Never will I harm you," I bellow. "You are wrong to say so!"

My scaleplates are rising, my tail begins to pound. Through the mists I hear his gasps.

I recall dragging a heavy black thing to my Cave.

Chill cold, kill cold . . . In the cold I killed you.

Leelyloo. He did not resist.

Great is the Plan. He accepted all, perhaps he even felt a strange joy, as I feel it now. In the Plan is joy. But if the Plan is wrong? *The winters grow.* Do the fatclimbers have their Plan too?

Oh, a hard thinking! How we tried, my redling, my joy. All the long warm days I explained it to you, over and over. How the winter would come and change us if we did not hold the warm. You understood! You share, you understand me now, my precious flame—though you can't speak I feel your sharing love. Softly . . .

Oh, yes, we made our preparations, our own Plan. Even in the highest heat we made our Plan against the cold. Have other lovers done so? How I searched, carrying you my cherry bud, I crossed whole mountain ranges, following the sun until we found this warmest of warm valleys on the sunward side. Surely the cold would be weak here, I thought. How could they reach us here, the cold fogs, the icy winds that froze my inner Me and drew me up the Trails into the dead Caves of Winter?

This time I would defy!

This time I have *you.*

"Don't take me there, my Moggadeet!" You begged, fearful of the strangeness. "Don't take me to the cold!"

"Never, my Leeliloo! Never, I vow it. Am I not your Mother, little redness?"

"But you will change! The cold will make you forget. Is it not the Plan?"

"We will break the Plan, Lili. See you are growing larger, heavier, my fireberry—and always more beautiful! Soon I will not be able to carry you so easily, I could never carry you to the cold Trails. And I will never leave you!"

"But you are so big, Moggadeet! When the change comes you will forget and drag me to the cold."

"Never! Your Moggadeet has a deeper Plan! When the mists start I will take you to the farthest, warmest cranny of this cave, and there I will spin a wall so you can never never be pulled out. And I will never never leave you. Even the Plan cannot draw Moggadeet from Leelyloo!"

"But you will have to go hunting for food and the cold will take you then! You will forget me and follow the cold love of winter and leave me there to die! Perhaps that is the Plan!"

"Oh, no, my precious, my redling! Don't grieve, don't cry! Hear your Moggadeet's Plan! From now on I'll hunt twice as hard. I'll fill this cave to the top, my fat little blushbud, I will fill it with food now so I can stay by you all the winter through!"

And so I did, didn't I my Lilli? Silly Moggadeet, how I hunted, how I brought lizards, hoppers, fatclimbers and banlings by the score. What a fool! For of course they rotted, there in the heat, and the heaps turned green and slimy—but still tasting good, eh, my berry?—so that we had to eat them then, gorging ourselves like babies. And how you grew!

Oh, beautiful you became, my jewel of redness! So bursting fat and shiny-full, but still my tiny one, my sunspark. Each night after I fed you I would part the silk, fondling your head, your eyes, your

tender ears, trembling with excitement for the delicious moment
when I would release your first scarlet limb to caress and exercise
it and press it to my pulsing throat-sacs. Sometimes I would unbind
two together for the sheer joy of seeing you move. And each night
it took longer, each morning I had to make more silk to bind you
up. How proud I was, my Leely, Lilliloo!

That was when my greatest thinking came.

As I was weaving you so tenderly into your shining cocoon, my
joyberry, I thought, why not bind up living fatclimbers? Pen them
alive so their flesh will stay sweet and they will serve us through
the winter!

That was a great thinking, Lilliloo, and I did this, and it was
good. Fatclimbers in plenty I walled in a little tunnel, and many,
many other things as well, while the sun walked back towards
winter and the shadows grew and grew. Fatclimbers and banlings
and all tasty creatures and even—Oh, clever Moggadeet!—all
manner of leaves and bark and stuffs for them to eat! Oh, we had
broken the Plan for sure now!

"We have broken the Plan for sure, my Lilli-red. The fatclimbers are eating the twigs and bark, the banlings are eating juice
from the wood, the great runners are munching grass, and we will
eat them all!"

"Oh, Moggadeet, you are brave! Do you think we can really
break the Plan? I am frightened! Give me a banling, I think it
grows cold."

"You have eaten fifteen banlings, my minikin!" I teased you.
"How fat you grow! Let me look at you again, yes, you must let
your Moggadeet caress you while you eat. Ah, how adorable you
are!"

And of course—Oh, you remember how it began then, our
deepest love. For when I uncovered you one night with the first
hint of cold in the air, I saw that you had changed.

Shall I say it? Your secret fur. Your *Mother-fur.*

Always I had cleaned you there tenderly, but without difficulty
to restrain myself. But on this night when I parted the silk strands

with my huge hunting claws, what new delights met my eyes! No longer pink and pale but fiery red! *Red!* Scarlet blaze like the reddest sunrise, gold-tipped! And swollen, curling, dewy—Oh! Commanding me to expose you, all of you. Oh, how your tender eyes melted me and your breath musky-sweet and your limbs warm and heavy in my grasp!

Wildly I ripped away the last strands, dazed with bliss as you slowly stretched your whole blazing redness before my eyes. I knew then—*we* knew!—that the love we felt before was only a beginning. My hunting-limbs fell at my sides and my special hands, my weaving hands grew, filled with new, almost painful life. I could not speak, my throat-sacs filling, filling! And my love-hands rose up by themselves, pressing ecstatically, while my eyes bent closer, closer to your glorious *red!*

But suddenly the Me-Myself, Moggadeet awoke! I jumped back!

"Lilli! What's happening to us?"

"Oh, Moggadeet, I love you! Don't go away!"

"What is it, Leelyloo? Is it the Plan?"

"I don't care! Moggadeet, don't you love me?"

"I fear! I fear to harm you! You are so tiny. I am your Mother."

"No Moggadeet, look! I am as big as you are. Don't be afraid."

I drew back—Oh, hard, hard!—and tried to look calmly.

"True, my redling, you have grown. But your limbs are so new, so tender. Oh, I can't look!"

Averting my eyes I began to spin a screen of silk, to shut away your maddening redness.

"We must wait, Lilliloo. We must go on as before. I don't know what this strange urging means; I fear it will bring you harm."

"Yes, Moggadeet. We will wait."

And so we waited. Oh yes. Each night it grew more hard. We tried to be as before, to be happy, Leely-Moggadeet. Each night as I caressed your glowing limbs that seemed to offer themselves to me as I swathed and unswathed them in turn, the urge rose in me hotter, more strong. To unveil you wholly! To look again upon your whole body!

Oh yes, my darling, I feel—unbearable—how you remember with me those last days of our simple love.

Colder . . . colder. Mornings when I went to harvest the fatclimbers there was a whiteness on their fur and the banlings ceased to move. The sun sank ever lower, paler, and the cold mists hung above us, reaching down. Soon I dared not leave the cave. I stayed all day by your silken wall, humming Motherlike, *Brum-a-loo, Mooly-mooly, Lilliloo, Love Leely.* Strong Moggadeet!

"We'll wait, fireling. We will not yield to the Plan! Aren't we happier than all others, here with our love in our warm cave?"

"Oh, yes, Moggadeet."

"I'm Myself now. I am strong. I'll make my own Plan. I will not look at you until . . . until the warm, until the Sun comes back."

"Yes, Moggadeet . . . Moggadeet? My limbs are cramped."

"Oh, my precious, wait—see, I am opening the silk very carefully, I will not look—I won't—"

"Moggadeet, don't you love me?"

"Leelyloo! Oh, my glorious one! I fear, I fear—"

"Look, Moggadeet! See how big I am, how strong!"

"Oh, redling, my hands—my hands—what are they doing to you?"

For with my special hands I was pressing, pressing the hot juices from my throat-sacs and tenderly, tenderly parting your sweet Mother-fur and *placing my gift within your secret places.* And as I did this our eyes entwined and our limbs made a wreath.

"My darling, do I hurt you?"

"Oh, no, Moggadeet! Oh, no!"

Oh, my adored one, those last days of our love!

Outside the world grew colder yet, and the fatclimbers ceased to eat and the banlings lay still and began to stink. But still we held the warmth deep in our cave and still I fed my beloved on the last of our food. And every night our new ritual of love became more free, richer, though I compelled myself to hide all but a portion of your sweet body. But each dawn it grew hard and harder for me to replace the silken bonds around your limbs.

"Moggadeet! Why do you not bind me! I am afraid!"

"A moment, Lilli, a moment. I must caress you just once more."

"I'm afraid, Moggadeet! Cease now and bind me!"

"But why, my lovekin? Why must I hide you? Is this not some foolish part of the Plan?"

"I don't know, I feel so strange. Moggadeet, I—I'm changing."

"You grow more glorious every moment, my Lilli, my own. Let me look at you! It is wrong to bind you away!"

"No, Moggadeet! No!"

But I would not listen, would I? Oh foolish Moggadeet-who-thought-to-be-your-Mother. Great is the Plan!

I did not listen, I did not bind you up. No! I ripped them away, the strong silk strands. Mad with love I slashed them all at once, rushing from each limb to the next until all your glorious body lay exposed. At last—I saw you whole!

Oh, Lilliloo, greatest of Mothers.

It was not I who was your Mother. You were mine.

Shining and bossed you lay, your armor newly grown, your mighty hunting limbs thicker than my head! What I had created. You! A Supermother, a Mother such as none have ever seen!

Stupefied with delight, I gazed.

And your huge hunting limb came out and seized me.

Great is the Plan. I felt only joy as your jaws took me.

As I feel it now.

And so we end, my Lilliloo, my redling, for your babies are swelling through your Mother-fur and your Moggadeet can speak no longer. I am nearly devoured. The cold grows, it grows, and your Mother-eyes are growing, glowing. Soon you will be alone with our children and the warm will come again.

Will you remember, my heartmate? Will you remember and tell them?

Tell them of the cold, Leelyloo. Tell them of our love.

Tell them . . .*the winters grow.*

DAMON KNIGHT

1973: The Year in Science Fiction

Nineteen seventy-three was another year of continued growth in science fiction—"boom" would not be too strong a word. This in spite of *Publishers Weekly*'s annual figures, which show a 52 percent drop in s.f. titles compared to 1972. Unfortunately for all who rely on *PW*'s figures, the magazine stopped using its own data partway through 1972 and instead used the Library of Congress MARC II tapes. "In the latter [MARC II]," *PW* notes, "some mysteries, Westerns and science fiction books are listed and counted in general fiction."

In terms of money paid to authors, probably there had never been a better year. Ballantine bought the paperback rights to three novels by Arthur C. Clarke, two of them yet to be written *(Rendezvous With Rama, The Fountains of Paradise,* and *Imperial Earth)* for an unprecedented $500,000. (The hardcover editions will be published by Harcourt Brace Jovanovich.) Ballantine, recently acquired by Random House, also issued a large map of Barsoom in connection with its reissue of all the Burroughs Mars books.

The newsmagazine *Locus* counted 75 s.f. anthologies published during the year (66 percent of all s.f. titles, if *PW*'s figures were correct!), and Lester del Rey said at Toronto that s.f. accounted for 10 percent of all published fiction. This was at the Thirty-first

World Science Fiction Convention, the "Torcon," where Hugos were awarded to Isaac Asimov, Ursula K. Le Guin, Poul Anderson, and R. A. Lafferty for the best s.f. of the year.

Other conventions, too many to list, included the Infinity Con in New York City (Keith Laumer, guest of honor), the Balticon in Baltimore (Poul Anderson), Boskone X, Boston (Robert A. W. Lowndes), the Marcon in Columbus, Ohio (Gordon R. Dickson), the Lunacon in New York City (Harlan Ellison), the Disclave in Washington D.C. (Gardner R. Dozois), and the Bubonicon in Albuquerque, New Mexico (Robert Silverberg).

The first Scandinavian SF Film Festival was held in Copenhagen, and a week-long s.f. festival in Lille, France, was attended by 1,300. Science fiction was booming also in Germany, where agent Kurt Luif estimated that English-speaking writers are earning about $100,000 yearly in translation rights. In Poland, Stanislaus Lem received the Literary Award First Class of the Ministry of Culture, carrying with it a cash award of 50,000 zlotys. Here at home, Ursula K. Le Guin won the National Book Award for Children's Literature for her novel *The Farthest Shore* (Atheneum), the final volume of the Earthsea trilogy. The award was accompanied by a cash prize of $1,000.

The John W. Campbell Award, presented by Condé Nast to the best new s.f. writer of the year, went to Jerry Pournelle, with George Alec Effinger as runner-up. The John W. Campbell *Memorial* Award, juried by Leon Stover, Brian W. Aldiss, Thomas D. Clareson, Harry Harrison, and Willis McNelly, went to Barry Malzberg for his novel *Beyond Apollo* (Random House). In a letter to *Analog*, Poul Anderson bitterly protested this choice: "One can readily understand that the judges, dissatisfied with the Hugo and Nebula procedures, felt something else was needed, and established it. That's fine per se. What is not fine is their misappropriation of a great man's name."

The magazines continued to feel the competition not only of hardcover anthology series such as *New Dimensions* and *Nova*, but of the still newer commissioned theme anthologies, dominated by Roger Elwood. Elwood, almost unknown in science fiction until a few years ago, has contracted for more than sixty s.f. anthologies and has become s.f. editor for a number of publishers. A notice in the SFWA *Bulletin* gives a hint of his other activities: "He just recently signed a three-book contract with Avon—the subjects include: speaking in tongues (Pentecostalism), prison reform and athletics. Also under contract is a book about a reformed prostitute. . . . Elwood is working on a book about homosexuality, prostitution, gambling, pornography, abortion, and other subjects; he's writing it for Zondervan Publishing House of Grand Rapids, Michigan. Just recently, he signed a contract to edit for Pyramid a series of books about country-and-western music (he's also science fiction editor at that firm); and landed a major book on baseball star Hank Aaron for Chilton Books (where he's science fiction consultant). He is presently putting together a syndicated newspaper series featuring brand-new articles by Dale Evans Rogers, Anita Bryant and Hal Lindsey."

About the commissioned anthologies Sidney Coleman wrote in *F&SF*:

Nothing can stop a dumb idea whose time has come. . . . Ever since the ill-fated Twayne Triplets, this has been a known method of getting bad stories from good writers; nevertheless, its popularity continues to grow. Maybe it's just that publishers, a race subject to childish superstitions, believe that a book needs a gimmick if it is to sell. Perhaps at this very moment, another theme anthology is being born, in a conversation something like this:

EDITOR: Sam, give me some money. I'll put together a collection of original sf for you.

PUBLISHER: Sf? Oh, you mean sci-fi. What's the gimmick?

EDITOR: You'll love it. Listen to this: *Strange Fruits.* The blurb is "All New Tales of Alien Effeminacy."

PUBLISHER: No good. We bought the same idea from Elwood last month.

EDITOR: That's all right; I've got a million of them. How about *Wine of the Dreamers?* Four giants of science fiction accept the challenge of writing a story while dead drunk.

In spite of all this new competition, the magazines showed renewed signs of life. *Weird Tales* was revived by publisher Leo Margulies, under the editorship of Sam Moskowitz. A new slick magazine, *Vertex*, published in California, was an immediate success. New books and periodicals about science fiction appeared, notably *The World of Fanzines* by Fredric Wertham (Southern Illinois University Press) and *Science-Fiction Studies*, a semiannual journal edited by R. D. Mullen and Darko Suvin (Department of English, Indiana State University).

Our losses during the year included Professor J. R. R. Tolkien, who died at the age of eighty-one in England, September 2; Bruce Elliott, a former professional magician (New York, March 21); Leonard Tushnet, physician and Jewish scholar (New Jersey, November 28); and Walter M. Moudy, an attorney (Kansas City, Missouri, April 13). Other causes for sorrow were the decisions of the Drake, North Dakota, school board to burn copies of Kurt Vonnegut's *Slaughterhouse Five*, and of the California Board of Education to require the teaching of Genesis on a parity with the Darwinian theory of evolution.

Some further disappointments: Lancer Books filed for bankruptcy. *The Haunt of Horror* was suspended after two issues. Harry Harrison shelved his proposed anthology *The Year Two Million* because of unimaginative submissions. "I . . . will probably cancel the contract in the end," he said. "Don't blame *me.*"

In internal affairs, there was extended and sometimes acrimonious debate of a proposal for SFWA neckties (for men) and scarves (for the ladies). Nothing came of this, thank goodness, but Brigadier General Theodore R. Cogswell, editor of the SFWA *Forum*, was inspired to make the following remarks about required dress for the 1974 Nebula Awards Banquet in Hollywood:

"Black tie optional" means that shoes will be worn. Black shoes will be worn with black suits, brown shoes will be worn with brown suits. It would be appreciated if those arriving barefoot would check into the SFWA suite one hour in advance of the ceremony. Appropriately colored shoes will be available on a first-come first-served basis. Latecomers will have to make do with shoe blacking or browning as the case may be.

R. A. Lafferty may have summed it all up when he said, in an interview in *The Alien Critic*, that he is one of his own favorite writers "in spots." He explained: "A spot is really a blot, a stain, a blemish. The spots I like do appear to be those things, and in addition they slow down and break the rhythm of SF. But they are necessary. They are the generative spots, the original bits, and they will be less awkward every time they are borrowed and reworked. . . . There are clear-as-a-crystal writers of great reputation who will always remain spotless in this sense. There is not an idea or notion to be found in them that is not first found in others; none that would have been lost forever if they had not pinned it down. But some of us are spotted like sick leopards and we repel a little."

NEBULA AWARDS, 1973

The awards were presented at the annual Nebula banquet at the Century Plaza Hotel in Hollywood, April 27, 1974. Guests of honor included the Foreign Secretary of the National Academy of Sciences and Captain Edgar Mitchell, sixth man on the moon.

Voting for the Nebula Awards was as follows:

NOVEL

Winner: RENDEZVOUS WITH RAMA *by Arthur C. Clarke* (Harcourt Brace Jovanovich; serialized in *Galaxy*)

Runners-up: GRAVITY'S RAINBOW *by Thomas Pynchon* (Viking); THE PEOPLE OF THE WIND *by Poul Anderson (Analog);* TIME ENOUGH FOR LOVE *by Robert A. Heinlein* (Putnam); THE MAN WHO FOLDED HIMSELF *by David Gerrold* (Random House)

NOVELLA

Winner: "The Death of Doctor Island" *by Gene Wolfe (Universe 3)*
Runners-up: "Chains of the Sea" *by Gardner R. Dozois (Chains of the Sea,* Nelson); "Junction" *by Jack Dann (Fantastic);* "Death and Designation Among the Asadi" *by Michael Bishop (If);* "The White Otters of Childhood" *by Michael Bishop (The Magazine of Fantasy and Science Fiction)*

NOVELETTE

Winner: "Of Mist, and Grass, and Sand" *by Vonda N. McIntyre (Analog)*
Runners-up: "The Deathbird" *by Harlan Ellison (The Magazine of Fantasy and Science Fiction);* "The Girl Who Was Plugged In" *by James Tiptree, Jr. (New Dimensions III);* "Case and the Dreamer" *by Theodore Sturgeon (Galaxy)*

SHORT STORY

Winner: "Love Is the Plan the Plan Is Death" *by James Tiptree, Jr. (The Alien Condition)*
Runners-up: "With Morning Comes Mistfall" *by George R. R. Martin (Analog);* "How I Lost the Second World War" *by Gene Wolfe (Analog);* "Wings" *by Vonda N. McIntyre (The Alien Condition);* "A Thing of Beauty" *by Norman Spinrad (Analog);* "Shark" *by Edward Bryant (Orbit 12)*

DRAMATIC PRESENTATION

Winner: SOYLENT GREEN, screenplay by Stanley R. Greenberg (MGM)

Runners-up: *Catholics,* teleplay by Brian Moore (CBS Playhouse); *Westworld,* screenplay by Michael Crichton (MGM); *Steambath,* teleplay by Bruce J. Friedman (Hollywood Television Theatre)

CAROL EMSHWILLER

*The Childhood of the Human Hero**

Science fiction is an attitude about today and what tomorrow could become. Nothing definite, nothing more than an attitude. We think, rationally enough, that in twenty-five years we will be turning another century, the glorious year 2001 will be upon us. But who will be the men of that period? How are we molding them today to play their parts? Here is a glimpse of a boy who will then be a man. Your fingers are in the reality-clay, as are mine; together we are shaping his world. This then is "The Childhood of the Human Hero," the boy who will inhabit the world we are creating for him with the passing of each day.

*From Joseph Campbell.

❀

―――――――

❀

A little bit of you in him and a little bit of me and a little bit of him in you and I see a bit of my youngest brother. He's coming in, going out, coming in, going out, and it's another world outside which might be inner space which is outer space to him. "Captain, your ship is approaching a doomed planet at twice the speed of light."

He wants to order a pair of handcuffs at $2.95

A book on ventriloquism at 98 cents

He wants a realistic, plastic, plucked chicken, $5.99

A pair of sunglasses with one-way mirror lenses

A "patented 3–D hypno-coin" that comes free with 25 lessons in hypnotism

And one hundred stick-on stamps of the scariest movie monster

Mild-mannered boy wonder looks like any other average boy, but there's a trick to it. There's more than meets the eye and good deeds are being done every day in spite of appearances.

He has a secret identity.

Going into orbit around one hot world too many, he breaks pencils with a flick of the fingers of one hand and doesn't know he's doing it. He straightens paper clips trying to remember that France has a population of 51,400,000; that the major cities are:

Paris, Lille, Bordeaux, Marseilles; highest point, Mont Blanc, 15,-
781 feet; principal language, French.

He's the one with the new boots, just the kind he'd always
wanted; wide belt, black turtleneck sweater. Next year his hair
will be even longer because that's the only way you can tell the
kids in the Common Concern Club from the Young Americans for
Freedom.

When he grows a mustache (this much later), it'll be the long,
yellow/brown kind that curls up at the ends and he'll be smiling.

Say, did you know there's a new method that can give you
powerful muscles you'll be proud to show your friends in just ten
minutes a day? " Carry your great strength with prudence and
humility," I say, but you've broken another ballpoint pen writing
the answer to the problem of Farmer Brown who plows half an
acre in twenty minutes and Farmer Jones who has plowed thirty-
two acres in seventy-six hours.

He's coming in, going out, coming in, going out. It's another
world entirely outside and that waltz is really the original motion-
picture soundtrack from 2001.

I know you. I was a boy once myself, mother though I have
become, and I know it might as well be, maybe ought to be Chi-
chen Itza instead of Betelgeuse or some place with a lot of moons.
You'll lose all that, you know, Captain, next year or the year after,
but there will be greater losses, and that sonic blast was just a
stalling tactic to keep you busy while they roll in this monstrous
world. You have yet to face the bureaucratic creatures that crawl
through rocks and can hold you helplessly imprisoned in megaliths
even though you may be in telepathic contact with the big-
brained friends of this universe. There are things you'd never
suspect out here in reality land, and your night terrors are nothing
compared to them.

` You won't recognize him. I mean that man with the yellow/
brown mustache coming in for a landing on some different planet
farther in the future than you ever thought possible. He's of the
next century, you know, and will be at his peak by 2001. Did you

realize that yesterday when you asked me, "What does 'existential' mean?" and I couldn't answer so you knew? "Forget it," you said and I can't forget it, because without your existential superself you will certainly perish in wars of the future out among the satellites, overcome by cosmic thought patterns too convoluted for the human brain to contemplate, or, if not that, torn apart by humanoids in the death throes of their own identity crises, or exploded by technological advances available not only to the future but known already to the present and, if not one or more of the above, inevitably coarsened by Earthlings of your own kind. I can't save you, because even though thunder sends the cats under the bed and still brings you into my room where there can be no ghosts, no tigers, and monsters still shrivel up and die when I turn on the lights, my powers are fading. But I'm not—repeat, *not*—waiting for you to grow up, because that's another thing entirely.

"What's the size of a shark's brain?"

"What's the capital of Colorado?"

"What's the longest book ever written?"

"What's green and warty and lives at the bottom of the sea?"

For Mother, on Mother's Day, draw space ships.

Learn it, Dummy. 8×7, 8×8. "You're making me hate arithmetic," he says. Odd numbers, even numbers, two by two down school's light-green halls and he's been at it seven years. Even when there's a death, you know, we all go on more or less as though nothing had happened. Go back to those same old circumferences of circles, parallel lines down the middle of, and follow instructions. I'm telling you, you can do as you wish, see the dead laid out on display the old-fashioned way with a $50 blanket of roses just as Grandma wanted it, or not. It's up to you. But don't come to me after five o'clock because there's no changing your mind. There's a death deadline, but it's not what you think— falling down and losing your memory, getting up and falling down again, the sudden zap, zap, zap of ray guns. You've lost some of your best men, but you're miraculously safe. Captain, you're always so miraculously safe except in the dark.

"Slide inner front sprocket wheel (#17) over sprocket shaft, then place wheel retainer (#13) over end of shaft. Apply a drop of cement to end of shaft adhering retainer to shaft. Then cement outer front sprocket wheel (#18) to inner sprocket wheel by applying cement at notch on outer wheel."

"Look, Ma. Look, Ma."

(Don't bother me now.)

"Look, Ma, drop these seemingly innocent pellets into a glass of water and magically a worm will appear."

By 2001 I'll be dead.

No more "Look, Ma."

Inferno, mad inventor of instruments of torture and destruction, all your tricks are useless. They can't make him tell where his mother is hidden.

For those who dare! *Surprise Package.* Only fifty cents. Are you willing to take a chance on a secret? Listen then, the mother has both breasts and penis sometimes. She *has* to. There's no other solution to some of those knotty little problems of sexual identification; face them every day and see who wears the blue jeans. (Everybody does.) We won't tell you what *you* get, but because you're willing to gamble we'll give you much more than your money's worth. Satisfaction guaranteed. Are you willing to face the *real* green slime? Well, let's get this straightened out once and for all. Maybe the penis is just a realistic skin-colored spooky hand with red fingernails and big knuckles (ninety-eight cents). Imagine it poking out of your car door at sixty miles an hour, or out of a suitcase on the train. Imagine it on the piano keys, on the window ledge, peeking out of a grocery bag, opening a door. Comes with special adhesive. Sticks anywhere. Can be reused over and over and over and over.

What's green and squashed and lies in the gutter? That's a girl scout run over by a truck.

There are still some wishes left and crazy laughter and a secret handshake. But after a while you face life at your own risk.

When, in the course of human events, evidence comes to light of evil forces overpowering the good, give that boy three impossible tasks to do to restore the world to its proper place among the respectable planets. Steadfast and true. Honorable unto the death, of course.Helper of the helpless. Kind to animals. Honesty his best policy. Oh, incorruptible boy, I see the faint new moon float past your head one midafternoon. The clouds hardly moving and you, blasting off into one of those lazy Sundays with an Estes rocket. "Gentlemen, we're limping back to Aldebaran. We've slipped out of space warp and into real time. We're lost in an out-of-the-way section of deep space and who knows what evil lurks among the stars? . . ."

Back here we're waiting for all systems to be go, for all men to be safe and accounted for and in real time and serving a different purpose. It's another world going on outside and might be airless. Suit up, men, preferably in silver, then gasping (gasp, gasp), falling down. "Look, Ma, honorable unto the death."

What's green and squashed and lies in the gutter? Well, there's a war on and it's this world now and it could be you with your new yellow/brown mustache.

But that boy doesn't belong on this planet at all. Someday his real father and mother will come down to claim him and take him back where he belongs. He'll be homesick for his former Earth family for a while, but after a week or so it'll be all right. The new life will be hard, but rewarding. He will accompany his new father in a ship, preferably all in silver, and go from planet to planet doing one good deed every day, 365 good deeds every Earth year.

That last blast-off almost poked a hole right through the ceiling. "I wouldn't do that in here again if I . . ."

Beaming down while the cosmic energy still burns within him, shouts, "Wait, I know just what you're going to say and I don't want to hear it."

(But maybe it's just one of those imitation bullet holes at nine for fifty cents.)

Husband, ours is indeed an admirable boy, but don't expose his secret identity: "Seven toes to each foot and to either hand as

The Nebula Winners
1965–1973

The method of choosing the winners of the Nebula Awards is of the utmost simplicity. During the course of the year the active members of Science Fiction Writers of America nominate stories and novels as they appear in print. There is no limit to this list that grows to an unwieldy length as the year draws to an end. There is then a final nominating ballot and this time there is a limit in order that the final ballot be short enough for everyone to read everything on it. At every stage only the active members of the organization are permitted to vote. The final ballot and the winning stories are selected by writers, judging other writers. The stories in this volume, number nine of the series, were published in 1973. There is one new category this year, the first time there has been a major change since the beginning of SFWA. There is a Dramatic Presentation Award.

1965

Best Novel: DUNE *by Frank Herbert*
Best Novella: "The Saliva Tree" *by Brian W. Aldiss*
"He Who Shapes" *by Roger Zelazny* (tie)

Best Novelette: "The Doors of His Face, the Lamps of His Mouth" *by Roger Zelazny*
Best Short Story: " 'Repent, Harlequin!' Said the Ticktockman" *by Harlan Ellison*

1966

Best Novel: FLOWERS FOR ALGERNON *by Daniel Keyes*
                BABEL-17 *by Samuel R. Delany* (tie)
Best Novella: "The Last Castle" *by Jack Vance*
Best Novelette: "Call Him Lord" *by Gordon R. Dickson*
Best Short Story: "The Secret Place" *by Richard McKenna*

1967

Best Novel: THE EINSTEIN INTERSECTION *by Samuel R. Delany*
Best Novella: "Behold the Man" *by Michael Moorcock*
Best Novelette: "Gonna Roll the Bones" *by Fritz Leiber*
Best Short Story: "Aye, and Gomorrah" *by Samuel R. Delany*

1968

Best Novel: RITE OF PASSAGE *by Alexei Panshin*
Best Novella: "Dragonrider" *by Anne McCaffrey*
Best Novelette: "Mother to the World" *by Richard Wilson*
Best Short Story: "The Planners" *by Kate Wilhelm*

1969

Best Novel: THE LEFT HAND OF DARKNESS *by Ursula K. Le Guin*
Best Novella: "A Boy and His Dog" *by Harlan Ellison*
Best Novelette: "Time Considered as a Helix of Semi-Precious Stones" *by Samuel R. Delany*
Best Short Story: "Passengers" *by Robert Silverberg*

1970

Best Novel: RINGWORLD *by Larry Niven*
Best Novella: "Ill Met in Lankhmar" *by Fritz Leiber*
Best Novelette: "Slow Sculpture" *by Theodore Sturgeon*
Best Short Story: No award

1971

Best Novel: A TIME OF CHANGES, *by Robert Silverberg*
Best Novella: "The Missing Man" *by Katherine MacLean*
Best Novelette: "The Queen of Air and Darkness" *by Poul Anderson*
Best Short Story: "Good News from the Vatican" *by Robert Silverberg*

1972

Best Novel: THE GODS THEMSELVES *by Isaac Asimov*
Best Novella: "A Meeting with Medusa" *by Arthur C. Clarke*
Best Novelette: "Goat Song" *by Poul Anderson*
Best Short Story: "When It Changed" *by Joanna Russ*

1973

Best Novel: RENDEZVOUS WITH RAMA *by Arthur C. Clarke*
Best Novella: "The Death of Doctor Island" *by Gene Wolfe*
Best Novelette: "Of Mist, and Grass, and Sand" *by Vonda N. McIntyre*
Best Short Story: "Love Is the Plan the Plan Is Death" *by James Tiptree, Jr.*

The Authors

GENE WOLFE was born in Brooklyn, speaks with a modified Texas accent, and now lives in Illinois, where he is editor of the trade publication *Plant Engineering*. He sold his first story in 1965, and has appeared in most of the s.f. magazines and original anthologies in the intervening years. His novel, *The Fifth Head of Cerberus*, published by Scribners, won critical acclaim and was hailed as a science fiction classic on publication. A second novel, *Peace*, will be published by Harper & Row in 1975.

EDWARD BRYANT writes: "Started writing (after previous sporadic attempts) at the Clarion Workshop in 1968 . . . Selling regularly started after the second Clarion Workshop in summer of 1969. Since then have sold maybe 100 pieces (fiction, articles, reviews) . . ." Ed also writes: "I pray that you not share in your husband's bizarre delusion that I am thirty-three years old." *Among the Dead*, a collection of short stories, was published by Macmillan in 1973, and a second collection, *Cinnabar*, will be published by the same firm in 1975.

GEORGE R. R. MARTIN, born in 1948, has been writing as long as he can remember, and published his first story in 1971. After college, Northwestern, he worked with VISTA for two years in Chicago, and now flies around the country organizing chess tournaments. The tournaments are on weekends, leaving his weekdays free to write. In the three years he has been writing professionally he has sold nineteen pieces of short fiction and is now working on a novel.

BEN BOVA is currently editor of *Analog*. He is working on a "big novel for Random House," and also collaborating with Harlan Ellison on a TV movie, "Brillo." Also published this year is the juvenile collaborative work done with Gordon R. Dickson, *Gremlins, Go Home!,* St. Martin's Press. His book, *The Fourth State of Matter,* was honored as one of the top 100 science books of the year 1971 by the American Librarians' Association. *Starflight and other Improbabilities* was selected as a Junior Literary Guild book in 1973.

VONDA N. MCINTYRE graduated with college honors in biology from the University of Washington in 1970, but in 1969 she began to submit stories to magazines and when the two careers clashed, she dropped her course work toward her Ph. D. in genetics to become a writer. Another graduate of the Clarion Workshop, she became the program coordinator for Clarion West from 1971 through 1973. Her professional sales are at the dozen mark, and recently she completed a novel, *The Clouds Return.*

HARLAN ELLISON is probably the most honored writer in the field of science fiction, and to top that, this year he also won the Edgar, given by the Mystery Writers of America, for his short story, "The Whimper of Whipped Dogs." He lives in California where he writes short science fiction stories, TV scripts, movie scripts, articles, reviews. He has lectured at every Clarion Workshop, East and West, and in his "spare" time he makes flying trips to college campuses all over the country to lecture to overflow crowds.

NORMAN SPINRAD cooks Chinese food, makes clay animals, and serves as vice-president of Science Fiction Writers of America. His novel *Bug Jack Barron* created a stir in s.f. circles when it was published, and more recently he published *The Iron Dream.* In 1974 G. P. Putnam will publish *Passing Through the Flame,* and a history of science fiction, *Modern Science Fiction,* will be published by Doubleday-Anchor Books.

JAMES TIPTREE, Jr., writes: "Winning prizes is not the name of my game," and he was wrong. He also said: "I seem to recall I have a doctorate in a soft science and did some university chores." And he worked on a Chicago newspaper, and lived in India and Africa, and in the late sixties he started to write. To date he has had about forty stories published in most of the s.f. magazines, and in the original anthologies.

DAMON KNIGHT has written or edited over fifty books in the science fiction field. He has translated from the French, has written a book of critical essays, *In Search of Wonder*, and a biography of Charles Fort. Currently he is editing the *Orbit* series of original stories, working on number sixteen, to be published by Harper & Row.

CAROL EMSHWILLER's collection of stories, *Joy in Our Cause*, was published by Harper & Row in May 1974. Her short stories are more likely to be found in the literary magazines than in s.f. these days, but she is a contributor to the original s.f. anthologies. She studied art on a Fulbright scholarship, and then turned to writing. She teaches a course in writing in Wantagh, New York.

KATE WILHELM's most recent novel, *City of Cain* (Little, Brown, 1974), is her eighth novel. Forthcoming from Harper & Row are a collection of short stories, *The Infinity Box of Kate Wilhelm*, and a novel, untitled.